THE DEVIL'S COUNTRY

OTHER TITLES BY HARRY HUNSICKER

The Jon Cantrell Thrillers

The Contractors
Shadow Boys
The Grid

Lee Henry Oswald Mysteries

Still River
The Next Time You Die
Crosshairs

THE DEVIL'S COUNTRY

HARRY HUNSICKER

Published by Thomas & Mercer, Seattle

www.apub.com

Amazon, the Amazon logo, and Thomas & Mercer are trademarks of Amazon.com, Inc., or its affiliates.

ISBN-13: 9781503941908
ISBN-10: 1503941906

Cover design by Christian Fuenfhausen
Cover photography by Run Studios

Printed in the United States of America

To my mother and father, who gave me so much.
Foree Hunsicker
June 30, 1932–March 11, 2015
Harry Hunsicker Sr.
April 27, 1930–September 22, 2015

- IN THE WILDERNESS -

Need be, Molly decides to kill her children, then herself.

Death is better than what will happen if they are caught.

She clutches the stolen pistol with one hand, her daughter's arm with the other, and pulls the child toward the meeting place.

Sweat stings her eyes, trickles down the small of her back. Thorns from the mesquite trees claw at her skin and clothes.

The land is mean and unforgiving, like the men coming after her.

Her son is in the lead, maybe thirty yards ahead along the narrow cattle trail.

He is thirteen, not a boy anymore. He lopes with the endless stamina of youth, a slender, shadowy figure in the dense brush. Every few seconds he stops and turns their way, silently urging them on.

Molly struggles to catch up, but deep down she knows her efforts are wasted.

They will catch her because they must. Failure is not an option. Their faith, which was once hers, demands it.

She has seen too much, glimpsed at the secrets lurking behind the facade of the church.

Even worse, she has begun to understand, to truly comprehend the nature of where she has spent most of her adult life.

Understanding but without faith. Knowledge with no belief.

This is the ultimate sin, and they will make her pay the ultimate price.

Her only hope is to save her children.

With that in mind, she presses on, one foot in front of the other, pistol clutched tightly in her hand, the long skirt she wears hampering her progress.

Engines whine behind her as the pursuers zigzag their four-wheelers through the brush. Every second brings them closer.

Molly forces herself to move faster, lashing her half jog closer to a sprint. Her daughter struggles to keep pace, yelping as a branch slaps her in the face. Molly turns to check on her and stumbles over a fallen tree limb. She slams into the ground.

Dirt and cow manure soil her dress. Tears fill her eyes.

Futility rushes over her like water from a broken dam. The folly of her entire existence is laid bare. Everything she attempts eventually ends in disaster.

"Get up, Mama." The girl tugs on Molly's arm. "We have to hurry."

Her daughter is nine, but she's old beyond her time, well aware of the danger. The life that's been thrust upon her makes a person that way. This is perhaps Molly's biggest regret. A nine-year-old shouldn't have this much fear.

Molly gulps air. Her legs ache. She realizes she can't go on.

Even if she can reach the meeting point and the vehicle is there, the guards will track her down. Whatever safety they might find will be fleeting.

Silas and his men are everywhere. They see and hear everything.

Sometimes Molly wonders if they can sense even her very thoughts.

It's better to end the ordeal now. Avoid the pain and suffering to come. Let their souls be greeted by the Elohim.

The pistol is heavy in her hand.

It is the middle of the afternoon, but the sky has darkened, storm clouds gathering on the horizon. The air smells like rain, a welcome relief for this drought-stricken section of West Texas.

Her daughter kneels beside her, skin pale, teeth chattering despite the heat.

"Please, Mama. They're right behind us."

The child is beautiful. Auburn hair, big blue eyes, full lips. Molly wanted so much more for her. School and friends, boys to fret over. A life of her own choosing.

Molly stares at the gun. A silent prayer forms in her mind: *Dear Father in heaven. Please forgive me for what I am about—*

Thunder cracks in the distance, startling her.

Molly looks toward where she last saw her son.

The boy is standing on a limestone ridge, silhouetted against a dark sky.

He points to the other side of the ridge and shouts, "The pickup!"

Molly lets the girl help her up. She takes a deep breath and runs toward the meeting place, daughter by her side.

The whine of the four-wheelers' engines is louder.

Molly keeps running.

CRACK.

A rifle shot echoes across the land as she and her daughter scramble over the crest of the ridge. She checks her daughter in a panic, but the bullet found neither of them.

Below them is an old Chevy pickup parked on a gravel road, maybe twenty yards away. Her son is already there, opening the driver's door. Molly and her daughter run for the truck.

The ones who have gone before her arranged for the vehicle. The key will be under the floor mat, along with a mobile phone and a map to the nearest town. Safety.

Molly stares at the Chevy as she runs, hardly believing her good fortune. Things don't go right in Molly's world. People don't keep promises; events take the worst turn possible.

The rain begins. Fat drops splatter in the dust. Lightning jags across a purple sky.

Molly allows herself to feel a moment of relief. The rain will slow down the pursuers.

Another rifle shot rings out.

Her son cries out, grabs his shoulder. Blood oozes from between his fingers.

An invisible hand clenches Molly's throat.

Silas's men have caught up with them. They will kill the boy and then take away her daughter.

Her limbs shake, vision blurs.

A pain on her arm, like a bee sting.

She looks down, afraid she'll see blood.

The girl is pinching her.

"Mama. We have to get to the truck. *Hurry.*"

Molly pushes away the hysteria and sees that her son is holding the key to the pickup aloft at the end of his unwounded arm.

The sky grows darker still. Sheets of rain begin to fall.

Mother and daughter run for the truck as Molly says a silent prayer of thanks.

- CHAPTER ONE -

I value my privacy.

A quiet corner and a good book. A cup of coffee or a beer.

That's not too much to ask, is it?

Not after what I'd been through, certainly.

The bar was called Jimmy and Dale's Broken Promise. It had low ceilings and even lower expectations, as good a place as any to spend an hour or so out of the heat.

I was sitting by the beer taps, reading a paperback copy of Edward Gibbon's classic, *The History of the Decline and Fall of the Roman Empire*, nursing a mug of Coors.

Other than the bartender and myself, only three people were present. A woman at a table in the back by the jukebox and two cowboys by the front, wearing Stetsons, throwing darts.

I'd counted customers when I'd entered, rated each as to what kind of trouble they could cause. Made sure of where the exits were.

Old habits.

The bartender was named Jimmy, and I surmised he was also the owner. I'd thought about asking what had happened to Dale and the broken promise, but that was dangerously close to putting down roots, so I'd just ordered the beer and started reading.

Two pages later, my mug was down maybe a half inch.

Jimmy wandered over, polishing a glass with a towel. He was in his midforties, a few years older than I, and sported a Joe Dirt–style mullet.

"We're running a special on Goldschläger," he said. "You want a shot?"

I shook my head, continued reading.

A moment passed. Jimmy finished with one glass, began shining another.

"You working at the feedlot? Haven't seen you around here before."

The flat-screen over the bar was tuned to the Weather Channel and showed a line of thunderstorms advancing toward the tiny town of Piedra Springs, Texas, the location of Jimmy and Dale and their broken promise.

There's an art form to being polite but not encouraging conversation, a thin line to be traversed. Act friendly but not engaging. Don't be an asshole or a chatterbox.

"Just passing through."

I flipped the page to a new chapter: "The Tyranny of Caracalla and the Usurpation of Macrinus."

Due to changes in my employment situation, I'd decided to catch up on some of the stuff I'd missed out on over the years—books not read and roads untraveled being the first two.

"Passing through Piedra Springs?" Jimmy chuckled. "Don't that beat all."

The town was in a desolate, hard-to-reach section of West Texas, the badlands between Odessa and Sonora, a long way from anywhere that mattered.

Not many people just stumbled upon Piedra Springs. You either had business there or were trying to avoid business somewhere else. Or you were just wandering, like me.

He pointed to my nearly full beer. "You OK on your drink?"

"I'm fine, thanks." I didn't look up from the book.

Another two pages had gone by when the girl by the jukebox glided to the bar, carrying an empty glass.

She was in her early twenties, with small bones and delicate features, a doll relegated to a high shelf because the children's playtime was much too rough.

She pushed the glass across the bar and asked for a refill, vodka on the rocks.

While the bartender made the drink, she turned her attention my way. "Hi there."

I finished the paragraph. Waited a moment. Looked up.

"Hello." I immediately returned to the book.

"Whatcha reading?"

I put down Gibbon, wondered if there was a place in town where I could just get a cup of coffee and not have to talk to people. "A history book," I said. "About the Romans."

She wore a leather headband, a pair of faded jeans, and a low-cut peasant blouse, tie-dyed.

"You don't look like a history buff." She leaned against the bar. "Or a Roman."

The movement displayed more of her cleavage, which seemed to be the point.

She said, "You look like you just got out of the army or something."

She was actually sort of correct. My hair was short. I stood a little over six feet, weighed a fit 180 pounds, arms and shoulders stretching the T-shirt I was wearing.

I'd been discharged from the Texas Rangers almost eight months before. I'd been a Ranger for nearly a decade, going into some of the worst places East Texas had to offer.

I didn't tell the girl any of that. I just shrugged and picked up Gibbon again.

A moment later, she said, "You ever been to Italy?"

"Italy, Texas?"

"No, silly. The other one. The real Italy."

I debated my answer. The line between being friendly and an asshole was getting thinner.

"Leave him be, Suzy." The bartender put her drink on a napkin. "The man just wants to read his book."

I made a mental note to leave a healthy tip. Then I gave both of them a polite smile and went back to the Romans.

Jimmy told her how much the drink would be.

She patted her pockets.

"My purse. It's back at the table." All innocence. "I'm sure I've got some money left."

I looked up from my book. Jimmy was staring at her with the look bartenders reserve for young women who try to scam themselves free drinks.

"We talked about this when you came in," he said. "You told me you could pay your tab this time."

He wasn't angry, and I understood why.

It was hard to get mad at a girl like Suzy. You instinctively knew she was doing the best she could and that was never enough.

"There's money in my purse." She stood up straight, chin high.

Jimmy and I stared at her. She made no move toward the table where her handbag was.

I sighed and put down the book again. Despite my years as a cop, I was a sucker for lost causes, stray pets, and people who couldn't quite fit into the groove of life.

A waif with no money, looking like she'd been conceived in the back of the Grateful Dead's tour bus, in a bar called the Broken Promise.

Pretty much the definition of a lost cause, right there.

I pulled out a twenty. "Here. Allow me."

Jimmy took the cash, and the woman climbed onto the stool next to mine.

"Thank you, kind sir." She took a sip of vodka. "I thought my friend was going to be here by now."

I picked up Gibbon and tried to find my place. Tried to ignore her without being impolite.

"It's kind of a date," she said. "I haven't seen him in years. We hooked up online."

I didn't reply. Kept reading.

"He used to be in my cousin's Al-Anon group." She clinked the ice in her glass. "This was up in Abilene."

The words on the page became a blur, the sound of her voice making them hard to process.

"He's been in Austin for the last month or so." She paused. "An unfortunate misunderstanding with the local authorities."

I stopped reading. "He's been in jail?"

"Only for a short period." Her eyes were wide as saucers. "He says that he's a political prisoner. People can't handle the truth of his views."

I rubbed the bridge of my nose, tired all of a sudden.

On the TV, the thunderstorms were getting closer.

"You seem like a nice person, Suzy. Maybe you could try and meet somebody at a homeless shelter or a methadone clinic."

She rattled the ice in her drink and stared off into the distance. "Everybody deserves a second chance, don't you think?"

I wondered if there was a bus leaving later. The destination didn't matter.

She shifted her weight so that our knees were touching. After a moment, I shifted away.

One of the cowboys who'd been playing darts approached the bar, ordered two more beers. The crown of his hat peaked higher in the rear than in the front, the crease sloping toward the wearer's face, what's known as a Tom Mix–style Stetson. His friend's hat was similar.

He tilted back the Stetson and eyed Suzy with the look men reserve for women who are easy pickings.

She'd been in the back, alone. Now she was at the bar, with someone she obviously had just met. Might as well have had a sign around her neck that read PUTS OUT ON FIRST DATE.

Then the cowboy looked at me.

I looked back, settled behind the flat, unblinking stare that used to make the tweakheads and gangbangers in certain parts of the Lone Star State run for shelter. It still had some utility, evidently. The cowboy paid for the beers and headed back up to his friend at the dartboard.

Suzy stayed at the bar and drank, humming to herself softly. She didn't try to talk to me anymore, so I opened my book and continued to read.

A page and a half later, a gust of wind swept through the bar as the front door opened and a man in his forties entered. His scalp was clean-shaven, and he had a swastika inked on his forehead and what looked like teardrop tattoos under each eye. He stood by the entrance, blinking, letting his eyes adjust to the dim light.

I glanced at Suzy over the top of the book, kept my voice low. "You can go out the back."

She stared at the man, index finger running around the rim of her glass.

"Nobody would blame you." I flipped the page.

The man with the shaved head sauntered toward the bar. I looked up from my book. His skin was sallow, eyes flat and cold, a mackerel on ice.

She slid off the stool, wobbly on her feet. "Thanks for the drink."

Mr. Swastika stopped a few feet away from us, head cocked to one side.

"Hello, Suzy. Been a long time." His voice was ragged, like he'd been shouting a lot or smoking meth. "How're you doing, girl?"

"Peachy, baby. How about you?" She moved toward the man, her body language open and inviting.

Mr. Swastika ordered a pitcher of Bud Light. He carried the beer to the back, Suzy trailing after him. They sat at her table by the jukebox.

I watched them for a few moments, wishing I'd picked a different place to spend an hour reading about the Romans, a different town, even. But I'd been tired of being on the bus, and Piedra Springs had a nice ring to it, so here I was.

Twenty minutes later, the pitcher was empty. Mr. Swastika stood up. Suzy did the same, wobblier than before.

They headed toward the exit. Suzy looked over her shoulder at me as she went. Her expression was mournful but resigned. Or maybe that was my imagination.

A red band scrolled across the bottom of the TV screen, a tornado warning for the county where Piedra Springs was located.

I opened the book, read a few lines. Then I closed it.

Jimmy wiped down the bar with a rag. "She does stupid stuff like that on a regular basis."

I didn't reply.

"I'd advise against trying to help her," he said.

I looked toward the front door.

"But if you want to anyway," he said, "I'll keep your beer cold."

- CHAPTER TWO -

I stuck a cocktail napkin in the paperback. "Whatever you do, don't lose my place."

Jimmy nodded.

On the TV, the thunderstorms were almost to town.

I strode to the front exit and stepped outside onto Main Street, the only commercial avenue in town, ten or twelve blocks long.

It was late in the afternoon, the middle of June, but the sky was black, thunderclouds rolling in from the west. Dust and litter blew down the street, chased by a cool wind that smelled like ozone and sage.

Piedra Springs was tiny, a population of maybe five thousand if you counted dogs and cats. At the moment, nobody was on the street, not people or animals.

The county courthouse and bus station were at one end of Main Street, Jimmy and Dale's at the other, across from an old motor hotel built during the Eisenhower administration. The Comanche Inn, where I'd checked in about an hour before.

A car door slammed not far away.

The automobiles on the street appeared empty, so I headed to the narrow parking lot between the bar and the local feed store.

Nothing in the parking area except three vehicles and a battered pay phone mounted to the wall of the bar.

The first vehicle was a twenty-year-old Chevy pickup with no one inside.

It was parked next to a newer version of itself, a late-model extended-cab Chevrolet, gray with tinted windows.

The third vehicle was a battered Ford van across the lot from the two pickups. The van had a Confederate flag bumper sticker.

Rain began to fall, a few drops here and there. A thin mist of steam rose from the surface of the parking lot, cold water on hot asphalt.

The van's rear lights winked on as the engine chugged to life and exhaust spooled from the muffler.

The vehicle backed out of its spot and started toward Main Street.

Nothing was stopping its departure but me, standing in the middle of the parking lot, blocking the way.

The dash lights gave Suzy and her date an eerie glow, almost purple.

Mr. Swastika stared at me, a confused look on his face, no doubt thinking something along the lines of, *What is this idiot doing? Am I going to have to give him a beat down right here in the parking lot?*

Suzy stared at me, too, her eyes soft, a sad little smile on her face. After a moment, she mouthed something to me, what looked like, *I'm OK. Thank you.*

The wind grew louder, and I realized I was in Piedra Springs, a town I'd never been to before, and not in a police station back in Dallas, weeping over the news that my wife and children had been murdered.

I stepped aside.

You can't save everybody. If Suzy wanted to bump uglies with a Charles Manson wannabe, who was I to stop her?

The van drove past.

Mr. Swastika nodded once, a simple acknowledgment that I had let him pass. He wasn't offering thanks, but he wasn't gloating, either, and I wondered if he realized how close he'd come to tumbling down into the black canyon at the center of my being.

Suzy waved as the van turned onto Main Street and headed west.

I watched the taillights get smaller as thunder cracked and the rain fell harder.

That's when the woman appeared.

She must have been crouched by the front of the older pickup, out of sight.

She was otherworldly, like a time traveler from 150 years before. Her hair was in a bun. The dress she wore looked like something from *Little House on the Prairie*, a flowing skirt that reached her ankles, the sleeves covering her wrists. The material was ripped and soiled.

"Please help me," she said. "They're going to kill us if you don't."

- CHAPTER THREE -

The woman in the old-timey dress moved away from the old Chevy, and I saw two figures behind her, a boy in his early teens and a girl a few years younger. The boy held one arm like it hurt.

The wind blew harder, whipping our clothes.

"What happened?" I said. "Are you all right?"

"We escaped." The woman's voice was shrill. "They're coming after us."

"Who's coming after you?" I said. "What are you talking about?"

"Aren't you the one we're supposed to meet?" she asked. "I tried to call."

"I'm not supposed to be meeting anybody, ma'am." I paused. "Take a deep breath, and tell me what's going on."

She stared at me, mouth agape, an astonished look on her face.

The boy spoke for the first time. "The men. That's who's after us."

Blood coated his arm. He trembled, teeth chattering.

"Have you been shot?" I said.

The woman and the boy stared at me despondently, faces weary. This was the end of the line for them, and for whatever reason, I was their last hope.

The girl moved to the woman's side, clasped her arm.

She was about ten, yet somehow already well on her way to being a stunningly beautiful young woman. Creamy skin, high cheekbones, long limbs hidden by a dress as shapeless as the woman's. In a few years she could be a model or an actress, gracing the covers of magazines.

If she got out of this parking lot.

I pointed to the bar. "Let's go inside and call the police."

Terror filled the woman's eyes. She shook her head. "No-no-no."

"I'll stay with you until—"

Around the front corner of the bar, two figures appeared. They wore jeans and work shirts that were of a modern design, hats pulled low against the rain. The hats were distinctive, crowns creased and sloped Tom Mix–style, high in the back, low in the front.

The cowboys from the bar, the ones playing darts at the front.

They approached us, stopping a few feet away, and I realized I'd made an error in judgment when I first saw them.

They weren't a couple of guys playing darts after a hard day punching cows. They were hired muscle, thugs. The way they carried themselves and stood apart from each other—not too close, not too far, either, hands loose by their sides.

The one who appeared to be the leader had a thick mustache that grew down either side of his chin.

He said, "We're here, Molly. Everything is OK."

The woman looked at the men and then back at me, an expression of abject horror on her face.

"Let's be quick about it," the man with the mustache said. "Your boy needs a doctor."

"Don't let them take us." The woman held out a hand in my direction. "Please."

I stood between her and the cowboys, looking back and forth between the two groups.

Lightning jagged across the sky, followed almost instantly by a thunderclap.

"C'mon, Molly." The man with the mustache began to ease around my side. "It's time to go."

"No." Molly pressed her back against the old Chevy, clutching the children. "Stay away from me."

The man looked at his partner. Some sort of wordless communication passed between the two. The partner began to flank out on my other side.

Another crack of thunder. Then the rain slackened and the sky took on a greenish tint, the quiet before the real storm began.

"She doesn't want to go with you," I said, watching them take their positions. "You boys need to walk away before you get hurt."

The partner laughed, shook his head slowly.

The man with the mustache said, "You're not involved in any of this. You should keep it that way."

"They're going to kill us," Molly said. "Please help."

Her children whimpered behind her.

I was unarmed except for a folding knife in my waistband.

On the ground at my feet lay a piece of brick and a broken broom handle, the latter maybe a yard long, one end jagged and sharp.

The two men had stopped about six feet away from me, which was a mistake.

I couldn't fault them, however. They were hoods, not professionals.

There is a rule that every cop knows.

The Thirty Foot Rule. Ten yards, the length needed for a first down.

If you were fewer than thirty feet from an adversary, a determined attacker could cross that space in a matter of a second or two, while you were still clearing your gun from its holster. I had no idea if these guys were armed, but only six feet away, it wouldn't matter.

I picked up the broom handle.

From the direction of the courthouse came the wail of a civil defense siren, a tornado warning.

Molly began to cry. The children did as well.

There's another rule that's specific to the Texas Rangers, hard-edged people who are used to working alone, a rule they don't talk about much but has been used to save many a Ranger's life.

If you think the situation is about to get nasty, attack first.

The partner glanced toward the street. Then he reached under his shirt as the man with the mustache said, "Put the stick down and ge—"

I took a quick step toward the partner and smashed the broom handle across his nose.

The gun that was barely in his grasp dropped to the ground. He grunted, reached for his face, and I shoved the jagged end of the broom handle into a spot right above his navel. The wood punctured his flesh, penetrating maybe a half inch into the man's abdominal muscles. No permanent damage, just a lot of pain and blood.

He fell backward, landing on his ass with a thud.

The man with the mustache swore, reached under his shirt.

I charged and met him as he brought up a pistol. Got one hand on the gun, twisted, felt something like a finger bone crack. Not mine, fortunately.

He screamed.

I kept pushing, ramming him against the exterior wall of the bar.

The pistol clattered to the asphalt.

He swung at me with his uninjured hand. Missed.

I kneed his groin.

He doubled over.

I grabbed his throat and slammed his head against the brick wall.

He fell to the ground, all the fight gone out of him like a switch had been thrown.

From a long way off came what sounded like a freight train at top speed, a high, steady howl. The tornado was coming.

Adrenaline from the fight made my limbs shaky. The rain had almost stopped, but the wind was furious.

I looked around for the woman and her children, but they were nowhere to be seen. They must have run off while I'd been dealing with the two cowboys.

I picked up the guns and tossed them on the roof of the bar.

The woman and her offspring could have escaped one of two ways—the alley or the street.

I jogged to the street, looked in both directions, debating which way to go. There were no people visible. Everything was shut up tight against the storm.

A swirling mass of clouds covered the western horizon. Beneath the mass, a funnel appeared.

I ran back into the bar.

- CHAPTER FOUR -

Jimmy stood just inside the front door when I entered.

The place was empty.

"What happened out there?" he said.

On the TV by the bar, big red letters flashed across the screen: SEEK COVER! A TORNADO HAS TOUCHED DOWN WEST OF PIEDRA SPRINGS.

"Do you have a storm cellar?"

Jimmy didn't answer. He looked at the television and then at me. He seemed to be having a hard time processing what was going on.

A lot of people in tornado country are like those who live where hurricanes are prevalent. They either talk of riding out the storm or subscribe to the it'll-never-happen-to-me theory. They're fearless until the moment Mother Nature's fury actually arrives. Then they are paralyzed.

"We need to get somewhere safe," I said. "This is the real deal."

"The storeroom." He pointed behind the bar. "That's the best place."

Jimmy and Dale's was constructed from cinder blocks and had very few windows. A pretty good design for surviving tornadoes, if the storm didn't spawn a biggie like an F-5, a monster cyclone with a base that could reach a half mile wide.

I propped open the front door with a chair. This would equalize the pressure between inside and out, keep what windows there were from imploding and the roof from crashing down. In theory, anyway.

I jogged to the bar, grabbed my book, and followed Jimmy into the storeroom, a twenty-by-twenty room filled with shrapnel. Hundreds of liquor bottles. Cases and cases of beer.

Jimmy stared at all the glass. "What should we do?"

Two sofas were against one wall. They were identical, old and worn, armless, wide enough to hold three sitting people or one lying down.

"Get on the floor."

I scooted one of the sofas away from the wall.

Jimmy did as instructed, lying on his stomach.

I tilted the sofa on top of the man, forming a barrier over him about the size and shape of a coffin. Then I flipped the second sofa and crawled underneath. Not perfect but better than nothing.

Outside, the freight-train sound had gotten louder. The end of the world.

Which put me in mind of a day nine months before. The end of another world, the day my family was taken from me. Through force of will, I closed the door on that day and chose another.

●   ●   ●

Years before that, when we were young and happy and life held the promise of a thousand cloudless days, I held her in my arms.

My wife, the reason for everything. Alpha and omega. The beginning and the end of my existence.

We were two-stepping to a Bob Wills song in a dance hall outside of Fort Worth. Sawdust on a wood floor, the twang of a steel guitar, Lone Star and Shiner Bock in ice-filled tubs.

"What are you thinking about?" She squeezed my hand.

I didn't answer. A lot was on my mind. Impending fatherhood will do that to a man.

"It'll be OK," she said. "People have been having babies for a long time now."

She had eyes the color of jade and skin that smelled like lavender soap. In the dim light, those eyes twinkled, mischievous and innocent in the same moment.

When she looked at me like that, I felt captivated and beguiled, entranced. Her gaze left me adrift in a sea of warmth and grace, the core of who she was.

"I want it all to be perfect," I said.

"Nothing's ever perfect, Arlo." She rubbed her cheek against mine. "But we'll make it work, you and me. And whoever this turns out to be." She smiled down between us at the life we'd made. "We should start thinking of names."

I was drawing a blank. That's what she did to me. I held her close. "I love you."

The music stopped. The crowd clapped, called for another song.

She kissed me. "I love you, too, Arlo."

• • •

The air around me smelled like leather and stale beer.

Everything was dark. I couldn't see.

Then, light and a voice.

"You OK?" Jimmy stood over me, holding a flashlight.

We were in the storeroom of his bar. He'd moved the sofa off me.

The dance with my wife had been a decade ago, seven months before our first child had been born. Our son.

"What happened?" I blinked.

"Storm passed. We made it."

I stood. My legs were shaky.

"You OK?" He aimed the light at my face. "Looks like you've seen a ghost or something."

Perceptive, that Jimmy.

I left the storeroom.

The bar was empty and dark, the front door still propped open.

Jimmy followed me outside.

Sunlight streamed through the rapidly diminishing cloud cover.

The power appeared to be off for the whole town, and debris and tree limbs littered Main Street, but all of the buildings remained intact. There were no collapsed walls or broken windows. The cars that had been parked along the curb were still there, too, dotted with leaves and trash.

I strode to the side of the building, the area between the bar and the feed store.

The parking lot was empty.

The two Chevy pickups—one old, one new—were gone, as were the two injured cowboys.

I jogged to the rear of the parking area, looked down the alley in either direction.

No living thing was visible. There was nothing to see at all except dumpsters and the backs of buildings.

"What are you doing?" Jimmy stood at the edge of the lot by the street.

I stared up at the sky but didn't reply.

Jimmy pulled out a phone, tapped on the screen. "Weather Channel says it was a small one. Looks to me like it zipped straight down Main Street. Didn't hit nothing." He grinned. "We just rode that sucker out."

I walked back to the front of the bar.

From the back of the building came a popping noise. A moment later, the neon **OPEN** sign in the front window of Jimmy and Dale's flickered on.

The air was hot and humid. I wiped sweat off my brow.

"You want another beer?" he asked. "On the house."

"Maybe later." I headed down Main Street to search for Molly and her children.

- CHAPTER FIVE -

I walked to the far end of Piedra Springs and back, stepping around downed tree limbs and scattered garbage left by the storm, stopping at each cross street, looking for any sign of the woman and her children.

I saw the First State Bank, a limestone and marble building in the center of town. The bank sat between a shuttered movie theater called the Hippodrome and an old dry-goods store that was now a defunct antique mall. I saw a high-school-age boy wearing a Dallas Cowboys jersey, riding a bike. I saw farmers driving pickups filled with hay bales. I saw a three-legged dog eating garbage.

What I didn't see was a woman in a prairie dress and her two children, one of whom was injured.

At the outset, I was pretty sure my efforts would end up being futile, but I felt like I ought to do something to make sure they were safe.

Fifteen minutes later, I was back where I'd started, in front of the bar.

A diner was across the street, next door to the Comanche Inn.

Earl's Family Restaurant occupied a one-story adobe building with an enormous pitched roof and windows that looked out over Main Street.

Bright-red paint decorated one of the windows, advertising the *especials de la maison.*

Meat loaf. Double-battered chicken-fried steak. Earl's Famous Enchiladas.

I decided to check if someone at the restaurant had seen Molly leave the parking lot or, failing that, knew who Molly was or where she lived. Maybe I'd get something to eat at the same time. So I walked across the street, book under my arm, and entered. A bell on the door jangled.

It was a little before seven in the evening. Half the tables and booths were full. Mothers and fathers with their children. Senior citizens. Men who'd spent the day tilling the land or working livestock.

I realized I should have come here to read instead of Jimmy and Dale's. Everything would have been different if I'd done that.

A waitress in her forties with blue eye shadow and fake lashes as long as my thumbnail seated me in a booth by a window. Several people at nearby tables smiled and nodded hello, friendly like they tend to be in the western part of Texas.

The interior of Earl's was decorated with pictures of John Wayne and World War II bombers. The air smelled like cooked onions and a deep fryer that was a few months past needing its grease changed.

Snippets of conversation drifted my way, talk about the tornado and the price of sorghum.

The waitress brought me a glass of water and a menu. I couldn't imagine the enchiladas at a place called Earl's would be very good, famous or not, so I ordered the meat loaf and an iced tea, unsweetened. As she jotted down my order, I said, "You been in Piedra Springs long?"

"How do you define 'long'?"

"You know a woman named Molly? She's around thirty. Wears old-timey dresses."

The waitress scratched her chin, then shook her head.

"What about Earl?" I said. "Do you think he might know her?"

"Earl died three years ago. I'll ask in the kitchen, but I bet they don't know, either."

I thanked her, opened Gibbon, and started reading.

Twenty minutes later, I was halfway through my meal and just getting to the part about Macrinus and his Usurpation when a Vietnamese man in his late forties entered the restaurant.

He wore a crisp khaki uniform with a badge on the breast, brown Roper boots polished to a high gleam, and a semiautomatic pistol on his hip.

The sheriff.

The waitress who took my order greeted him, as did several customers. He took the booth next to mine, sat so that we were facing each other. The waitress brought him a cup of coffee. He added sugar and cream and then looked me in the eye like cops tend to do.

He said, "How you doing, partner?"

"Fine." I put down the book. "And you?"

"The four-twenty from Abilene, right?" He had a Texas drawl as strong as new rope. The accent seemed off-kilter coming from a Vietnamese guy.

"That's correct."

He was referring to the bus I'd arrived on. An observant man, this sheriff.

"Greyhound runs only three a day through here," he said. "Wasn't hard to figure out."

I nodded politely, and we were both silent for a moment, sizing each other up.

"You look like you might be in the same line of work as me," the sheriff said.

Cops always recognize one another. The way a person holds his head, scans the room, never quite relaxes, it's pretty obvious. They say people who've been in prison can do the same.

"I was with the DPS." I paused. "Now I'm not."

The Texas Rangers are a division of the Department of Public Safety, so my answer was technically correct. I didn't feel like getting into the details. Most people don't leave the Rangers unless they retire or die.

He cocked his head like he was waiting for an explanation as to why a man in the prime of life was no longer in law enforcement. When none was forthcoming, he said, "What brings you to town?"

There were a lot of answers I could've given.

I didn't think he'd be impressed with my plan to read several of the great history books while exploring the nether regions of our fair state. I also didn't want to tell him that movement was what had kept me reasonably sane these past few months after my family died.

So I shrugged and said what I always did in these circumstances: "Just passing through."

He took a sip of coffee and rubbed his chin, appearing lost in thought.

An elderly couple—the man wearing a short-brimmed hat and Buddy Holly glasses—stopped by the sheriff's seat and discussed the storm.

I returned to Gibbon and the Romans, finished my meal.

A few minutes later, the sheriff appeared by my table. He pointed to the other side of the booth. "You mind?"

"Not at all." I put the book down again. "Please."

He sat but didn't speak. He just looked at me like I was a fork in the road and he was trying to figure out which way to go.

"What can I do for you, Sheriff?"

"You were across the street earlier, right? At Jimmy and Dale's."

I nodded, liking his conversation starter not at all.

"Slow afternoon over there, I would imagine. Not many customers."

27

I shrugged but didn't say anything.

The sheriff tilted his hat back, looked out the window.

The seconds stretched to a minute. Neither of us spoke.

The technique was old but effective. See what a person would say during a long period of silence. Most people feel uncomfortable in that type of situation. They want to fill the void, which means they might say something useful, reveal a nugget of information that they might not otherwise let slip.

I'm not most people, though.

After about two minutes, the sheriff said, "There're these two old boys I don't much care for. Right about now, they're probably a half hour from the emergency room in Odessa."

I'd been wondering where the nearest medical facility was. I figured it had to be either Odessa or San Angelo, each at least a hundred miles away.

"What I heard, they were at Jimmy's earlier." He paused. "About the same time you were."

I kept quiet, didn't take the bait.

"One of 'em has a broken nose and a hole in his gut. Somebody jabbed him with a stick," the sheriff said. "The other got his bell rung pretty good."

"Why don't you care for them?" I asked.

"Huh?"

"These two guys. How come you don't like them?"

Silence.

The sheriff picked at his thumbnail for a few moments. Then: "I got my reasons. But that's not what we're talking about right now."

"What are we talking about?"

"These two fellows and how they come to get themselves banged up."

"Maybe they were out in the tornado?"

The sheriff didn't reply. He gave me a blank stare instead.

"Let's talk about why you don't like them, then."

"When you're sheriff, you can tell the pony what trail to take." He leaned forward, elbows on the table. "Right now, I need to know if you saw these two old boys at Jimmy and Dale's earlier today."

I didn't reply.

"They're white guys in their thirties," he said. "Both of 'em wearing cowboy hats with a crease that's low in the front. One's got a Fu Manchu mustache."

After a moment, I said, "Yeah, I saw them."

"And you had an altercation with them in the parking lot?"

His voice had a slight upturn at the end of the sentence, so maybe he was asking instead of stating what he already knew.

In any event, I'm not real big on self-incrimination, so I didn't reply.

"Did you ever stop to think that they might have friends?" the sheriff said.

As a matter of fact, I had. But I was more concerned with why a woman, standing in the rain with her wounded son and terrified daughter, was deathly afraid of those two men.

"Who would those friends be?" I asked.

No answer.

"Let me guess," I said. "Other people you don't care for."

"I don't know you from Adam, but here I am, trying to do you a solid." The sheriff shook his head.

The waitress brought my check.

"You left the bar for a spell," the sheriff said. "Jimmy, he stuck his head outside. Apparently he saw you going all Steven Seagal on those two."

"Jimmy must have infrared vision," I said. "It was as black as midnight and pouring rain."

The sheriff shrugged.

"I wouldn't trust Jimmy as far as I could spit," I said. "Never believe a man with a mullet."

"You're a pistol, aren't you?" he said. "Ate up with the smart-ass syndrome."

An eighteen-wheeler loaded with cattle lumbered down Main Street, trailing a cloud of diesel exhaust.

"Here's how this is gonna work." He tapped his index finger on the table. "You're gonna be on the first bus out of here tomorrow morning."

"The nine fifteen to Pecos," I said.

He nodded. "And since you'll be leaving, I won't feel obligated to arrest you."

His offer seemed reasonable. My usual MO was three days tops in any given town, then back on Greyhound or the side of the road with my thumb out. I figured that might be too long in Piedra Springs, given the inquisitive sheriff and the two thugs I'd beaten up.

Leaving meant I wouldn't be able to look for Molly, however, and that bothered me.

"Do we have a deal?" he asked.

I waited for a beat. Then nodded.

The sheriff smiled. He scooped up the bill. "Allow me. I insist."

"Thanks." I marked my place in Gibbon with the cocktail napkin. "When Jimmy was running his mouth, did he happen to mention the woman?"

The sheriff put some money on the table and arched one eyebrow.

"Her name was Molly," I said. "Late twenties, maybe early thirties. White, about five eight, a hundred ten or so."

"Doesn't ring a bell. I know just about everybody in the county. Only Molly I recollect is in her seventies, lives on a ranch north of town."

I slid out of the booth. "This Molly dresses like a schoolmarm. Looks like she's about to get on the wagon train for Californy."

Maybe it was my imagination, but I thought I saw a flicker of recognition cross his face. Then his expression became deadpan.

"You know who I'm talking about, don't you?"

"First bus out tomorrow," he said. "We have a deal, remember."

"You never said if Jimmy had seen the woman or not."

A moment of silence followed by a flash of emotion in the man's expression. Anger, quickly squelched.

"You're staying at the Comanche, aren't you?"

I nodded.

"In the morning. I'll give you a ride to the bus station."

I picked up my book. "Before I leave, I'd like to make sure the woman is OK."

"There's nobody in town named Molly." The sheriff shook his head and left.

- CHAPTER SIX -

Outside the diner the air smelled clean and fresh. Peach-colored clouds stretched across the horizon toward the setting sun. Looking at the town, you'd have had a hard time believing a tornado had passed through only an hour or so before.

The sheriff was waiting for me on the sidewalk.

"How come you picked Piedra Springs?" he said. "We make the middle of nowhere look like Times Square."

"Greyhound stopped here. I was tired of being on the bus." I paused. "How come you won't tell me about Molly?"

"Already did. I don't know anybody who fits that description."

The kid in the Dallas Cowboys jersey rode by on his bike, smoking a cigarette. We watched him until he disappeared.

"I never caught your name," the sheriff said.

I didn't reply.

"Quang Marsh." He held out a hand.

I shook. "Arlo Baines."

He gave me a curious look, the name clearly triggering a memory. Maybe he remembered an article in the paper or a segment on the local news, something about either the murder of my family or the subsequent deaths of those responsible. Maybe he'd had coffee with a state trooper who'd told him the story.

"Have a nice evening, Mr. Baines." He smiled. "I suggest you go to your room and stay there until morning."

I told him good night and crunched across the gravel in the empty parking lot of the Comanche Inn.

My room was on the back side of the building, out of view from the manager's office, which fronted Main Street. The furnishings were old but clean. A lumpy mattress. Threadbare carpet.

I stepped inside, clicked the dead bolt, and sat in the easy chair by the dresser, *The History of the Decline and Fall of the Roman Empire* in hand.

I read until it was time to go to sleep, and I tried not to think about my family or the woman named Molly and her children.

• • •

I woke before dawn, as was my habit. I showered, packed my rucksack, and went to Earl's for breakfast.

They had waffles, which made me think this was going to be a good day.

A new waitress was on duty, a woman in her fifties with hair dyed the color of eggplant. I asked her if she knew a woman named Molly. Turns out she did, the senior citizen north of town. That was her mother's second cousin.

I thanked her and placed my order: a waffle along with two scrambled eggs and three sausage patties. Minutes later, the meal arrived. I ate. Drank a half pot of coffee and an orange juice.

After breakfast, I headed back to the motel to read some more. I figured to give the Romans a half hour or so and then I would wander around town and look for signs of Molly and her children until it was time to catch the bus to Pecos.

I rounded the corner of the motel and saw Sheriff Quang Marsh standing in front of my room, banging on the door. His squad car was parked at an angle in front of my room, engine idling.

I called out to him: "You looking for me?"

He stopped banging and stared at my face like cops do when dealing with a suspect, the friendly demeanor from last night long gone.

"Little early to go to the bus station, isn't it?" I said. It was only seven fifteen.

"We're not going there just yet."

"How come?"

"You didn't tell me you were a cop killer," he said.

"That's because I'm not."

He was referring to the men who'd murdered my family.

They weren't cops, no matter what their credentials indicated. They were something that stuck on the bottom of your shoe and smelled bad. In any event, I hadn't even been charged, despite what the homicide squad had trumpeted to the media before the forensics came back.

Sheriff Marsh pointed to the vehicle. "Get in the back. We're going to the station."

The back of his unit was designed to hold prisoners. No inside door handles, a wire cage protecting the riders in the front.

"Five years since the last murder in this town," he said. "And then you show up."

"What are you talking about?"

He opened the rear of his squad car. "Pretty sure we found the woman you've been asking about, your friend Molly."

- CHAPTER SEVEN -

The interview room at the Piedra Springs sheriff's office was in the old courthouse at the end of Main Street. The room doubled as a conference area where officers met before going on shift. It had gray carpet and walls painted a pale green, dotted with human resources posters.

Several deputies hovered just outside, but Sheriff Marsh and I were the only ones in the room. We sat on opposite sides of a long folding table. The air smelled like coffee and copier toner.

"Tell me what happened," I said.

"That's not how this works. I'm the one who asks the questions."

He leaned back in his chair, arms crossed. Except for the fact that he was Vietnamese, he looked like the crooked sheriff in a bad seventies crime movie, the redneck lawman who'd just busted an innocent coed.

I waited, hands folded in front of me.

The sheriff said, "Tell me what you did last night."

"You mean after you saw me go to my motel room?"

He didn't answer.

"I read for a couple of hours and then went to sleep. By myself. This morning I got up and had breakfast, then headed back to my motel. Which is where you came in."

"Did you have contact with anyone during that period?"

"None whatsoever."

He jotted some notes on a yellow pad. Then: "One of my men found the body of a Caucasian female at 3:07 this morning." He paused. "The corpse was still warm."

I didn't respond.

"She was in the alley behind the bar where you were yesterday."

I stared at a bulletin board on the far wall, at a flyer for the upcoming Fourth of July parade. I wondered where I would be in July. Hopefully not in Piedra Springs.

The sheriff opened a file. He pulled out a sheet of paper, slid it across the table. "Is this the person you were asking about?"

The picture had been taken with a camera phone, reproduced on a color office printer.

The woman named Molly, the one who'd been so fearful of being killed, lay on her back in a puddle of water, unseeing eyes staring at the camera. The water had a reddish tint from the blood. The blood came from the gaping wound across Molly's throat.

"Yes. That's her."

I wanted to know about her children but didn't ask. These were tricky waters, and it was best to let the sheriff guide the conversation for the time being.

He flicked on a small digital recorder. "Can you account for where you were between two and three this morning?"

"I was in my room, alone." I pointed to the recorder. "You should have had that on from the start."

During my last two years with the Texas Rangers, I'd been a homicide investigator, called into places like Piedra Springs, small jurisdictions that couldn't afford a dedicated crimes-against-persons division.

Locals always did stuff like forgetting to turn on the recorder or contaminating the crime scene. Or worse, railroading a suspect.

He left the recorder running, walked across the room. He poured himself a cup of coffee.

"I'm good, thanks," I said. "Had enough at breakfast."

"You have a history of violence." He spoke without turning around. "You show up in town, and a few hours later there's a murder. You can see how this is gonna play out."

Anger boiled in my stomach. Memories from nine months before that would never go away.

"You don't know anything about my history," I said. "Don't act like you do."

He stirred sugar into his cup but didn't say anything.

"I have a history of being falsely accused," I said. "They tried to stick me with the murder of the men who killed my wife and children. Tried and failed."

"Sometimes the simplest answer is the right one." His voice was soft.

I took several deep breaths, tried to control the fury.

Images of my family flashed in my head, our last Christmas together mixed with three coffins in a row, the result of the evil that had come into our lives.

"You have children, Sheriff? You know what it's like to lose a loved one to violence?"

He returned to the table and sat down, a faraway look in his eyes.

"My father was a GI. Big ranching family over in the next county." He took a sip of coffee. "My mother was Vietnamese, worked for the Americans in Saigon. She died in a reeducation camp when I was five."

Score a point for Sheriff Quang Marsh in our undeclared game of who'd endured more pain and suffering.

We were silent for a moment.

"Any witnesses?" I asked.

"I'm not at liberty to discuss the case with a person of interest."

Translation: no. If there'd been witnesses, he would have led with that.

"You planning to charge me?"

I didn't see how he could. There wasn't even circumstantial evidence linking me to the death. But this was a small town that hadn't seen a crime like this in years. A man just off the bus with no ties to anybody would make a perfect suspect. A nice, neat package, albeit one unburdened with bothersome details like facts or evidence.

He took another sip of coffee but didn't say anything.

"What about her children?" I asked.

A blank stare.

I described the boy and the girl. "Any sign of them?"

"She was found alone. Don't know anything about any kids." He shuffled some papers, read a few lines. "You said her name was Molly."

"That's what one of the cowboys called her."

"One of the people you assaulted?"

I didn't reply.

"Do you know her last name?"

I shook my head. "She was afraid of those two guys, the ones you don't care for. You should look at them and their friends."

"You telling me how to do my job?"

I shrugged. "Just offering a suggestion."

A moment passed. Then he chuckled. "You are a piece of work. That's for sure."

"Did you check her prints?"

He nodded. "Nothing came up."

That was an odd turn of events. Just about everyone's prints are on file somewhere.

The FBI's database had records for more than 120 million people, 40 million of them with no criminal history. In addition, the State of Texas captured the thumbprints of anyone who had ever applied for a driver's license or an ID card.

"So she's not from Texas," I said. "And she's never been arrested. Maybe when you run her picture on the local news, you'll get a hit."

"I'm gonna need the blade you keep in your waistband." He pointed to my right hip.

"You are planning to contact the media, right?" I removed my Spyderco, slid it across the table. "That's standard procedure in a Jane Doe case."

He used a pencil to maneuver the knife into an evidence bag. Then he sealed the bag and marked it with his initials.

"Maybe you could just put her description in the local paper," I said.

"The *Piedra Springs Gazette* shut down ten years ago."

"How about the papers in Midland or Odessa?"

"That's the big city. You know what an ad up there costs?"

I didn't say anything. The price of advertising shouldn't be part of the equation. The murder of an unidentified woman was a news story, free coverage. His subtext was clear. He didn't particularly care to find out who the woman was.

He slid the evidence bag into the file and then looked at the door leading to the hallway like he was making sure it was closed. He leaned across the table.

"There's still time to catch the bus to Pecos."

I didn't say anything, running over in my mind the possibilities of a trap. I thought about the guys in the hospital in Odessa, the ones who were after Molly. Whoever they represented seemed like the most logical suspects. Unfortunately, no one had seen them with Molly but me.

"For your own good," he said. "You need to be on that bus."

I wondered about his sudden concern for my well-being.

What's the worst that could happen? He'd smear the victim's blood on my knife? Then put out a statewide BOLO on me? That was pretty bad, but somehow it didn't seem like Sheriff Quang Marsh's way of doing things.

I shook my head. "I'm not leaving until I find out what happened to the children."

He nodded slowly, like that was the answer he'd been expecting. "Then I bet we'll meet again."

"Who was Molly?"

He stood. Stuck the file that contained my knife under his arm.

"The guys in the parking lot," I said. "What do they have on you?"

He left the room, and I was alone.

- CHAPTER EIGHT -

I poured a cup of coffee and then sat back down in the empty conference room to formulate a plan.

My goal was simple—find the two children who had been with Molly. Make sure they were safe. They'd been as scared as she, the boy wounded.

Molly had been found by herself, throat slit. That meant one of three things.

One, her kids were killed somewhere else.

Two, the killer had taken them.

Three, they'd escaped.

My best educated guess was either two or three.

If the killer had wanted to murder them, he would have done so in the alley, along with the mother. For some reason, the person responsible struck me as a pro, better than the two guys I'd taken out. A pro wouldn't want to leave behind two crime scenes, double the chances of a forensics land mine exploding in his face.

So the odds were good that the children were still alive. Which meant someone had to find them, i.e., me.

This was an investigation, my wheelhouse. I didn't have a badge, but that almost seemed like a plus in this instance. Sometimes rules got in the way.

I made a mental list—interview potential witnesses, check out the crime scene, do a door-to-door. The basics of any case. Run down leads. Build a narrative.

A deputy entered the room, a heavyset guy in his twenties with red hair and a thick mustache.

"You need to *vámonos*," he said. "This ain't no Applebee's. You can't just sit here all day."

"How about I finish my coffee?"

The deputy looked at the cup in my hand—marked Piedra Springs Sheriff's Department—and the coffee urn on the far wall.

"Where'd you get that?" he said.

"There's still half a pot. Don't worry."

He squinted at me for a moment. Then: "We're fixing to have a meeting about the murder." He pointed to the door. "You need to git."

"Did you know the victim?" I remained sitting. "Ever see her around town?"

He frowned, obviously unsure of how to act with someone who looked like a cop and might or might not be a suspect. After a moment, he shook his head.

"What about her children?" I described the boy and the girl.

"Nobody knows anything about any children." He looked again at the coffee urn. "She was a damn drifter. We're probably never even gonna find out her name."

The official version was being constructed, piece by piece.

Molly was going to be described as a homeless person, a vagrant.

That meant nobody would notice if she went missing, so why expend too much energy trying to find out who she really was? As for her kids, well, there was only one person who claimed to have seen

THE DEVIL'S COUNTRY

them, a guy from out of town whom no one knew, technically homeless, too.

If he caught the next bus, and the official record didn't mention the presence of the children, then pretty soon it would be like they didn't even exist.

Noise in the hallway, feet shuffling, people talking. Officers gathering for their big meeting about the murder of Jane Doe.

I drank the last of my coffee. "Has Sheriff Marsh called the Rangers yet?"

Right about now, Marsh should be on the phone with the Texas Rangers, putting in a request for help with the murder, talking to the major in charge of Company E in El Paso. The major would begin the process, sending a message to the nearest substation, an office in Midland.

Midland would send an investigator, someone like me, a seasoned law enforcement officer who would look at everything with fresh eyes but without the prejudices of the locals.

The only prejudices he would have would be toward the solitary person of interest, a euphemism for suspect, a former Texas Ranger who'd brought shame upon the division when he'd been accused of murdering three police officers.

"Why would we get them involved?" the deputy said.

"Oh, I dunno . . . maybe to find out who killed the woman?"

The deputy crossed his arms. "You finished with your coffee yet?"

• • •

It was a little before nine in the morning. Outside the courthouse, the air was still and cool, the sun not yet hitting town with its full intensity.

I headed east toward Jimmy and Dale's and the parking lot where I'd last seen the woman named Molly. There was a fair amount of traffic

3

on Main Street, a half dozen pickups, double that of sedans. All of them American made. Rush hour.

That's what made the Bentley stand out, an expensive import in a pond of domestic vehicles. The automobile was the color of onyx, polished to a high gleam. It drove sedately down the street and then parked in front of the bank.

I slowed, stopping in front of the Dollar General Store across the street. After a few moments, when no one got out of the Bentley, I continued on.

A few hundred feet later, in front of a vacant store that had at one time been the local pharmacy, I stopped again.

A Toyota Prius, another out-of-place vehicle, was parked in front of the closed drugstore. The automobile had a small bar-code tag on the rear driver's side window, indicating it was a rental.

The driver's door opened and a woman exited.

She was in her midthirties, lean like a runner. She wore expensive-looking jeans that had been faded and ripped at the factory, a beige sport coat over a white T-shirt, and lime-green Chuck Taylor shoes.

An astute observer, such as a former investigator like myself, might surmise that she was from out of town.

"Hey. How you doing?" She spoke without smiling. Like small talk didn't come easily.

I stared at her, trying to figure out what a woman in designer jeans and hipster shoes was doing in Piedra Springs.

She stared back, unblinking. Her eyes had a way of looking at you like they were peering deep inside your head, a light shining in the dark corners you'd rather not have exposed.

"I'm fine," I said. "How are you?"

She pulled a small backpack from the passenger seat, slung it over her shoulder. "You know where the local appraisal district office is?" Her accent indicated she'd grown up a long way from Texas, somewhere in the northeast.

"No, sorry. I'm new in town."

In Texas, every piece of real estate was recorded and tracked by the county appraisal district for tax purposes. Owner's name, property location, value, that sort of thing. The appraisal district office seemed like a perfectly normal place for a woman from the East Coast to be asking about. She was probably researching a cattle ranch to buy.

Out-of-state Rancher Lady in her green Chuck Taylors and I stared at each other for a few moments.

"Where do you eat around here?" she said. "You been in town long enough to know that?"

"Earl's. Try the enchiladas." I headed toward the bar where I'd last seen Molly and her children.

- CHAPTER NINE -

Before I got to the bar, I stopped at the feed store and bought a new knife.

They had a good selection, kept in a glass counter between GPS tracking devices for livestock and the bovine antibiotics.

Gerbers and Bucks. Bone-handled Case XXs for the traditionalist. A handful of Spydercos and Benchmades.

I selected a Spyderco Endura with a 2.75-inch blade, half-serrated, half-plain-edged, and paid the elderly man behind the counter in cash.

"Heard you had some excitement last night." I stuck the knife in my waistband.

"Will there be anything else?" The old man wore overalls and a perpetual scowl.

"In the alley," I said. "Police must have been everywhere."

No response, just a blank stare.

I wanted to get the old man talking, to ask if he'd seen anything amiss in the area behind his store. I decided to try another avenue.

"Nice place you've got here." I smiled, tried to look nonthreatening.

The store was small but well stocked. On one side of the room were sacks of cattle feed next to big green blocks of salt and plastic barrels of deworming solution. The other side was devoted to items that might be needed by a working ranch or a busy dominatrix. Ropes and riding crops. Bridles and saddles. Rolls of barbed wire.

His scowl deepened, lips like two worms mashed together. "If there's not anything else," he said, "I've got inventory to tend to."

"Do you know a woman named Molly?" I described the victim and her two children.

Dead silence.

"She was killed behind your store last night."

More silence. Then: "You got any idea how old I am?"

I shook my head.

"Seventy-eight this last March."

I didn't reply. No sense rushing the man. I figured if you're pushing the big eight-oh, you've earned the right to take your time getting to the point.

"Best lesson I've learned in all that time is to mind my own business."

"I'll mark you down as a 'Negative' for knowing Molly."

Another moment of silence. He rearranged some pens on the top of the counter.

"You know what's good for you," he said, "you'd get out now."

I wondered if he meant his store or the town itself.

Everyone else in Piedra Springs had been friendly until this guy. Was he just a jerk or had something changed?

"Have a nice day." I smiled and left.

Next door, Jimmy and Dale's Broken Promise had a CLOSED sign in the window, but the door was unlocked, so I stepped inside.

All the chairs rested on top of the tables. Jimmy was mopping the floor. The air smelled like pine disinfectant.

"Heya, Jimmy. How's it going today?"

He jumped back, clearly startled, the mop handle pressed against his chest like it was a barrier. "Wh-what are you doing here?"

I sat at the bar. "Thought we could talk about what happened last night."

He didn't say anything.

"Did you hear about the woman?" I asked.

He began mopping again. "The one that got killed?"

"Yeah. Her."

He turned to a fresh section of floor. "I got work to do."

"Need any help?"

He didn't answer, just mopped faster.

"What time did you get out of here last night?"

He jammed the mop in the bucket, sloshing water everywhere. Then he resumed swabbing the floor, wiping back and forth furiously, the long part of his mullet swinging from side to side.

Molly's body had been found a little after three, still warm. Bars in Texas had to stop selling alcohol at two. They could stay open until whenever, but the booze had to stop flowing 120 minutes after midnight, which was when most shut down.

There was a lot of activity involved with shutting down for the night. You had to close out the register, restock the beer coolers. Make sure everything was shipshape. Then you had to lock up and turn on various alarms. I figured all of that might take forty-five minutes. Say, until a little before three.

"Did you go out the back way last night?" I asked.

He scooted the bucket to a different section of the bar, the area by the jukebox.

"I'm wondering if maybe you saw something when you left."

He stopped working and stared at the jukebox. He spoke without turning around. "You need to leave, OK?"

Jimmy had been a chatterbox last night, my new BFF. Now, he was like the guy at the feed store. Unfriendly, on the edge of hostile.

48

"What about her children?" I asked. "Have you seen or heard anything about them?"

Jimmy mopped furiously but didn't speak.

"You saw her children last evening, didn't you?"

No answer.

"A boy and a girl," I said. "You probably forgot to mention them to the sheriff when you were talking about me and those two guys in the cowboy hats."

He closed his eyes, muttered to himself.

"So who were those two guys anyway?" I asked.

He took several deep breaths, almost hyperventilating but not quite. His face was flushed.

"You OK, Jimmy? You're not looking so good."

"I just want to run my bar." Emotion choked his voice. "Is that so hard to understand?"

I didn't reply. We weren't that different. I just wanted to sit in a corner and read. Not be bothered. That raised the question: Was someone other than me interfering with Jimmy and his goal of just running his bar? Did that someone have anything to do with the death of Molly and the disappearance of her children?

He jammed the mop in the bucket so hard the latter tipped over, spilling liquid across the floor.

I slid off the barstool and took the mop from his hand.

He offered no resistance.

I sat the bucket upright and began sopping up the spilled liquid.

"You don't got to do that," he said.

I kept mopping.

He pulled a chair from a table and sat, shoulders slumped.

"Molly, or whoever she was, is dead," I said. "But her children, odds are good they're still alive somewhere."

He didn't say anything.

"Somebody needs to find those kids." I wrung liquid from the mop into the bucket. "And I'm afraid I'm the only one who's going to be looking."

Jimmy stared at the floor. "You ever wonder how things come to be the way they are?"

I shrugged but didn't reply. Most of the spilled liquid was back in the bucket. I decided to clean some of the floor. I began mopping by the bar, my back to Jimmy.

"Like that story about the frog and the water that starts to heat up real slow," he said. "You wake up one day and you're cooked. Hardly even noticed it getting hot."

"Tell me about last night, Jimmy." I didn't look up from my task.

One trick I'd learned as an investigator was to engage yourself in an activity while you conducted an interview. The subject would focus on what you were doing and be more likely to answer questions. I'd interviewed a CPA in Longview one time, got him to confess to killing his estranged wife with a garden hoe. I'd been sewing a button on a shirt during the interview.

The technique didn't work all the time, however.

"You need to leave," he said. "I'm not supposed to be talking to you."

"Who told you that?" I stopped mopping.

No answer.

I turned around.

He had a small pistol in his hand, not pointing at anything in particular, just in my general direction. He held the weapon like it smelled bad.

"You gonna shoot me, Jimmy?" I leaned the mop against the bar. "Did somebody tell you to do that, too?"

"I just want you to go. That's all." He put the gun on the table. Wiped his eyes.

"OK." I eased toward the front door. "But I'll be back."

"I know." He sighed heavily.

- CHAPTER TEN -

I left Jimmy sitting in his bar, a morose look on his face and a gun he clearly didn't want to use resting on the table.

Outside, the day had gotten warmer. The sky was cloudless, a pale, washed-out blue that promised a hot afternoon.

I stood in the shade by the front door of the bar and thought about where to go next.

Across the street, the breakfast rush at Earl's had ended. Only a handful of cars were parked in front, including the Toyota Prius driven by the out-of-town woman in the green canvas sneakers.

Jimmy's place was at the end of the block. The bar and the feed store shared a parking lot. The building next to the feed store was two stories tall, space for stores on the ground floor, offices up top. The structure was obviously vacant and looked like it had been built in the thirties.

I decided to check out the murder scene itself, the alley behind the bar. So I walked around the corner of the building and into the parking lot, the place where all this mess had started. Suzy and her date and the white van, the woman and the two children.

There wasn't a white van in the parking lot this morning.

Instead, there was an onyx-black Bentley.

The British auto was facing the alley, idling.

A man stood at the front of the Bentley, staring at the ground. He wore a black suit and white shirt. His hair was dark brown, almost black, and neatly trimmed. He was not tall or short, maybe five eleven, average build.

I walked between the wall of the bar and the Bentley. A figure sat in the passenger seat, an older-looking man eating an ice-cream cone.

The man in front of the Bentley didn't look up, though he must have heard me approaching. He continued to stare at the cordoned-off area, the spot where Molly had died.

I stopped a few yards away and took stock of where the murder had occurred.

Crime-scene tape ran from the back of the bar to the feed store, then across the alley, where it attached to the rear of another building.

In the middle of the area was a rust-colored stain about the size of a large pizza box.

The dark-haired man in the black suit was tieless, shirt buttoned at the collar. He was in his forties, with a face that was long and thin, a pointed jaw that matched his nose.

After a moment, he looked over at me and said, "Are you familiar with death?"

Not exactly the greeting I expected. Not, "Good morning. Hey, what about this weather? Can you believe somebody got killed right here?"

"Yes," I said. "More so than I care to be."

A single, errant gust of wind rustled through the parking lot. A crumpled piece of newspaper blew across the crime scene.

"The first time I saw a dead body was in Kuwait in 1991," he said. "The Iraqis left seventeen in a house in Jahra. All women and children."

His voice was soft, accent hard to place, the cadence formal, almost stilted.

"Hard thing to see," I said.

"Tears flowed from me that day." He clasped his hands in front of his waist.

Another piece of trash blew down the alley.

"The poem by John Donne." He looked up. "'Every death diminishes me.' I learned the truth of this statement in Kuwait."

We were silent. The boy from yesterday rode his bike into the parking lot from Main Street. He screeched to a stop a few yards on the other side of the man with the dark hair. The kid wore the same Dallas Cowboys jersey, No. 22, Emmitt Smith.

The man and I looked at him.

The kid stuck a cigarette in his mouth, lit it. "I heard somebody got killed. That's some cray-cray shit right there, let me tell you what."

He was older than I'd thought originally, probably closer to eighteen. He was small, though, and pale, like he didn't eat very well.

"Her name was Molly," I said. "Did you know her?"

The man strode to the boy and yanked away the cigarette, dropped it on the asphalt. "Smoking's bad for your health," he said.

"Screw you, old man." The kid gave us both the stink eye.

"This gentleman asked you a question." Mr. Bentley pointed to me. "Did you know the person who died here?"

The teen suggested Bentley Man perform an anatomical impossibility, a certain body part be inserted into a certain orifice. Then he rode off, middle finger held high.

"Kids today." I shook my head.

"The breakdown of the family unit," the man said. "No respect for their elders. Children running around like hooligans."

"I blame the Internet."

The man looked at me with a quizzical expression on his face for a moment. Then he stuck out his hand. "My name is Silas."

I shook, introduced myself. His skin was soft, grip firm. Up close like this, I could smell the Old Spice aftershave coming off him.

"Did you know the victim?" he said. "Molly . . . that's what you said her name was?"

"I met her briefly last night." I turned away from the bloody asphalt, looked at the Bentley. "Nice car. You live around here?"

Two unrelated statements, one a question. An easy way to keep someone off balance, see what they comment on first. The problem with this technique was that guys who own Bentleys usually aren't thrown off balance by some dude asking questions in the parking lot of a bar.

"God has blessed me and my family greatly, Mr. Baines." He handed me a business card. Plain black lettering with the man's name—Silas McPherson—and an address on a county road. Below that was a single phone number and an e-mail address. "Come see me before you leave town."

"How do you know I'm not from here?" I stuck the card in my pocket.

"An educated guess." He smiled.

"I'm not leaving for a while."

He cocked his head to one side.

"Molly had two children with her." I gave him a brief description. "They're still out there somewhere. I'm not leaving until I find them."

"If you need my assistance, please let me know. I have certain resources at my disposal that might help."

I glanced at his Bentley again.

The older man in the passenger seat was staring at a phone. For some reason, maybe because he appeared smaller than Silas, I got the impression he was the subordinate, an aide-de-camp.

"Do you know where the body is?" Silas asked. "Molly's."

The man in the passenger seat looked up from the phone. His eyes found mine. He smiled, a timid expression on his face. It was hard to tell because of the windshield, but it looked like one cheek was bruised or discolored somehow.

"If no one claims her," Silas continued, "I'd like to see that she gets a decent burial."

I looked away from the man in the passenger seat. "A burial?"

"Even the least among us deserves a proper resting place, don't you think?"

- CHAPTER ELEVEN -

I told Silas McPherson good-bye and left him in the parking lot, standing in front of his Bentley. I wondered what one did in such a desolate part of the world to earn enough money to buy that car. Oil or cattle, maybe. Or perhaps he made his fortune elsewhere and chose to live in the region for the peace and quiet and fine-dining options such as Earl's Family Restaurant.

A curious man, that Silas McPherson.

Yesterday, I'd seen a public library on a side street, closed at the time. The library would be open now, hopefully, and would have an Internet-connected computer.

The next step in this type of investigation was a door-to-door, asking people along either side of Main Street if they'd seen anything. The same for the street on the other side of the alley. With the number of places that were out of business, I didn't imagine that would take very long.

Also, after my encounters with Jimmy and the guy at the feed store, I wanted to learn a little more about the town of Piedra Springs and my new pal Silas. A few minutes on a search engine seemed like a good way to get up to speed on both topics.

I turned west on Main Street, walked past the feed store.

From the front window, the old man who'd sold me the knife watched me go, a sour expression on his face. Evidently, he had finished his inventory chores.

I waved and continued past the empty building.

The library was two blocks away, on Maple.

The next cross street was gravel, little more than an alley.

First Avenue, that's what it was called. I didn't recall seeing a Second or Third Avenue, and I wondered if the founding fathers of Piedra Springs had realized they were never going to be as big as New York, so they just stopped with First.

The four buildings at the intersection of First Avenue and Main Street were all empty. Dust covered their windows. Padlocks and chains dangled from their doors.

For some reason, the hairs on the back of my neck stood up. I walked slower and rolled my shoulders, trying to keep loose and ready. For what, I didn't know.

Maybe the beer bottles on the sidewalk bothered me. Maybe it was because the air smelled like old cigarette butts and stale urine. Maybe it was the slight sense of movement just out of my view.

Who's to say?

In any event, I wasn't all that surprised when they appeared, right as I got to the corner and was thinking about how easy it was for a town to go downhill when people used the sidewalk as a toilet.

There were three of them.

The middle guy was Suzy's date from the night before, the ex-con with the swastika tattoo on his forehead.

He had two friends with him, pale-skinned men in their thirties who looked like they were on their way to a Klan rally. The guy on the left wore a T-shirt with a Confederate flag on the front over a caption that read, IT'S A WHITE THING. YOU WOULDN'T UNDERSTAND.

The guy on the right had a tattoo on his forehead as well. Simplicity was its own virtue, I suppose, because his message to the world was a single word: RACIST!

They stood shoulder to shoulder, blocking my way.

I smiled, kept my tone friendly. "You fellows are on your way to the Barack Obama Appreciation Dinner?"

Dead silence.

The guy in the Confederate flag shirt looked at Suzy's date. "What the hell is he talking about, Chigger?"

"Chigger?" I said. "Is that your name?"

Suzy's date, now ID'd by his nom de guerre, flexed his fingers and glared at me.

"You dissed me last night," he said. "Messing with that girl's head, telling her I ain't good enough and shit."

Mr. Confederate Flag pulled a blackjack from his back pocket. The guy with the one-word tattoo slid a pair of brass knuckles over his fingers.

"Time you learn some respect," Chigger said. "A nice little tune-up, that'll do you good."

There was no one else on the street at that moment. Just the three human skid marks and me, all of us standing on a sidewalk that smelled like piss.

They were about ten feet away, clustered too close to one another.

I walked toward them, hands clasped over my breastbone, a non-threatening stance but one from which an attack could be undertaken quickly.

"Look, uh, Chigger. I'm sorry about last night."

Five feet to go.

Chigger smiled, flexed his fingers again, clearly looking forward to what was to come.

I kept walking. "See, I was having a bad day and—"

I feinted toward Mr. Confederate Flag. Then I uncoiled my arm like a striking snake and popped the guy on the right. The tips of my fingers squished into his eye.

The blow wasn't hard, but it didn't need to be. Eyeballs, they're really sensitive. No permanent damage, just a lot of pain.

The guy screamed like a hyena stuck in a blender. He staggered backward, hands to his face, and stumbled off the curb, landing on his back in the gutter.

I was aware of this only through my peripheral vision. As soon as my fingers had connected with his eye, I'd turned toward the man in the Confederate flag T-shirt.

He was standing still, which was the wrong move, rearing back his arm to hit me with the blackjack.

I kicked him in the knee with the sole of my shoe, another blow that didn't require a lot of force in order to be effective.

I can't speak for everyone else, but I imagine they heard what I did: the tendons in his knee snapping like a banjo string yanked too tight.

Note to self: next time don't use that much force.

He howled and fell to the ground, landing on an empty quart bottle of Schlitz. The bottle broke, instantly bloodying his arm.

Chigger, the smartest of the bunch, had jumped back. He was now out of reach.

"Where's Suzy?" I walked toward him. "For your sake, I hope you didn't hurt her."

He looked at his friends, no doubt wondering how his carefully laid plans to beat the crap out of me had fallen apart so quickly.

He pulled a pair of nunchakus from his back pocket, two heavy wooden batons connected by a piece of chain about eight inches long. The weapon of choice for generations of *Dungeons & Dragons* aficionados, kung fu enthusiasts, and others who lived in their parents' basements.

Across the street, a squad car stopped. No one got out.

"Be careful with those things," I said. "You're liable to hurt yourself."

Chigger swung the chucks around his head, over his shoulders, a redneck Jackie Chan.

I stepped back, looked around for a weapon. The broom handle from last night would have been perfect, but there was nothing similar within easy reach.

"What's the matter?" he said. "You scared of little old Chigger?"

Without warning, he swung for my head.

I jerked away but felt the weapon whizz by my scalp.

He chuckled, bounced on the balls of his feet, moved closer.

I eased back, shoes crunching on broken glass.

Mr. Flag, still on the ground, grabbed at my leg.

Chigger used the distraction as an opportunity to move in for the kill.

I raised my hand to ward off the blow, risking a broken arm instead of a concussion.

But the strike never came. Instead, Chigger screamed and dropped the nunchakus as my face burned and my vision hazed over.

I backed away, wiping my eyes until I could see.

Chigger, his face as red as a tomato, stood a few feet away, tears streaming down his cheeks.

The woman in the green canvas shoes was on the street, aiming a spray canister at him. She looked at me and said, "Are you all right?"

"Yeah, I'm good."

Chigger, temporarily blinded, moaned and accidentally stepped off the curb. He lost his balance and fell on top of the guy with the injured eye.

"Thanks for the help," I said. "But I had him just where I wanted him."

"Really?" She lowered the canister.

"More or less." I took several deep breaths, tried to slow my heart rate.

The woman looked across the street. I followed her gaze.

Sheriff Quang Marsh was leaning against the hood of his car, watching us, making no move to intervene.

The woman said, "How come he's just sitting there?"

"He's trying to make a point. We had a difference of opinion over when I would leave town."

She stuck the pepper spray in her backpack while I felt the adrenaline from the fight subside and anger take its place.

"A little advice," she said. "Don't beat up the sheriff. That's a losing proposition."

"I'll keep that in mind." I paused. "You always help people you don't even know?"

A wry smile crossed her lips, and for a moment she looked like a younger version of herself, softer, not so businesslike.

"I've been looking for you," she said. "The enchiladas at Earl's. They sucked."

- CHAPTER TWELVE -

Sheriff Quang Marsh watched as I strode across Main Street toward him. He was still leaning against the side of his squad car.

I paused in the middle of the road as the Bentley drove by between us.

The sheriff turned his attention to the British auto, watching the vehicle disappear to the west.

I finished crossing the street. The woman in the green canvas shoes followed me.

I stopped in front of the sheriff. "What the hell kind of cop are you, anyway?"

"What are you talking about?"

"Those guys attacked me. You just sat here and watched."

He peered toward where Chigger and his two buddies lay in front of the empty building.

"From over here," he said, "looked like you made the first move."

The woman pulled out a notepad and pen.

"Besides, everything worked out OK." He paused. "After your lady friend helped you with the last one."

The woman snorted. Scribbled on her pad.

"Usually a guy like you would have his deputies rough me up," I said. "Not contract out the job to a bunch of idiots."

He arched one eyebrow. "A guy like me?"

My face still burned. I wiped away tears. That's one of the dangers of using pepper spray. The mist tends to drift with the wind, causing collateral damage.

"I didn't contract out nothing," the sheriff said. "You got into that mess on your own."

Across the street, Chigger was standing now, leaning against his friend I'd popped in the eye. They were clustered around their buddy with the damaged knee.

"Guess I'd better call an ambulance." The sheriff sighed. "You're keeping the Odessa ER busy, that's for sure."

The woman glanced at me before continuing to jot on the notepad.

"That reminds me," I said. "How's the search going for Molly's children?"

Silence.

"You haven't looked at all, have you?" I said.

"There's a twelve-thirty bus going to San Antonio." He adjusted his gun belt. "The county would be more than happy to buy you a ticket."

"Who's Molly?" the woman asked.

The sheriff and I turned our attention her way. The sheriff said, "And who are you? I don't believe I've had the pleasure."

"Hannah Byrne. I'm a journalist." She paused. "With the *New York Times*."

The sheriff didn't say anything. His lips pursed, eyes squinted.

Cops hate reporters. All the questions, the Freedom of Information requests. The accountability. Hard to do good police work when there's some bleeding heart peering over your shoulder, second-guessing your every move.

"So you're not looking to buy a ranch?" I said.

"Huh?" She lowered her notepad.

"You asked about the appraisal office. Figured you wanted to buy a ranch."

"Do I look like a rancher?"

"Not really, but I try not to judge people by their appearances."

The sheriff cleared his throat. "Uh, what's the *New York Times* doing in Piedra Springs?"

"Working on a story," she said.

"What kind of story?" Sheriff Marsh asked.

"The decline of small-town America. So who's Molly?"

The sheriff stared at her, face blank. No one spoke for a few moments.

I filled the silence. "Molly is the name of a Jane Doe found last night with her throat slit."

Hannah scribbled furiously. "When's the last time you had a murder, Sheriff?"

Marsh didn't say anything.

"Five years ago," I said. "Isn't that what you told me, Sheriff?"

Marsh shot me a look full of daggers and venom.

"Can I get the name of your public information officer?" When he didn't answer, Hannah looked up.

"The county barely has money for coffee," I said. "They sure don't have the resources for a media relations person."

Sheriff Quang Marsh took a deep breath and hitched his thumbs in his gun belt. "An unidentified woman was found murdered this morning," he said. "Evidence gathered at the scene indicates she was a prostitute and that she got sideways with a customer."

"What evidence?" I tried to contain my anger. "What are you talking about?"

Not only was the woman going to be painted as a vagrant, now she was being labeled as a prostitute, a doubleheader in terms of someone people wouldn't care about.

If you wanted to be invisible in America, completely out of sight of mainstream society, be a homeless hooker.

"You need anything else, ma'am, drop by the courthouse." Sheriff Marsh tipped his hat.

"What about her children?" I said. "You can't just leave them out there."

Marsh ignored me. He smiled at Hannah, got into his squad car, and drove away, heading down Main Street.

I swore, kicked at the dust in the road.

Across the street, the three hoods had disappeared, skulked away to lick their wounds and plot revenge, no doubt. A pickup rattled past, headed out of town. Several Mexicans sat in the back, laughing with one another. Other than that, Piedra Springs was as quiet as a tomb.

"Tell me about the children," Hannah said. "What's your connection?"

I didn't reply. My face burned, though that was no longer from the pepper spray.

"What about the victim? Were you two friends?" Her tone was sharp, a reporter's pressing voice. Any hint of softness long gone.

I considered telling her the story—the men threatening Molly, her wounded son. But talking to reporters doesn't come easily to someone like me. So I stayed silent.

Hannah tried another gambit. "That sheriff's an interesting guy. What do you know about him?"

"You really doing a story on the decline of small-town America?"

She didn't reply, which was answer enough.

- CHAPTER THIRTEEN -

Eight Years Ago

There's a moment in a man's life when all that is good and hopeful is distilled into one instant. A feeling unlike any other. The strongest narcotic in the world, a flush of well-being that fills your body with warmth and light, the goodwill of those who came before you and the hope you have for the generations who will follow.

I'm talking of course about when a man holds his child for the first time.

My daughter. She was twenty minutes old, face wrinkly and sticky from afterbirth, tiny body swaddled in blankets.

She was beautiful, so wonderful and precious and full of promise that her mere presence left me tearful as I sat on the edge of the bed next to my wife.

Across the room, our son, two at the time, was playing with his grandfather, my father-in-law. The boy didn't understand what all the fuss was about. We'd told him there was going to be a new addition to the family, his baby sister. We'd impressed upon him how he was going to have to look out for her as they grew up.

That had been in the abstract. The day of her birth was the reality, and, all things considered, he'd rather play on Grandpa's phone.

"She's beautiful, isn't she, Arlo?" My wife stroked the newborn's tiny head.

I nodded, unable to speak.

"One of each," she said. "That's what we always wanted."

I kissed my daughter's temple.

A single tear slid from my cheek, dropping to the infant's forehead as a nurse entered the room and told my wife the baby needed feeding.

Frank, my father-in-law, hoisted the boy onto his shoulders. "Let's take a walk, little man. Give your sister time to have her first breakfast."

They left, and I handed the infant to my wife.

"Go with them, Arlo." She pointed to the exit. "You can't forget your firstborn just because someone new came along."

I looked at the door and then back at the baby.

"We'll be all right." My wife winked at me. "I promise."

"Won't be long." I slid off the bed.

Frank and my son were in the waiting room at the end of the hall, looking out the window above the hospital parking lot.

Frank was in his fifties, with silvery hair and a tennis-court tan. He was wearing a navy-blue polo shirt, pressed khakis, and boat shoes. He looked like he'd just come from the country club, which he probably had.

My boy grabbed his grandfather's phone again and scampered to a chair a few feet away. I watched him play with the device, remembering his birth in this very hospital not that long ago.

Frank stuck a piece of gum in his mouth. Sunlight reflected off the Rolex on his wrist. Frank always carried about him an aroma of Wrigley's Doublemint and Polo aftershave, to my mind the smell of prosperity and privilege.

"I sure am proud of you, son," he said. "That's a nice little addition to the family you've got there."

"Thank you."

The tears had stopped, but my heart still felt bigger than normal, about to swell out of my chest.

"You've treated my girl right, made her happy," he said. "From one man to another, I appreciate that."

I gave him a nod of thanks.

He chewed his gum, the sinews in his jaw flexing against his tan skin.

I waited for what was to come. There was always something else with Frank. He was a successful man, the president of a bank, a pillar in the community. Driven and competitive, continually in motion, always working on the next deal.

"How long are you planning to keep playing cops and robbers?" he asked.

I looked at my son across the room, wondered what his other grandparents would have thought of him. Of me and the life I'd fashioned.

My father and mother had been killed in a car wreck when I was twenty. I was an only child. My wife and my son and daughter were all I had. All I needed, too.

"I've applied to be a Texas Ranger," I said.

"Good Lord, Arlo." Frank sighed, smacked his gum. "You're bound and determined to make my girl a widow, aren't you?"

"I'm good at what I do. The Rangers will only make me better."

"The people you have to deal with. Common criminals. Murderers." He shook his head. "Aren't you afraid of bringing that home?"

I didn't answer. The gun tucked under my T-shirt, the weapon I always carried when off duty, felt heavy in my waistband.

We'd had variations on this conversation before, and I never knew how to explain the reality to a man like Frank. Being a cop was to be part of something larger than yourself. A fraternity, a group of people who would look after you and yours if the regular channels failed to do so. I tried one more time.

"You like what you do, don't you, Frank?" I said. "And you're good at it, too, right?"

He didn't answer.

"So how would you feel if someone told you to stop being a banker?"

He stared out the window. "Every day at work you wear a bullet-proof vest. What kind of life is that?"

"I'm a cop, Frank. It's my kind of life."

"You can be head of security at the bank." He turned away from the window, looked me in the eyes. "Make four times what you're earning now."

My parents had taken out substantial life insurance policies, money that I had never touched, left invested. I wasn't in the same league as my father-in-law, but I didn't lack for finances.

I shook my head.

"OK. Fine." Frank sighed again, just a little too loudly, and I realized that I'd been played like a tourist at a three-card monte game.

He pulled a notecard out of his back pocket. "Since you're dead set on staying in this line of work, how about you do me a little favor?"

Across the room, my son—Grandpa's phone in hand—squealed with laughter at whatever was on the screen.

My turn to stare out the window. I wished I were back in the room with my newborn daughter.

Frank held up the card. "This fellow wants to do some business with me. I need to find out if he's legit."

I took the card. Looked at the name, a man who owned a chain of strip clubs, among other, less savory business ventures.

Legit was in the eye of the beholder, I supposed. Always looking for the next opportunity, Frank on occasion dealt with people who were less than upstanding members of the community. The deal came first; the details were secondary.

"Follow him around for a day or two," Frank said. "See who he hangs out with."

"I'm not a private investigator." I returned the card.

"No, you're not." Frank smoothed back his hair.

I felt a weight settle on my shoulders.

"Do it for my daughter, then." Frank stuck the card in the pocket of my T-shirt. "Imagine you're doing her a favor, if that makes you feel better."

- CHAPTER FOURTEEN -

I spoke my wife's name out loud, the first time in weeks. Two syllables carried away on a hot breeze drifting through Piedra Springs, Texas.

The image of my infant daughter that day in the hospital was overpowering, the smell of her skin competing with the odor of Wrigley's Doublemint and Polo aftershave, the latter an odor I now associated with the darkness that is in every man's soul.

"What did you say?" Hannah Byrne looked at me with a quizzical expression on her face.

We were standing on Main Street, across from where the three hoods had attacked me. The day was heating up. Not a cloud in the sky.

"My father-in-law," I said. "He could sell life insurance to a dead man."

"What are you talking about?"

"You have any children?"

She looked at me for a second, then shook her head.

"Tell me about this big story you're working on," I said.

A few seconds passed. Then she said, "How about you tell me what your name is first, cowboy?"

I was wearing a black T-shirt faded to dark gray, a pair of Levi's, and lace-up work boots. Not exactly cowboy attire, but she was from out of town, so I decided not to call her on it.

"Arlo," I said. "Arlo Baines."

"You don't look like an Arlo."

"What do I look like?"

"I don't know." She sounded genuinely confused by me.

High overhead, a jet streaked across the sky, gray contrails stark against pale blue.

"The way you took down those guys," she said. "That was pretty impressive."

"Every now and then I get a little wood on the ball." I wiped sweat off my brow. "It's getting hot. See you around."

I headed for the library, my original destination.

She followed after me, canvas shoes slapping on the asphalt.

"Hey. Wait up."

I kept going.

"I want to know about Molly."

"Ask the sheriff." I reached Maple Street.

The library was to the right, across from a large brick building encircled by a chain-link fence. The First Presbyterian Church of Piedra Springs, now abandoned. A marble cornerstone read, FOUNDED 1879.

I stared at the church for a moment before walking on toward the library, a two-story limestone structure.

"You looking for something to read?" Hannah called out.

I stopped on the sidewalk in front of the library. Two granite columns were on either side of the entryway. Above the columns was a white plaster gable with words molded into the surface: CARNEGIE—1906.

"You know who that was?" Hannah stopped beside me. "Andrew Carnegie?"

There was a slight tremor in her voice, like she needed to clear her throat or her emotions were getting the better of her.

"He was a Scottish-American industrialist," I said. "What they used to call a robber baron. Made millions in the steel industry."

"Look at you. Being all knowledgeable." The tremor was gone.

"My parents were history professors." I began walking up the library steps.

Hannah called out to me again. "You know of any Russians or Eastern Europeans in town?"

I kept climbing. "In this town? You've got Piedra Springs confused with Houston."

"*Bratva.* Do you know what that means?"

I stopped halfway up, looked back at her.

"Russian mafia," I said. "Roughly the equivalent of a made man."

She nodded. "You're a cop, aren't you?"

"Was. Past tense. What's the Russian mob got to do with this dinky little town?"

"Two guys in New York. Both named Boris, but the bigger of the two, this guy tipped the scale at three and a quarter; they call him Fat Boris."

"What's the other one called? Regular Boris?"

"No, he's just plain 'Boris.' Anyway, these two are . . . *were* big-time into money laundering and cybercrimes. You know—identity theft, credit card hacks, that sort of thing."

I nodded.

She continued her story. "A week ago, the Borises were found in a dumpster in Queens."

I stared at the abandoned church across the street, wondering what was coming next.

"Their throats were slit. Just like your friend Molly's."

I didn't say anything. On average, fifty people were murdered every day in the United States. Surely a small percentage of those died from knife wounds to the neck.

"So what's that got to do with your being in West Texas?"

"Fat Boris, he had a burner phone in his pocket," she said. "The only number in the registry traces back here to Piedra Springs."

"Maybe he was looking to buy a ranch."

She didn't say anything.

"Could be spoofed," I said. "That's the most likely explanation."

Telemarketers had perfected ways to trick caller ID, to make a phone number in Vegas appear like it was in Florida; they called it spoofing. Hackers and other illegal operators often used the same techniques.

"I checked. The number's legit. Belongs to a pay phone across the street from that god-awful restaurant."

"The phone by the bar," I said. "Jimmy and Dale's."

Hannah nodded.

"That's the sum total of your story?" I said. "Morbidly obese Russian thug has friends in small West Texas town?"

She didn't say anything. The expression on her face indicated there was more, but she wouldn't be giving it up anytime soon.

I wondered what would bring the attention of somebody like Fat Boris to Piedra Springs. What scam is there to run in a place all but devoid of people and businesses?

"I'm staying at the Comanche Inn." She told me the room number. "Drop by when you're ready to talk about Molly."

- CHAPTER FIFTEEN -

The Piedra Springs Library was cool and quiet, the air thick with the musty smell of old paper and lemon furniture polish.

Books were everywhere, and I immediately felt comfortable and relaxed.

The house where I'd grown up had been full of the printed word, too. Works of history and political science, volumes on philosophy and anthropology. Novels, both classic and popular.

At the time, I'd not appreciated having ready access to so much wisdom and knowledge. I'd been a jock, an enigma to my soft-spoken parents, more interested in girls and football than in first-edition Hemingway novels and the complete works of Herodotus in the original Greek.

Now, I was a different person, but the books were gone, as were my parents. As was everyone else in my life who'd been important.

I looked around. There wasn't much else in the library other than printed materials and a small selection of DVDs. There certainly weren't many people, only two patrons that I could see. A Mexican guy in a rumpled suit reading the Sunday issue of the *Dallas Morning News* and an elderly Anglo man, leafing through an unabridged dictionary.

The librarian, a woman in her seventies, was perched behind the front desk. She was friendly, but she didn't know anybody named Molly, even the woman north of town.

She showed me to a computer terminal at the end of the reading table, opposite the old guy with the dictionary.

"Internet service isn't very good on this side of town," she said. "Cuts off a lot."

"Oh, for a good fiber-optics line." I smiled.

"Fiber what?"

"Never mind." I sat down at a computer that was at least a decade old.

The Internet connection was indeed dial-up slow, but within a few minutes, I had managed to learn a fair amount about Piedra Springs, *piedra* being Spanish for "stone."

The town had thrived up until the last few decades of the twentieth century, the population nearing ten thousand, almost double what it was today.

The primary industries were ranching and farming, the latter mostly north of town where the soil wasn't too rocky. Unfortunately, one too many droughts and the consolidation of family spreads into larger, agribusiness holdings had hurt employment and driven people to larger metropolitan areas.

The economic deathblow had come about fifteen years ago when the single biggest employer in the area, a prison in the south part of the county, had closed. The very remoteness of the area that made the place suitable for a correctional facility had made it too difficult to find qualified workers.

None of this helped explain the presence of a terrified woman in a prairie dress and the two thugs after her.

Across the table, the old man cleared his throat loudly, the sound like a goose being strangled. He looked at me like I was making too much noise by clicking the keys of the computer. After a moment, he opened the dictionary to a new section.

I returned my attention to the computer and googled Sheriff Quang Marsh.

Nothing out of the ordinary came up there, either.

A LinkedIn page that hadn't been updated in a while. A PDF newsletter announcing Marsh as a speaker at a conference in Abilene next month. Several pictures of the man in gym shorts, coaching a children's softball team sponsored by the First Presbyterian Church. One of the players was a girl about eight years old with the same Asian features as Quang Marsh, his daughter no doubt.

The date on the photos was three years ago. I wondered when the church had ceased operations. Probably not long after.

Next, I searched for Silas McPherson, but there were too many hits to sift through.

So I entered his name in quotes followed by a qualifying word: *Texas*. Still, there were pages and pages of results, many of them old census records and other historical documents from a hundred years ago.

I pulled out the business card he'd given me and entered the address. Nothing came up.

The search engine's mapping software placed a pin in the far southwestern part of the county, on a small road where no street view was available. The nearest thoroughfare with a view, a state highway a few miles to the east, showed nothing but an endless sea of rocky terrain, barren and bleak, except for the occasional mesquite tree and outcropping of cacti.

A satellite overview indicated no buildings at that location or nearby except for a large complex to the south, marked PIEDRA SPRINGS STATE CORRECTIONAL FACILITY—CLOSED.

Again, this set of facts was not all that remarkable. The satellite imagery that was freely available on the Internet was not in real time. A building could have been constructed on that road since the last flyby, though why on earth anyone would have a home or office in such a remote area was beyond me.

One last bit of data to forage for, the phone number on Silas McPherson's business card.

I entered the digits, pressed the "Search" button.

A business name appeared at the top of the page, ZL Enterprises, followed by an address in Midland. No indication as to what kind of company ZL Enterprises was or what type of commercial activity the firm engaged in. Just a name and an address associated with that phone number, neither of which matched what was on the business card.

I opened another browser page, copied "ZL Enterprises" into the search box. Pressed "Enter." And waited. And then waited some more.

After about half a minute, I tried to navigate to a new page just to see if everything was working properly. The browser went blank, followed by a one-line message: NO INTERNET CONNECTION.

Across the table, the old man looked up from the dictionary. "You think that machine has all your answers, do you?"

"Excuse me?"

"It's not working, is it?"

I stared at him for a moment and then shook my head.

"The information superhighway has a crack in it." He chuckled in appreciation of his joke.

"You know how to get back online?" I punched "Enter" again.

"Not hardly."

I looked toward the front desk. The librarian smiled at me and then got up and shuffled to the women's restroom.

"We're a long way from anywhere," the old man said. "Phone lines get damaged, power goes out. Pretty much on your own."

He was wearing a faded denim shirt, khaki trousers, and a long gray ponytail. A thick scar ran across one side of his forehead.

"You live in Piedra Springs?" I tried to reload the search page. Nothing.

"Most of my life. My great-granddaddy was born here in 1891."

"You know a woman named Molly?" I looked up, described the person I'd seen the night before. Told him about the children.

"Molly?" He stroked his chin. "Had a mule with that name one time. A right fine animal. Good teeth." He paused. "Does your Molly have good teeth?"

Oh joy. An elderly comedian. Just what my day needed.

"Beats me," I said. "Wrong species anyway."

A period of time passed. I restarted the computer to no avail while the old man continued reading from the oversize dictionary.

The Mexican in the rumpled suit carefully folded his newspaper and left. The librarian returned to the front desk. She was about thirty feet away, out of earshot.

Across the table, the old man flipped a page loudly. "I saw what you did to Chigger and his posse."

I looked up. "So you know he had it coming, then?"

"Chigger's had it coming since the day he dropped out of his mama's cooch in a gas station bathroom."

"When I have some free time, I'll feel sorry for him. Right now I'm trying to find the children who were with Molly."

I took a closer look at the old man's head. The scar was deep, tracking a slight indentation in the skull. I wondered if some of his wires had been crossed by whatever had happened to him.

"Next time you ought to just kill him," he said. "Save everybody a truckload a' trouble."

"I'm not a murderer."

He stared at me for a long few seconds. "Your eyes say something different."

"You're creeping me out." I stood. "See you around, pops."

"Where you going?" He leaned back. "Don't you want to see Suzy?"

- CHAPTER SIXTEEN -

The old man pushed himself out of the chair. He wore flip-flops held together with duct tape. The knees of his khakis were patched with different-colored pieces of cloth.

"You friends with Suzy?" I said.

"Let's go out the back." He pointed to a passageway between two bookshelves.

"Why not the front?"

"You scared to go into the alley with me?" he said. "After what you did to Chigger's crew?"

I didn't move. "Tell me about Suzy. What's your connection?"

"Me and her grandpa, we roomed together at Texas Tech."

The bell over the front door of the library tinkled.

"We might ought to hurry," the old man said.

The entryway was out of view from the reading table. The front desk was not.

The librarian nodded toward whoever had just entered, a friendly, welcoming gesture. She said something that was not quite audible from my location, a greeting probably.

I could make out only one word—*sheriff.*

The old man shuffled toward the rear exit. I waited an instant and then followed.

A few seconds later, we were behind the library on a narrow gravel track that ran perpendicular to Main Street.

Even the alley was desolate. No dumpsters or stray dogs, no bags of trash. Certainly no people.

He walked north, away from Main Street. I followed.

We crossed over to the next block. On one side of the alley was a relatively new strip mall, at least by the standards of Piedra Springs, built probably in the 1970s. On the other was a vacant, overgrown field.

From the rear, the strip mall appeared unoccupied, the back doors marked with the names of businesses that had long since gone away.

Robby's Shoe Store. Tiger Tan. Big Pam's Burger Shack.

The old man stopped at the last unit, a nail salon. He fished a key from his pocket, unlocked the dead bolt.

"Hold up, pops." I pressed a hand against the door, kept it from opening. "Tell me what's on the other side."

"Name's Boone. Not Pops." He rubbed the scar on his forehead. "Dr. Boone, if you're being formal."

"What kind of doctor?"

"Veterinarian. Specialized in large animals. Horses and cows, mostly."

"What happened to your head, Dr. Boone?"

"You don't have to call me that. I was joking. I'm retired now."

He looked like he wanted to say something, but the words wouldn't come. Instead, he leaned against the side of the building.

"You OK?"

"Headaches. They come and go." He closed his eyes. "I'll be all right in a sec—"

He fell, and I managed to catch his arms before he hit the ground. I eased him down so that he was lying flat on his back—standard procedure when someone loses consciousness, get the blood going to the brain.

I checked his vitals, which were good—pulse strong, airway clear. He was not in any immediate danger.

Someone on the inside of the nail salon opened the door a crack.

I stood, kicked the door in the middle, and then jumped to one side, back pressed against the wall.

A yelp from the interior.

I waited.

A few seconds passed. Then, movement. Feet shuffling. Heavy breathing.

"Boone? Are you all right?" A woman's voice, one I recognized.

Suzy.

I stepped away from the wall.

She stood in the doorway, staring at the old man on the ground. She was wearing the same clothes as last night. Her face was even paler, skin drawn around the eyes and mouth, except for one side where a bruise had formed high on her cheekbone.

"Hello, Suzy. How are you doing today?"

She didn't reply. She glanced at me and then back at Boone.

"How'd the date with Chigger go?"

"What's wrong with him?" She pointed to the old man.

"Beats me." I peered over her shoulder toward the interior. "Who else is inside?"

"Nobody." She rubbed her nose.

"Are you OK?"

"What do you care?" She stuck out her lip, all pouty.

"You got anybody else giving a damn about you right now?"

Silence. Boone stirred at our feet, groaning.

"Let's get him inside." I helped the old man stand.

The interior was dark and looked like it had been abandoned years before in midmanicure.

Along one wall were three workstations, each with jars of crusted polish and baskets of dusty cotton balls. On the opposite wall was a sofa and a coffee table. Old newspapers had been taped over the front windows. Cobwebs were everywhere.

Suzy and I maneuvered the old man onto the sofa. He was conscious now but not really awake.

"How are you feeling, Boone?" I checked his pulse again. Normal.

He mumbled something indecipherable.

"What's wrong with your head?" I asked.

No answer. I looked at Suzy. She shrugged but didn't say anything.

Outside, a car door slammed.

"Don't go down south tonight," the old man said. "The border ain't no good place to be."

"What's he talking about?" I asked.

"Dunno. He doesn't make much sense sometimes."

He snorted like he was mad but then closed his eyes.

"Where are we?" I looked around the room.

"Right now? This here is Boone's place." She pointed to the old man on the couch.

"He owns a nail salon?"

"Uh-uh. He owns the building." She paused. "Hell, he owns about half of downtown."

I glanced at the figure on the sofa.

He appeared to be sleeping, snoring softly. He looked like someone you might find passed out in a bus station toilet stall, proof that you should never judge a book by its torn dust jacket.

From the street came the sound of a second car door shutting.

I strode to the window. A corner of one of the newspapers had come undone. I peered through the hole.

A gray Chevrolet pickup with an extended cab was parked in front of the building across the street. The building was small, maybe two

or three offices total. A sign in the front window read PIEDRA SPRINGS
COMPUTER REPAIRS.

At the rear of the pickup stood two men.

They were of average height and build, wearing jeans and work
shirts. Completely unremarkable except for what was on their heads—
straw cowboy hats with Tom Mix creases.

Just like the two men who'd tried to take Molly and her children
last evening.

I watched the two guys and debated what to do. I was in enough
trouble already with the local authorities, and I didn't particularly want
to have another run-in with Sheriff Quang Marsh.

Suzy stood by the old man on the couch, looking lost and pissed
at the same time.

She put me in mind of another girl, one from a long time ago.
Made me wonder whatever had become of her, and if she'd been the
beginning of something bad or the end of something good.

- CHAPTER SEVENTEEN -

Five Years Ago
Interstate 35, just outside of Hillsboro, Texas

The truck stop was not the kind of place that advertised clean restrooms and hot coffee. It was the kind of place that drivers talked about in code on Internet forums, a location to score crank or weed or a lot lizard, the latter a prostitute who scurries from rig to rig like a reptile.

I'd been assigned to a human trafficking task force the feds were running, an operation designed to stop the flow of women from south of the Rio Grande to the brothels of North America, at the time a large ancillary source of cash for the drug cartels.

We'd busted a driver with a trailer full of Guatemalan teenagers, and the feds were doing the paperwork while I checked out the other eighteen-wheelers on the premises.

The last vehicle wasn't a truck. It was a late-model Mercedes, an S-class sedan.

The driver was Caucasian. Midforties with slicked-back hair and a starched, white, button-down shirt. An expensive gold watch on one wrist, a matching bracelet on the other.

He rolled down his window.

"What's the problem, Officer?"

"I need to see your license, sir."

I stood a little behind the driver's door. The angle made it easy to see the man's hands but hard for him to use a weapon against me.

"Did I do something wrong?" He made no move to get his license. "I'm just sitting here."

His tone was pleasant but forceful, the way he might address a waiter who'd forgotten to refill his water glass.

"Sir, I need to see your ID."

He nodded toward the cluster of federal agents. "Looks like you got your hands full over there. Why you messing with me?"

His tone was less pleasant. People in expensive cars were used to getting their way.

"No one's messing with you." I paused. "But you need to show me your license *now*."

The front passenger seat was empty.

I sensed movement behind the tinted windows in the rear. I stepped back, put my palm on my weapon.

"Out of the car. Right now."

"Whoa there, buddy." He held up his hands. "Let's not get carried away."

"Who's in the backseat?" I drew the gun.

The cartels were known to employ extra guards, third parties who traveled separately and were not easily identifiable as being part of the smuggling operation.

A white guy in his forties in a luxury automobile didn't fit that profile, but a lot of law enforcement officers were dead because they let down their guard at the wrong time.

He stared at the muzzle of my gun. There was no fear in his eyes, only a mild sense of irritation at his time being wasted.

"My daughter's in the back," he said. "You gonna shoot her, too?"

"Not unless I have to. Now get out of the vehicle."

He stared at me for a long few seconds. Then he opened the door with one hand, the other held so it was in view.

I kept my gun aimed. "Real slow and we won't have a problem."

He pulled the handle and swung open the door. His movements were precise and cautious. After a moment, he stepped out, hands up.

I flung him around the open door and onto the hood of the car, facedown.

Then I peered in the back of the Mercedes through the windshield, gun at the ready.

The girl was maybe fifteen but more likely not, certainly too young to drive yet. She appeared unarmed.

She was wearing a plain white T-shirt that was smudged with dirt like she'd been rolling on the ground. She was thin, her skin pallid, pupils dilated. Her face was dirty, too.

"What's your name?" I asked.

No answer.

"That's Emily," the driver said. "It's OK, sweetie," he shouted. "Everything's gonna be all right."

I lowered my gun. "Are you OK, Emily?"

Silence. The girl didn't even look at me. She just stared straight ahead.

I holstered my weapon and gave the man a quick pat down, pulling a cell phone from his front pocket and a wallet from his back. In the billfold, I found his license. I dropped both wallet and phone on the hood next to the man's head but held onto the license.

"Talking, that's not her thing," the driver said. "She's autistic."

The man's name was Dirk Wilson, home address in a ritzy part of Dallas. I read his particulars into my radio, asked Dispatch to run a check for wants and warrants.

"She looks junked up," I said.

The man didn't say anything.

"Has she taken any drugs?"

"What kind of father do you think I am?" He sounded angry.

I tossed his license on the hood. "The kind of father who brings his daughter to a place like this."

Across the parking lot, the Guatemalans had emerged from the trailer and were blinking into the bright light, staring at their new surroundings. It was July, the middle of the afternoon. I could only imagine the smell coming from the trailer.

"You're making a big mistake, Officer." Dirk Wilson shook his head. "You have no idea the trouble you're getting yourself into."

There was the line I'd been waiting for. Cops were always making "big mistakes."

"What kind of work are you in, Mr. Wilson?" I picked up the man's phone.

"I'm in the real-estate business. I'm a developer. Can I get off the hood of my car now?"

The device was password protected.

"Not yet." I held on to the phone. "Tell me why you're hanging out at this particular truck stop. You thinking about building a shopping mall here?"

"I was just getting some gas. No law against that, is there?"

The pumps were a hundred yards away, close to the highway entrance. The Mercedes was parked by the back fence. The ground was littered with cigarette butts, broken beer bottles, and more than a couple of used condoms.

My radio squawked, Dispatch calling. Dirk Wilson was clean. No wants or warrants.

I pulled him off the car. "Lean against the hood. Keep your hands visible."

"Thank you, Officer"—he peered at my nametag—"Baines."

"The girl, Emily," I said. "Is she on any prescription medication?"

He smoothed his shirt and smiled at me like he was thinking of a joke, something not all that funny, just mildly amusing.

"A Texas Ranger. You think that makes you a big man or something?"

"So she's not on any meds as far as you know?"

No answer. Just a smirk.

"Does she have any ID?"

"She's fourteen. Of course not."

I peered in the backseat. "Can you tell me your name, honey?"

Silence.

"Do you know where you live?"

"I cannot believe you are doing this." Wilson shook his head. "She's autistic. She can't talk."

The girl crossed her legs, one arm draped across the seat back, a faint smile on her lips. Her eyes were no longer quite as glazed. They were hard and cold.

In that moment she appeared older than her years, aware of her sexuality in ways that a fourteen-year-old should not be.

I looked at Dirk Wilson. "Where is she on the spectrum?"

"Huh?"

"She's autistic, right?"

He hesitated, then nodded.

"So where does she fall on the spectrum? Does she have Asperger's? Or Rett syndrome?"

No answer. A hint of fear crossed his face before being replaced with anger.

"The last one," he said. "She has, uh, Rett syndrome."

We were both silent for a moment. A police helicopter flew overhead.

"She doesn't have ID," I said. "She looks like she's doped up, but you can't or won't tell me if she's on any meds."

"Where are you going with this, Baines?"

Some officers would look at the facts, taking into account the obvious social standing of the man, and let him go. Others, like me, would follow the more prudent route and call CPS so they could sort everything out.

I started to answer the man, to tell him I was sorry but I was going to have to verify that the girl was in fact his daughter and that she wasn't in any peril, either from her own actions or those of others. I was going to tell him there was too much that didn't add up about the situation so I would be getting Child Protective Services involved.

An abundance of caution, that was the phrase I planned to use in my report.

That was what I planned to tell the man.

But his phone—still in my hand—rang, and my father-in-law's name popped up on the screen.

Three minutes later, I let Dirk Wilson drive away with the girl.

She watched me from the rear window as the big Mercedes sped across the parking lot, and I wondered what would become of her.

- CHAPTER EIGHTEEN -

From the window of the abandoned nail salon, I stared at the two guys across the street, standing by their gray pickup in front of the computer shop.

They weren't the same people who'd tried to assault me the night before, but their clothing was similar, their hats identical. They were hard-looking—faces weathered, arms ropy with muscle. Men who would give others pause, make people cross the street.

Unlike the nail salon, the computer repair business appeared to be a going concern. An **OPEN** sign hung in the window, and a couple of cars were parked in front.

"Suzy," I said. "Come here for a second, will ya?"

She sauntered to where the gap in the newspaper was. Boone, the old veterinarian, was still on the couch, eyes closed.

I pointed to the hole. "You know who those men are?"

She peered outside. Shook her head.

"Two guys with the same kind of hats," I said. "They were in the bar last night."

She looked again. "This is Texas. Lots of people wear hats."

"Cowboy hats exactly like that, the crease higher in the back than in the front?"

She didn't say anything.

"They were driving an extended-cab, gray Chevy, just like that one. That ring a bell to you?"

She didn't answer. Instead, she took a sharp breath, leaned closer to the hole.

I pushed her away, looked outside.

Chigger—face still red from the pepper spray—stood in the doorway of the building across the street, talking to the two men.

"What's he doing over there?" I said.

"Maybe he got a job. He's good with computers. Least that's what he told me last night."

Whatever his skill set, at the moment Chigger didn't appear to be very happy. The two cowboys kept pointing to their pickup. Chigger kept shaking his head.

Suzy ripped another hole in the paper so she could see what was going on, too.

"I hope they kick his ass," she said.

"What did he do to you?"

Silence.

"Tried to warn you," I said.

A choked sob.

I pulled away from the gap in the newspaper. "Sorry. I didn't mean to—"

"His phone." She wiped her eyes. "He wanted to take pictures."

"What kind of pictures?"

"You know . . . while we were doing it."

A moment of silence passed.

I said, "Did he rape you?"

"That's an ugly word." She crossed her arms. "Why would you say something like that?"

92

I looked back outside, where Chigger and the two men were continuing their discussion.

"Besides, I probably led him on," she said. "I'm always doing that,
seems like."

"You *led him on* to give you a black eye?"

No answer.

Some people couldn't be saved, even from themselves. Especially
from themselves.

I described the woman from last night and told Suzy what had
happened to her. Asked if she knew anybody named Molly who looked
like that. She told me no.

While I debated what to do next, the men by the computer store
flanked out just like the others had the day before, going on either side
of Chigger. They clearly wanted him to get in the truck, and he just as
clearly did not want to. But he didn't go back inside, either. Probably
realized there wasn't anywhere he could run to if they were determined
to take him.

I strode to the front entrance.

"What are you doing?" Suzy said.

I flipped the dead bolt and stepped outside. The blinds on the door
rattled, the sound loud in the stillness of the day.

The two men and Chigger turned and looked at me.

I marched across the street, hands loose at my sides like Gary
Cooper in *High Noon*. Except I was carrying a folding knife, not a
six-shooter.

"What the hell are you doing here?" Chigger's eyes were wide.

"Go inside," I said. "Your friends and I need to have a little visit."

Silence. The two thugs looked at me like I was from Pluto. After a
moment, they turned their attention back to Chigger.

The leader, a heavyset guy with a goatee, said, "Don't go inside,
Chigger. That'd be a bad move."

Even though the temperature was well into the nineties by now, Chigger shivered.

Mr. Goatee said, "If you go inside, I'll torch the building. You'll have to come out then."

Chigger looked at me, his expression filled with fear.

I sighed heavily, not believing that I was going to have to defend this Aryan douche canoe. "Nobody's torching anything, cowboy."

Neither man spoke.

I looked at the two thugs. "Last night some of your friends tried to kidnap a woman named Molly."

Up until now, they had been moderately relaxed. At the mention of the name "Molly" they stiffened and looked at each other.

"She got away," I said. "Along with her two children."

The guy with the beard nodded once. His underling walked to the driver's side of the pickup and got behind the wheel.

I stepped between Chigger and Mr. Goatee. Chigger was about six feet behind me, standing to one side of the building's front steps. Goatee was the same distance in front of me.

"Somebody—I'm guessing your two friends—killed her a few hours later."

The guy behind the wheel of the pickup cranked the engine.

Mr. Goatee shook his head. "You are intervening in matters that don't concern you."

His diction and word choice were odd.

"What are you?" I said. "A college professor in your off hours?"

"Divine matters," he said. "Righteous retribution awaits you."

"Whatever floats your boat, God Man. But one way or the other, I'm going to find those children and make sure they're safe."

Mr. Goatee was a pro, much better than the two clowns last night. He moved like a finely tuned, extremely fast machine, pulling a gun from the rear pocket of his jeans, a black, semiautomatic pistol.

There was no time to react other than to drop to the ground as his arm brought the weapon toward me.

I was moving much too slowly, like a flat stone drifting downward in a pool of warm water.

The muzzle arced closer and closer. I represented a huge target, and he stood only six feet away. No way was he going to miss.

He didn't.

Two rapid shots, so close together they sounded like one long boom.

The bullets found their mark, striking Chigger in the torso.

I finally landed on the pavement right about when Chigger died. He staggered a couple of steps and fell on top of me.

His blood was warm and sticky. One of his arms draped across my face.

I tried to move the limb, but somebody grabbed my hand and pressed my fingers around a hard object, a piece of plastic shaped like a pistol grip.

I yanked my hand away.

Metal clattered by my head.

I managed to shove Chigger's arm off my face and saw the pistol a few inches away.

Mr. Goatee ran to the passenger side of the gray pickup.

I reached for the gun but stopped once he got in the Chevy. No sense putting even more of my prints on the thing. A moment later, the pickup sped away.

And that's how Sheriff Quang Marsh found me a few seconds later.

Hand poised over the gun used to kill the guy on top of me.

- CHAPTER NINETEEN -

They put me in jail this time, deep in the basement of the courthouse.

They took my new knife, my wallet and watch, and the belt I was wearing. A deputy I'd never seen before fingerprinted me and swabbed both my hands to determine if I'd fired a weapon recently.

When he was finished, he stuck me in a cell. A few minutes later the red-haired deputy who'd run me out of the conference room earlier brought me a hand towel and a bar of soap and told me to clean myself up. There was a sink-toilet combo in the corner, so I washed off as much of Chigger's blood as possible. Then I rinsed out my T-shirt. When I was finished, I hung the shirt to dry on the bars of the cell.

About an hour later, the same deputy brought me lunch—a bologna sandwich, a bag of chips, and a bottle of water.

I took the food and said, "I want to talk to a lawyer."

The deputy left without speaking.

I ate. Then I waited.

Another couple of hours went by. It was maybe three or four in the afternoon when the redheaded deputy came back and told me to put on my T-shirt. I did so even though it was still damp along the seams. The deputy cuffed my hands and led me upstairs to the conference room.

This time two people were sitting at the table: Sheriff Quang Marsh and a man in his fifties, the latter wearing a starched khaki shirt, a straw cowboy hat, and an ivory-gripped semiautomatic pistol on his hip.

The guy in the hat was a Texas Ranger named Aloysius Throckmorton, one of the most vocal of my colleagues in demanding my dismissal from the organization. He thought of me in the same terms that a pest-control man would have a cockroach—something nasty that needs to be eradicated.

Throckmorton was old school, as hard as granite, with all the warmth of a concentration-camp guard. Rumor had it that he once used a machete to hack off the kneecaps of an abusive pimp and then left the man to the mercies of the street, specifically his stable of battered prostitutes. This was in El Paso, where stranger things had happened, so most people believed the story to be true.

A clear plastic bag sat in front of Sheriff Marsh. The bag held a gun that looked like the one used to kill Chigger. Next to the bag rested several sheets of paper.

The deputy sat me in the chair across from the two officers. He didn't remove my cuffs.

Throckmorton pulled a can of snuff from his back pocket. He put a pinch in his mouth and said, "Afternoon, Arlo. How you doing today?"

"I want to talk to a lawyer."

"People in hell want ice water," Throckmorton said. "Don't mean they get it."

I rattled the handcuffs on my wrists. "This any way to treat a former colleague?"

Throckmorton smiled. "Protocol. You understand how it is."

Sheriff Marsh stared at the far wall, his face blank.

"Two murders in twelve hours." Throckmorton shook his head. "That's some kind of record around here, I bet."

I didn't respond. No lawyer, no talking.

"And you're up to your ears in both of 'em." He spit into a Styrofoam cup. "Hell, you got in a fight with the second vic not an hour before he got shot."

My T-shirt felt itchy from air-drying. The fabric still had a faint smell of blood and sweat, along with a heavier odor of cheap soap.

Throckmorton looked at Sheriff Marsh. "You know about my boy here, don't you?"

The sheriff continued to stare at the far wall.

"Killed three police officers." Throckmorton paused. "And got away with it."

I took slow, deep breaths. It wouldn't have taken a fortune-teller to predict that the Texas Ranger would bring that up. A cop killer who walked—that was my personal brand in certain law enforcement circles. Even though crooked cops had murdered my family, to many fellow officers, that hadn't mattered, since those responsible had been popular and well connected politically, certainly more than I was at the time.

For a moment I debated telling the rest of the story, about my father-in-law's fingerprints being found on the gun, not mine. But I decided that under the circumstances, the less I talked about fingerprints on guns, the better it would be.

I glanced at the papers in front of Sheriff Marsh, recognized them.

"I see you have the results of the gunshot residue test," I said. "So again, how about taking off these cuffs?"

He pulled a page from the bottom, held it up for me to see.

Two enlarged fingerprints.

One was clear and easy to see, whirls and ridges as distinctive as roads on a map. It probably came from my personnel file at the state.

The second was smudged, hard to read, a partial print. Not something that could be used definitively to identify who'd held the item in question. The second one no doubt had been lifted from the murder weapon.

I didn't say anything.

The gun used to kill Chigger was a Glock. The grip was stippled on all four sides, dotted with hundreds of tiny bumps. Stippling made a gun easier to hold but harder to retrieve a good fingerprint.

Throckmorton put down the paper with the prints in front of me. "You want to tell me about this?"

Sheriff Marsh got up without speaking.

I watched him walk to the window on the far wall. Once there, he just stood in front of the glass and stared outside. I turned and faced Throckmorton.

"Let's talk about the results of the gunshot residue test instead."

Throckmorton didn't reply. A muscle in his jaw twitched, but his eyes were unblinking.

"My guess is the test was negative," I said.

No response.

"And the partial print." I nodded toward the paper. "That looks like a low-probability match, probably ten percent or less."

Throckmorton pulled the other papers closer. He read the top page. He didn't say anything.

The nearest criminal defense attorney was probably two hours away. The nearest good one—El Paso or Fort Worth—would need the better part of a day to drive here.

I decided to cooperate. A little.

"You want to know what happened?" I asked.

Throckmorton looked up, face blank. He didn't speak.

I described the two men and the pickup truck, a late-model Chevy, extended cab, gray, parked so that I'd not been able to get a look at the license plate.

Throckmorton pushed away the papers and listened.

I related the conversation between the men and the victim, as well as Chigger's obvious reluctance to go with them. I described how the guy with the goatee pulled a gun and fired twice into Chigger before driving away. I didn't say anything about how he'd forced my hand to grasp the pistol. No sense giving them any more info than was absolutely necessary at this point.

I told Throckmorton about Chigger and Suzy and their date the night before. Said Suzy could corroborate everything because she'd been watching from the abandoned nail salon.

Sheriff Marsh spoke from behind me. "We searched that building. It was empty."

"What about the old man?" I turned around. "What about Boone?"

"The old vet?" Marsh snorted. "That mush-head never leaves his house. What the hell would he be doing there?"

Throckmorton looked at the sheriff. "How about the pickup? You know anybody in town who drives a rig like that?"

"Shitballs," Marsh said. "Whose team are you on? Nobody in the county has a truck like that. He's making it all up."

"So let's go over the stuff that you know to be true." I ignored the sheriff, spoke to Throckmorton. "You've got a partial print that might or might not be mine on the murder weapon."

Silence. Throckmorton read the papers again.

"You've got a gunshot residue test that probably shows only a few trace particles on my hands," I said. "Consistent with someone six or seven feet away firing in my direction."

Throckmorton looked at me and then over my shoulder at Sheriff Marsh.

Marsh swore.

Throckmorton heaved a sigh and looked back at me. "Let's talk about the dead hooker from last night. The one you were chattin' up."

"I've known a hooker or two in my day," I said. "She wasn't one."

Throckmorton spat into his cup again.

I continued. "Let's talk about her children."

Another muttered curse from behind me.

"A boy and a girl," I said. "Ask the sheriff why he doesn't want anybody to find them."

The blow came from nowhere, a blinding starburst of pain on the side of my face.

One moment I was sitting in the chair, talking to Throckmorton, the next I was on the floor, wiggling my jaw to see if it would still work.

"Who the hell do you think you are?" Sheriff Marsh stood over me, fist raised. "Coming into my town and killing people."

From the other side of the table, the sound of a chair scooting back.

Marsh leaned down and struck me again in the face, the opposite side this time.

I saw the punch coming, so I rolled away and avoided the worst of it.

That was good for my face but not for my temper.

Now I was mad. I kicked at him with one foot, connecting with his leg. He fell, landing a few feet away with a thud.

He stared at me, eyes like slits, anger coming off him like a wave. He pushed himself up, grabbed an ASP baton from his belt.

I kicked at him again but missed.

He extended the metal baton to its full length.

I was helpless. On the floor, hands cuffed behind my back.

Throckmorton appeared in view. He grabbed the baton. "Back off, Marsh."

The sheriff took several deep breaths, regained his composure. "Let's get this piece of shit back in the cell where he belongs."

Throckmorton pulled me to my feet.

"What's the charge?" I asked.

"Assaulting an officer," Marsh said. "Let's start with that."

"I assaulted you while I was handcuffed?" I said. "Isn't that the point of handcuffs?"

Throckmorton shrugged.

"I want a lawyer."

Sheriff Marsh headed toward the door. "I'll get a deputy to take him downstairs."

Throckmorton shook his head. "We ain't putting anybody back in the cell right now."

Marsh stopped, an astonished look on his face. "Come again?"

"You don't have enough," Throckmorton said. "If we put away this bastard, I want to make sure we do it right this time around."

Marsh spun on me, his face purple with rage. "Get out of my town, Baines. Take the bus or rent a horse. I don't give a shit how. Just get out. *Now.*"

Throckmorton, a curious look on his face, stared at the sheriff. Then he pulled a key from his belt and unlocked my cuffs.

I touched my cheek. A spot of blood came away on my palm. Marsh must have backhanded me with the first blow and his ring broke the skin.

"Arlo's not going anywhere," Throckmorton said. "He's still a person of interest. We need to keep him close."

Sheriff Marsh clenched his fists. A vein in his neck throbbed.

Throckmorton looked at me. "If you leave the county, I'll throw you back in a cell so hard your grandkids will feel it."

I didn't say anything. Sheriff Marsh had attacked me when I'd mentioned the children to Throckmorton. The altercation had the effect of abruptly stopping that particular conversation. Now he was in a lather to get me out of town even though the proper protocol, as pointed out by Throckmorton, would be to keep me around.

The children were the key.

"All right, I'll stay," I said. "But no more talking without a lawyer."

Silence.

"When I come for you," Throckmorton said, "ain't no lawyer in the world gonna be able to save your ass."

- CHAPTER TWENTY -

The red-haired deputy handed me a manila envelope full of my personal belongings.

We were in the main office of the sheriff's department, a large area on the ground floor of the courthouse. No other deputies were around. The sheriff had remained in the conference room with Throckmorton. He'd sent a text, authorizing my release.

"What happened to your face?" the deputy said.

"Sheriff Marsh didn't like it when I asked about the dead woman's kids."

"She didn't have kids," he said. "She was a hooker."

"What the hell does that mean? You think prostitutes can't have chi—" I squelched my anger. Took a deep breath. "So what's Marsh's connection to the guys in the hats?"

A blank stare, like he was trying to understand what I meant.

"And why is everybody so worried about Molly?" I said.

I didn't really expect an answer, but he struck me as being a few bars short of full cell coverage, so I figured *what the heck.*

The deputy crossed his arms. "Why don't you quit asking question and just leave town?"

"I'm a person of interest in a murder," I said with no small amount of satisfaction. "The Texas Rangers won't let me."

He frowned.

"Thanks for bringing me lunch." I headed for the door.

•   •   •

Outside the courthouse, the air was hot and dry. It was a little after four thirty in the afternoon, and the town was preparing to shut down.

A man in a western-style brown sports coat stood on the sidewalk, talking on a cell phone. When he ended his call, I asked him if he knew where the county appraisal office was. He directed me to a one-story brick structure a couple of blocks away, just off Main Street.

The building was small but new, with a handicap ramp running along the front and a large flagpole set in the lawn.

An elderly man wearing a Snoopy necktie and a short-sleeve dress shirt was lowering the flag when I walked up the sidewalk leading to the entrance.

According to the sign by the door, the appraisal office's hours were from nine to five, Monday through Thursday. It was now 4:50 p.m. on a Wednesday.

I entered anyway.

A woman wearing a pair of oversize rhinestone eyeglasses and a pink pantsuit sat behind the front desk, reading a romance novel. She was in her seventies with hair the color of steel wool, done up in a towering bouffant. The nameplate on her desk read OPAL SMITH.

"We close in ten minutes." She flipped a page.

"I need to do a search on an address."

"Can you do that in ten minutes?" She glanced up.

"Probably."

She squinted through the glasses. "What happened to your face?"

"I fell down."

She didn't say anything. A frown formed on her lips.

"Do you know a woman named Molly?" I described last night's murder victim.

"That the person who got killed?"

"Yeah. Her."

The old man in the Snoopy tie came inside carrying the folded flag.

"Ten minutes, Opal." He disappeared into a room marked EMPLOYEES ONLY.

"You probably should get on with your search." She pointed to an area behind her desk.

There were six computer workstations, two rows of three facing each other, the monitors in separate study carrels so that they were shielded. Beyond the workstations were rows and rows of chest-high filing cabinets, each one topped with stacks of massive books that looked like oversize photo albums. Plat maps and real-estate records for the entire county.

"There's an instruction sheet by each terminal," she said. "Better get to it."

On the opposite side of the terminal row, two legs were visible at the middle station. The feet belonging to the legs were wearing lime-green Chuck Taylors. Hannah Byrne, the journalist for the *New York Times*, working on her story about Russian mobsters.

I started toward the nearest terminal, one not on Hannah's side.

"That woman who got killed," Opal said. "Sounds like one of them from the compound."

I stopped. "What compound?"

Snoopy Tie Guy stuck out his head, an angry expression on his face. "Damnation, Opal. You left the coffeepot on all day. Break room smells like charred ass."

HARRY HUNSICKER

"Oh dear." The woman patted her bouffant nervously. "I'll be right there."

He shook his head and disappeared back behind the employee door. Opal stood.

"The compound," I said. "Tell me what that is."

"You better hurry. We close in a few minutes." She disappeared into the break room.

I debated following her but decided I'd had enough trouble with the county government already. She'd have to come out eventually, and then I could ask.

So I strode to the nearest terminal and sat down. From the other side, I could hear the click of keys and the rustle of papers. I ignored that and went to work.

The instructions were clear, the interface surprisingly easy to use. There were three choices. Enter either the owner's name, the address of the property, or the account number.

I clicked the button to search for an address and entered "Elm Street," the location of the building with the nail salon, followed by the number range "1-9999."

The machine whirred for a moment. Then the results appeared, a dozen or so properties.

It didn't take long to identify the strip mall where I'd holed up with Suzy and the old man in the overalls.

A block off Main, 125 Elm Street. The owner was listed as Charles Harrington Boone, DVM, mailing address a street in the north section of Piedra Springs, about eight blocks away according to the mapping software that was part of the database. I copied down the address on a piece of scratch paper.

Snoopy Tie Guy came out of the break room. He went to the back of the public area and began turning off lights.

I clicked in the search bar again, this time intending to look up the address on Silas McPherson's business card.

106

I entered the data. Hit "Search."

Nothing happened. The page remained the same.

Snoopy Tie Guy continued to turn off lights, the room getting darker and darker.

I tried to refresh the page. Nothing.

Frustrated, I hit the "Back" button several times.

"We're closing up," he called out. "The network's off."

From the other bank of terminals, Hannah Byrne's head appeared. She looked at my face. "What happened to you?"

I didn't reply, intent on what I was seeing on the monitor. The search screen had returned to the original results, the properties on Elm Street. They must have been stored in the computer's cache.

"You get in another fight?" Hannah asked.

I ignored her, staring at the screen.

The property across the street from Boone's strip mall, 124 Elm, was an office building that housed a business called "Computer Repairs." The place where the two hoods had found Chigger.

What caught my attention was the owner's name—ZL Enterprises—followed by an address in Midland. The same name and address associated with the phone number on Silas McPherson's business card.

"Let me guess," Hannah said. "You ran into a door."

Snoopy Tie Guy appeared at the end of the row of terminals. "Y'all got to leave now."

I looked at him. "Is there any way I could stay a few more minutes?"

"Son, I'm already gonna be in trouble for having the AC so high today." He shook his head. "I keep the lights on much longer, there'll be hell to pay."

"Opal mentioned a place called the compound." I stood up. "Do you know anything about that?"

He frowned but didn't speak. A moment passed. Then: "Opal's not thinking too well these days." He moved to the far wall, turned off more lights. "Don't pay any attention to her."

Hannah lowered her voice. "The compound isn't something people around here talk about very much."

Snoopy Tie Guy didn't seem to hear her. He moved toward the front desk, where he began emptying the trash can into a plastic sack.

She pointed to the front door. "If you can make it outside without getting into a fight, maybe you and I could share a little information."

I watched her leave. Then I approached the guy in the tie and said, "Where's Opal? I'd like to talk to her if I could."

"She left out the back," he said. "Poor thing lives near Ozona— takes her a long time to get home."

I started to say something, but he interrupted. "She has tomorrow off, too. Won't be back until Monday."

I thanked him for his time and decided to take my chances with Hannah Byrne.

- CHAPTER TWENTY-ONE -

When I exited the appraisal office, Hannah Byrne was standing on the sidewalk, wearing a pair of Ray-Ban aviators. She'd removed her blazer and slung it over one shoulder. Her backpack hung from the other.

"What kind of cop were you?" she said.

Even though it was a little after five, the heat was still blistering, the sun high in the summer sky. Despite that, Hannah Byrne looked cool and unruffled.

"An honest one," I said. "Tell me what you know about this compound."

Other than the two of us, the street was deserted.

"That's not what I meant." She shook her head. "Who'd you work for?"

"Texas Department of Public Safety." I paused, then told her my branch of the DPS.

"A Texas Ranger," she said. "The Navy SEALs of law enforcement."

I shrugged. "We have our moments."

"Are you a religious person, Arlo Baines?"

That was a question I wasn't expecting. Completely out of place, vaguely intrusive, like asking if I bet on my favorite sports team or how old I'd been when I first had sex.

I thought about Sunday mornings with my family. Church more often than not, at the insistence of my wife. Then afterward we'd go to Luby's for lunch.

"Not anymore," I said.

"Does the name Sky of Zion mean anything to you?"

I shook my head. "Is that the compound you're talking about?"

She didn't reply. Instead she surveyed the empty street. "How do people live in this town? It's like the zombie apocalypse around here."

I realized her Prius wasn't anywhere to be seen. "Where's your ride?"

"Couple of blocks over. I like to move around on foot. Get the feel for a place."

That didn't make much sense in a town like Piedra Springs, a tiny little place where you could smell the poverty and decay from the inside of a vehicle speeding down Main Street.

"Tell me about the Sky of Zion."

"Let's get my car." She headed north, moving briskly.

Before I could react, she was ten feet away. I swore under my breath and followed. At the cross street, I caught up with her.

"I'm an atheist," she said. "Just so we're clear on that."

"Good for you."

She turned east and continued walking.

This was a residential neighborhood, not a nice one. Small, wood-framed houses with peeling paint, surrounded by rusted chain-link fences. Yards that were mostly bare dirt.

"Sky of Zion is a cult," she said.

I didn't reply.

"If you want to go to heaven, all you have to do is follow orders without questioning them and turn over all your possessions to the church."

"What's it based on?" I asked.

The line between cult and a legitimate if eccentric religion was thin. Giving all your money to the organization was a pretty big check mark in the yes-this-is-a-cult column.

"The official manifesto runs three thousand pages," she said. "A lot of it is written in a made-up language. Their belief system is . . . oh, let's just say it's hard to summarize."

I nodded but didn't say anything. Speaking about cults seemed to energize her, and I wondered why.

"That's a pretty big red flag, cult-wise," she said. "An inability to state concisely what your beliefs are. Christians, Muslims, Buddhists, whatevers—they can tell you their beliefs in a few seconds. Try that with a Mormon."

The woman named Molly had seemed otherworldly. Out of place in modern times. Sheltered, but not in a good way. Her membership in a cult made perfect sense.

Hannah Byrne continued her explanation. "The Sky of Zion's doctrine is a hodgepodge, the Old and New Testaments mixed with *Star Trek*."

A Honda rattled down the street, the old man from the appraisal office behind the wheel. He didn't acknowledge us.

"Something about a thirteenth tribe of Israel," Hannah said. "Their descendants are the true children of God."

A dog with a jagged scar on its side crossed the road in front of us. The animal was part pit bull and didn't look very friendly. We paused for it to get out of the street.

"The leader is called the Supreme Apostle," she said. "His word is law because he's considered a deity, the Son of God."

"What about Jesus?"

"Apparently he was just a warm-up act." She explained that most cults were essentially devoted to one person, an outsize personality, the charismatic visionary who promised his followers a better life.

Jim Jones and David Koresh. Sun Myung Moon. L. Ron Hubbard. Outsize personas who claimed the ability to communicate with the divine, to receive messages that only they could understand. The founder of the Mormon Church, on the lam from his creditors, downloaded divine communications via golden tablets only he could understand because he had magic spectacles.

The Supreme Apostle got his messages from the sky at sunset. The colors came from God. Only he could interpret what they meant.

I looked up. Dusk was still a couple of hours away. The clouds were big and white and fluffy, huge cotton balls in the sky. Far to the south, storm clouds were gathering.

Later the sky would be streaked with color, orange and pink, red and purple, hues so vivid that in a place like Piedra Springs, far removed from the pollution of a big city, the sheer intensity would make the breath catch in your throat.

"What's the *Star Trek* part?" I said.

"The Apostle came from a different galaxy on a special rocket ship. And angels are beamed around the universe." She paused. "The icing on the cake of a postmodern cult. Technology and religion fused together."

I was a fan of the original *Star Trek*, so I asked her about the galaxy and the spaceship.

"They're a little hazy on the details." She stopped in the middle of the block. "The important part is that the Son of God landed in a swamp outside of Ocala, Florida, in 1947."

On the far corner, the dog sat down and stared at us. Then it licked its crotch.

"So that means the original Apostle is dead," I said.

She nodded and explained that the mantle of priesthood fell to his offspring. This was another hallmark of a cult: the leadership function is often a family tradition, passed down from one generation to the next.

"You're pretty knowledgeable about all this," I said. "How come?"

She didn't reply. Her eyes darted toward the home nearest us, a tiny place that looked like something from a third-world shantytown.

It was in bad shape, siding patched with plywood and black plastic. The roof dipped like a swaybacked mule. The front door was either open or missing. A ragged screen did its best to keep bugs from flying inside.

"The Sky of Zion and their Supreme Apostle," I said. "What do they have to do with a pair of Russian mobsters named Boris?"

"The dumpster where they were found is across the street from the Zion's East Coast headquarters."

On the rotting porch sat a boy maybe two years old. He was playing with a stick and an empty soda can. He wore only a diaper, arms and legs streaked with dirt.

Hannah looked at the child. "Tell me again about the woman named Molly."

"Why are we stopped here?"

She didn't reply. She stood perfectly still and stared at the toddler, her expression blank.

"Do you know something about this house?" I asked.

"The Sky of Zion," she said. "They don't much like it when sheep leave the fold."

A woman darted out of the home. She was probably in her thirties but looked older. She was pale and gaunt. Her hair was in a bun piled high on top of her head, the exposed skin on her face and hands as dirty as that of the child's.

"Was Molly dressed like that?" Hannah spoke in a whisper, her voice husky.

The woman wore a filthy prairie dress that had been patched and mended too many times. Her feet were bare. She bent down and picked up the child. That's when she saw us.

Her lips pursed, cheeks bellowing with each breath.

She pointed a finger at Hannah. "Get thee behind me, evil one."

Her voice was ragged, not quite a shout. The child started to cry.

"What's wrong with her face?" I asked.

The woman's nose was misshapen, one side appearing to be damaged.

"She tried to leave," Hannah said. "That makes her an apostate. They've marked her."

I could see now that the woman had been mutilated. A knife had been inserted into her nostril, yanked outward.

Our appearance clearly was causing her a great deal of agitation. She shifted her weight from foot to foot, chest heaving like she couldn't catch her breath.

The child continued to cry.

The woman held out one hand, palm facing us, fingers splayed heavenward. She looked toward the sky. "Oh dear Lord. I beseech you. Release me now from this harlot of Babylon."

"Do you two know each other?" I couldn't imagine how, but there seemed to be a connection.

Hannah Byrne nodded. "That's my sister."

- CHAPTER TWENTY-TWO -

While I tried to absorb the fact that this reporter for the *New York Times* had a sister who was a member of a religious cult in this godforsaken town, another figure appeared in the doorway of the dilapidated house.

A man in his late thirties, wearing a pair of overalls that were as ragged and patched as the woman's dress. He was pale and skinny, too, like he wasn't getting enough to eat.

He appeared angry. He pointed a finger at Hannah. "What are you doing here? I told you to not come back."

"Hello, Joshua," Hannah said. "I just want to talk."

"Words of the serpent." He shook his head. "A forked tongue has no place in this home."

"What's happening with Jenny?" Hannah asked. "Is she all right?"

The woman in the dirty dress, Hannah's sister, screeched, a sound of pain like someone had driven a nail into her hand.

"The girl is of no concern to you." Joshua wagged his finger.

"She's my niece," Hannah said. "I want to make sure she's OK."

The woman disappeared inside with the child.

Joshua watched her go. "You've upset her."

"Maybe she's upset because she gave up her daughter," Hannah said.

"Jenny is blessed. She's a chosen one."

"Blessed?" Hannah's eyes grew wide with anger. "Are you out of your mind?"

"Faith is a gift from above. I wouldn't expect you to understand." He looked at me. "Who are you?"

"I'm a police officer." The lie slipped effortlessly off my tongue. "How about if we come inside and take a look around? Then we can sit down and talk."

"Elohim, protect me from the darkness." He raised both arms toward the sky. "Beelzebub walks among us."

I looked at Hannah. "I'll take that as a no."

Joshua reached a hand inside the doorway and pulled out a double-barreled shotgun, a side-by-side. The gun was as ragged as he and the woman in the dirty dress. The bluing on the barrel was worn away, and the stock appeared cracked, held together with black electrician's tape.

He cradled the weapon awkwardly in both hands, barrels pointing toward the ground.

I said, "Put down the gun, Joshua. We just want to talk."

He strode toward us. Every couple of steps, he glanced in either direction.

"I just want to make sure Jenny is OK," Hannah said. "Surely you care about your own daughter, too?"

He was almost to the edge of the yard. We were still in the middle of the street.

"Let's get out of here." I grabbed Hannah's arm.

"The power of Elohim makes the evil one flee," Joshua shouted. "Behold Elohim's grace."

I tried to pull Hannah toward the other side of the street. She wouldn't budge.

A man emerged from the house next door. He was skinny and pale, too, wearing overalls in similar condition.

Joshua glanced at him and then moved closer to us. When he was about five feet away, he whispered, "Will you bring her back?"

Hannah's eyes went wide.

"Please," Joshua said. "Save my daughter. Say you will."

"Yes." Hannah nodded once. "Yes, I will."

A door slammed nearby. Then another.

I looked across the street.

Two more men in overalls had appeared. They were a few houses down to the east, the direction we'd been headed. One was carrying a baseball bat, the other a garden hoe. They were out of earshot, but not by much.

Tears filled Joshua's eyes. "Thank you."

"She's at the compound, right?" Hannah kept her voice low.

The guys with the baseball bat and the garden hoe marched across their yards and took up position in the street toward the east end of the block. The man who lived next door to Joshua stood at the west end.

Joshua nodded. Then he raised the weapon, aiming in our general direction. He shouted, "I told you to get out of here."

"We're leaving." I grabbed Hannah's arm again, pulled her away.

This time she let me drag her toward the east end of the block.

The two men from across the street stood in the middle of the road, holding their respective weapons, trying to look tough. The guy on the left was missing an ear. The one on the right had his nose damaged in a similar way to the woman.

Hannah and I walked shoulder to shoulder between them.

Up close I could see they were dirty and malnourished. When we were a few feet past them, I stopped and turned around.

"How long has it been since either of you has eaten?" I asked.

No answer. Just sullen looks.

I pulled out my wallet and grabbed two twenties. "How about dinner on me?"

The men stared at the cash like it was a gold doubloon being offered by Lucifer himself. They wanted it; I could see that in their eyes. But they were afraid.

"There're no strings attached." I held out the money.

Neither man made any move to take it. After a moment, I folded the bills several times and placed them on the surface of the street.

The man with only one ear raised his garden hoe. "Be gone, evil one."

I pulled Hannah toward the end of the block as the two men watched us go.

- CHAPTER TWENTY-THREE -

Nine Months Ago

Belief is a strange animal. It makes people do things that are contrary to common sense, against the laws of nature.

Take, for example, my father-in-law, whose unshakable conviction that he was in charge of his own destiny, the master of his fate, led us all to the brink of destruction.

Some of us fell over the brink; the ones who survived were never the same.

The part that bothers me to this day was that our salvation lay in my hands, and I didn't even realize it.

I was weak. I chose a twisted version of familial duty over what was right. I think about that decision often, usually when the rocking of the bus makes reading hard, and I wonder what I would have done differently.

Would I have even been capable of choosing a different path?

My father-in-law's office was in a skyscraper in downtown Dallas, the fiftieth floor. The building was a monolithic shaft of glass, dark gray, located a few blocks from where Kennedy was killed.

The office was large and expensively decorated, as befitting a man of Frank's stature in the financial community. A desk the size of a Cadillac dominated one half of the room. The other half contained a sitting area, two leather couches bracketing a glass coffee table.

I stared out the window at the hazy wonder that was Dallas, a testament to commerce in action and powerful men who believed in building things using only their own daring ingenuity and mortgages with favorable loan terms.

A mahogany bookcase covered one wall, the shelves filled with leather-bound volumes that had never been read and framed pictures of Frank with various notables—governors and billionaires, several former presidents, more than a few film stars.

The largest photo, however, was a candid shot of the family—my wife and me, with both her parents and our two children, taken two years before at Frank's country club.

The other wall contained two items: a television tuned to a financial network and a bar.

Frank stood at the bar, a highball glass in hand, pouring himself a generous measure of vodka over a pair of ice cubes.

It was eleven in the morning.

I turned away from the window. "Why'd you call me?"

"How are my grandkids?" Frank drained half the drink like it was milk. "School OK?"

After a moment, I nodded. Both children were in private school, the tuition paid for by a trust Frank had established in their names.

"What was so urgent?" I said.

"You remember the guys I asked you about last year?"

"The Frisella brothers. You wanted to give them a real-estate loan."

He nodded. "You have a good memory."

The Frisella brothers were twins, originally from a small town in East Texas, not far from Shreveport, Louisiana. From a young age, the brothers had a burning desire to make their mark in the world, and they understood that ambitions such as they possessed could never be realized so far behind the Pine Curtain.

So they moved to Dallas while in their twenties. The move occurred, coincidentally, just as an investigation into the suspicious death of a pimp who owed the brothers money was heating up.

Now, two decades later, the Frisellas owned a large portfolio of shopping centers and office buildings. The shopping centers usually had as tenants one or more brothels masquerading as nail salons. The brothers were also silent partners in a half dozen used-car lots that laundered money for the South Louisiana mob and a chain of strip clubs that offered specials on lap dances and blow jobs every other Sunday.

"Do you remember what I told you?" I said. "About not getting in bed with them?"

"Arlo Baines and his self-righteousness." Frank drained the glass. "Were you born this smug or did you get sanctimonious working as a cop?"

We were silent for a moment, eyeing each other. I realized he'd probably had more than one drink already.

He rattled the ice cubes in his highball and looked away. He poured another inch of vodka and took a long sip.

"What's wrong, Frank?" I adjusted my gun belt and sat on one of the couches.

"The Frisellas won't make their payments."

His words hung in the air like cigarette smoke in a cancer ward.

The worst thing you could do in my father-in-law's universe was to not keep current with your loan. The structure of his very existence depended on borrowers making regular payments according to the terms of their mortgages.

To not pay was a grave sin, a heinous crime, akin to child molestation or voting for a socialist. The very notion was absurd.

Frank had the persona of a kindly uncle until someone failed to honor the terms of his loan. Then he became ruthless and cold, a shark going after a wounded swimmer. His weapons were made from paper but deadly in their own fashion—demand letters and default notices, foreclosure suits, everything administered with ruthless efficiency by his soldiers, a phalanx of high-priced attorneys.

The borrower's circumstances didn't matter. A sick child, a sudden illness, a contract that didn't make it in time. Nothing counted with Frank except getting paid.

This MO worked with 99 percent of his customers. Unfortunately, the Frisella brothers fell into that murky 1 percent.

I glanced at my watch. "I have to get back to work."

"I don't think you're understanding the gravity of the situation." Frank sat on the other sofa. "These are not exactly the kind of people who respond well when lawyers get involved."

I thought about all the things I could say, but I didn't want to be one of those I-told-you-so people or be accused again of being self-righteous. So I said, "It's one loan. Maybe you should just write it off and count your blessings."

He drained his glass of vodka. His face was so pale, I worried that he was about to have a heart attack.

After a few moments, he said, "It's not just one loan."

I sighed and rubbed my eyes.

"The bank's ratios are off," he said. "Way off."

"What does that mean, Frank?"

He stared at me like I was slow in the head. "The FDIC auditors, they conducted a random review of our books last week. They saw the numbers . . . the ratios."

I stared at him but didn't speak. My cell phone rang, and my boss's number flashed on the screen. I ignored the call, muted the ringer.

"Effing bean counters." He shook his head, an angry expression on his face. "Banks are supposed to make loans, right?"

Frank was a deacon at the North Dallas Baptist Church. He didn't believe in swearing, especially the F-word. Vodka in the morning, beer on the golf course, loans to East Texas mobsters—those were different matters.

"Too much debt on the books," he said. "Our loan-to-deposit ratio is too high."

I waited. There was more to come; I could tell by the look on his face.

"Too much *bad* debt." He spoke the last so softly I had to strain to hear the words.

He told me the rest of it, how the actual numbers were worse than what the FDIC auditors had seen. Something about certain figures on the bank's balance sheet being misreported to the feds over the last two quarters. How Frank's personal attorney said he should start calling the erroneous numbers a "clerical error" because there was now talk of a criminal investigation.

The kicker was that even with the misreported numbers being in the bank's favor, the ratio of bad loans to assets was at a critical point, almost to a level that would trigger a federal takeover of the bank. The tipping point would occur next week, when the Frisellas missed their third payment in a row and their loan was declared in default.

"They have to pay up." He stared at the floor. "If they don't, everything is gone."

I was unsure of what to do or how to respond. I said as much, not adding what I really thought—*You've made a bed of thorns and now you're going to have to sleep in it.*

"My daughter, the mother of your children." He wiped tears from his eyes. "What do you think it will do to her to see me in prison?"

I stood and walked to the window. The city glistened in the sunlight, ten thousand shards of broken glass.

"The Frisella brothers," he said. "Make them pay me. Please."

- CHAPTER TWENTY-FOUR -

Hannah and I made it to her rental car two streets over without incident.

The houses were nicer in this area of town. Not bigger but more well kept. Lawns instead of dirt. Paint jobs less than a decade old. Cars that looked functional.

On the horizon, the storm clouds had grown larger, another summer squall developing like yesterday's.

I got in the passenger side of the Prius and hoped there wouldn't be tornadoes. I didn't think Piedra Springs would fare very well with two strikes in two days.

Hannah slid behind the wheel. She started the vehicle and turned on the AC.

"Why is everybody so skinny?" I asked.

"They've all been kicked out for various reasons. They give everything they make to the church in order to buy their way back in."

I pondered the intricacies of the human mind.

People starving in a land of plenty. Emaciated of their own accord. So enamored with a belief system that didn't make sense, they were willing to die to regain their status.

Anorexia of the soul.

"Any government assistance they get," Hannah said, "food stamps, whatever, that goes to the church, too."

We were silent for a moment.

"Where is this compound, anyway?" I asked.

"This is my fight. I'll take you back to the motel." She put her hand on the gearshift.

I grasped her fingers, gently pulled them away from the knob.

"The girl I saw was shaping up to be a beauty. I'd hate to think of what might happen if no one's looking out for her."

"Do you have kids?" Hannah asked.

A moment passed. The sun was still shining, but thunder cracked in the distance, and the leaves on the trees had swung upward, indicating a shift in wind patterns. The storm was getting closer.

"I did."

She had the courtesy not to ask more questions. She looked behind us, in the direction of the block full of skinny apostates.

"How old is your niece?" I asked.

"Jenny just turned thirteen."

I didn't say anything.

Hannah continued to stare behind us, though there was nothing to see.

"I tried to warn my sister about the Sky of Zion. But she always saw the good in every situation."

"Joshua is her husband?" I asked. "Jenny's father? And that little boy's?"

Hannah nodded. "My sister wanted only one child, but the church elders said women should be fruitful."

Of course they did. Followers who have been recruited from the general public are more likely to question the theology. Better to raise your own.

"So where's the compound?"

"South of here. Maybe thirty miles as the crow flies."

I remembered the map I'd seen on the Internet. "The old prison."

"Yes, that's right."

"A fortress."

She nodded.

I pulled the slip of paper with Boone's information from my pocket. Entered the address into the Prius's GPS system. "This guy seems to know a lot about what goes on around town," I said. "I want to talk to him before we head south."

"You're planning to just go to the compound?" She sounded incredulous.

"Seems like a good place to start. Maybe Molly's children made it back there somehow. Seems pretty certain your niece is there, too."

She didn't reply. The sky darkened. A cloud of dust blew past the front window.

"How many other girls do you think are at that place, on their own?" I said.

"They'll see us coming from a mile away. We'll be sitting ducks."

Silas McPherson, the guy in the black Bentley, had given me a business card. The address was not far from the old prison. I wondered what his connection might be to the Sky of Zion. He'd certainly been interested in the site of Molly's murder.

Hannah put the car in drive. The engine was eerily quiet.

Two minutes later, we stopped in front of Boone's house, a large, two-story brick home in what passed for the upscale part of Piedra Springs.

For some reason, I wasn't surprised by what I found there.

I pointed to a spot in the circular driveway. "Park behind that black Bentley."

- CHAPTER TWENTY-FIVE -

On a block full of big, old homes, Boone's place appeared to be the biggest and the oldest, certainly the most impressive.

The house was made from stones the color of the earth, irregularly shaped, a roughly textured loamy brown, separated by veins of gray mortar.

The unkempt landscaping indicated the age and condition of the owner—grass that was overgrown, azalea beds filled with weeds, honeysuckle vines as thick as a man's wrist on the columns in front of the home.

No cars were in the driveway except for the black Bentley and Hannah Byrne's Prius.

Hannah and I exited her vehicle. The temperature was at least ten degrees cooler than when we'd started out only a few minutes before. Lightning flashed deep in the cloud bank behind the house. Thunder boomed a few seconds later.

Hannah pointed to the Bentley. "Wonder who that belongs to?"

I handed her Silas McPherson's business card. "That name mean anything to you?"

She shook her head, returned the card.

I stared at the home, imagining the life that might have once been in such a place.

Women in elegant evening clothes, dresses purchased at Neiman's in Dallas. Ranchers smoking cigars, drinking whiskey. A gathering place for the elite of the region.

Now the structure was old and worn, like the town itself.

"Who's the Supreme Apostle?" I asked.

"The last one anybody knows about was named Carlisle. He died in the late nineties, and there was a power struggle, different branches of his family fighting for the leadership role."

I continued to stare at the house as the wind blew harder.

"These days, nobody knows who's in charge," she said. "At least nobody on the outside."

We headed toward the front entrance, an oak door crisscrossed with iron.

"So it could be the guy who owns this car?" I asked. "McPherson?"

"Maybe. But I doubt it. I can't imagine the Supreme Apostle having business cards with his e-mail address on them."

When we stepped onto the porch, the door swung open and a man in a dark suit peeked out, the older guy in the passenger seat from earlier in the day. He was tieless, the clothes he wore similar to what Silas McPherson had been wearing. But the resemblance stopped there.

Silas had been nearly six feet tall, medium build, with attractive facial features.

This man was maybe five five and stocky like a wrestler. He wore thick, oval glasses atop a nose that was short and flat. His face was round like a pie tin, the temple and a portion of one cheek disfigured by a birthmark that looked like a puddle of red wine.

"You must be Arlo Baines," the short man said. "Silas told me about you."

I didn't reply.

"My name is Felix."

"Where's Boone?" I said.

"The heat was something today, wasn't it?" He looked at Hannah. "And who's the pretty lady?"

"I'm Mr. Baines's assistant." Hannah kept her tone even. "He doesn't like it when I talk much."

Felix cocked his head like he wasn't quite sure of what she'd said. After a moment he moved aside. "Please do come in. It's about to rain."

Hannah and I glanced at each other and then stepped inside.

We found ourselves in a large foyer that smelled like mold and Listerine. The walls were bone-colored plaster, cracked in places, the floors dark hardwood that needed waxing.

A wide staircase was in front of us, next to a hallway leading toward the back of the house. To the left was a formal dining room. To the right was a living area filled with furniture from the turn of the last century— heavy sofas with densely patterned upholstery, ornately carved chairs, dark woolen rugs.

"Who decorated this place?" Hannah asked. "The Addams family?"

"I thought you weren't supposed to talk much," Felix said.

She shrugged. "I'm not much for doing what men tell me."

He stared at Hannah with an expression that was a cross between quizzical and astounded, like she was a species from another planet or a talking gazelle.

A moment passed. Then: "Dr. Boone is upstairs," Felix said. "He's feeling indisposed."

"I'd like to see him anyway," I said.

"I'm afraid that's not possible." A hint of challenge in his tone.

I glanced up the stairway. A crystal chandelier with most of the bulbs burned out hung above the second-floor landing. The entire house was in shadows, dimly lit.

Felix pointed down the hall. "Silas is in the library."

I decided not to press the issue with this strange little man. No telling what was lurking in the nether regions of the old home. Better to take things one step at a time.

"After you." I tried to look friendly.

Felix smiled like he'd won a poker hand and waddled down the hallway. Hannah and I followed.

The library was on the right. The shelving overflowed with books. A worn leather sofa was in the middle of the room facing a desk made of dark wood that looked like teak.

Silas stood by a bay window, leafing through a ledger. He glanced at us and then turned his attention back to what was in his hand.

"Arlo Baines. Nice to see you again," he said. "You are friends with Dr. Boone, yes?"

"More like acquaintances."

Felix continued down the hall toward the back of the house.

Silas glanced at Hannah and then flipped a page. "You must be the reporter."

Hannah Byrne's eyes went wide. She didn't reply.

He looked up from the ledger. "Perhaps you can do a story on Boone, the scion of West Texas in the winter of his years."

Neither Hannah nor I spoke.

"An old man with no heirs." Silas shook his head. "So much property to dispose of."

"Why are you concerned with Boone's estate?" I asked. "Are you in the property business?"

Outside, a flash of lightning turned the yard a bright white. A second later, thunder crashed.

"My business," he said, "is none of your business." He flipped a page. "We should be clear on that, Mr. Baines."

Hannah pulled out her notepad, looked at Silas. "How do you spell your name?"

"You're not doing a story on me, are you?" Silas closed the ledger. "That would be a mistake."

She scribbled down something.

"Hannah Jane Byrne," he said. "The oldest daughter of Frank and Samantha Byrne. Born in Greenwich, Connecticut, in 1982."

His words were staccato, accent tinged with traces of the Midwest. Hannah looked up.

"Currently taking a leave of absence from the *New York Times*," he said. "An involuntary leave, I might add."

Hannah pursed her lips, eyes forming into slits.

"There were rumors of a breakdown in the newsroom." Silas stared out the window. "Idle gossip, I'm sure."

"Who the hell are you?" Hannah's tone was incredulous. "How did you know about any of that?"

Silas walked away from the window, chuckling softly. He tossed the ledger onto the desk. The rain started to fall, a few drops at first, then heavier. The light grew dim in the library, a lamp on the desk providing the only illumination.

"And here you are with my new friend Arlo Baines," he said. "Himself unceremoniously dismissed from the Texas Rangers."

"Look at you," I said. "Getting your Google on. You must have had a better Internet connection than I did."

"What do you want, Mr. Baines? I have a busy schedule."

"I'm still looking for Molly's children." I paused. "Why is it that I think you might know something about them?"

"These children you speak of are not mine to give."

A wonderfully ambiguous nonanswer. I decided to be more direct.

"Do you know where they are?" I asked.

He looked at me like I was a dog standing on two legs.

I followed the hunch forming in my mind and said, "You're looking for them, too, aren't you?"

"You annoy me, Mr. Baines." He had a sad expression on his face. "And I thought we'd get along so well."

Hannah glanced up like she'd heard something. She moved to the window, looked out.

"Sky of Zion," I said. "What's your connection?"

The question knocked him back for a moment. That was plain to see on his face. Silas McPherson wasn't used to people asking things that required real answers. I sensed that in his world, people followed orders. Or else.

"You are one of the unclean, Mr. Baines." His expression became cold. "I wouldn't expect you to understand."

From the other side of the room, Hannah banged on the window.

"Hey!" she shouted to someone outside.

Silas rushed to the window.

She turned to me. "I think it's the boy you're looking for."

Silas pressed his hands against the pane, peered outside.

"The weirdo with the glasses," Hannah said. "Felix. He's chasing the kid."

- CHAPTER TWENTY-SIX -

The words had barely left her lips before another bolt of thunder rattled the house.

Silas turned away from the window and faced me.

I stood in the middle of the room, blocking his path to the door. "Tell me about Molly and her children."

He opened his mouth as if he were going to respond. Then he lunged toward the door like he had a ballistic missile strapped to his back.

I could have tried to stop him, but he was moving like someone junked up on a bad combination of drugs—crack and angel dust, meth on top of bath salts.

I galloped after him, heading down the hall leading toward the rear of the house, Hannah right behind me.

We ran through what looked like a family dining room and into the kitchen.

The rear door was open.

I dashed outside.

The backyard was an overgrown mess—a lawn that was more weeds than grass, bordered by pyracanthas and oleanders growing as thick as bamboo.

At the rear of the property was an outbuilding, what looked like a garage and guest quarters. The door to the structure was open.

Silas McPherson stood in the middle of the yard, swiveling his head, looking in all directions.

Rain splattered on the shoulders of his suit, drops permeating the woolen fabric.

I headed toward him, and he charged toward the side yard, heading to the front of the house.

Hannah stood by the corner of the house, holding a piece of firewood.

Silas was paying attention to me, so he didn't realize she was there until it was too late.

He saw her at the last instant, right as she swung the hunk of wood toward his head. He managed to get his right hand up in time to block to blow.

That was good for his head, bad for his hand.

I was only a few yards away. Despite the rain, I could see clearly what happened.

The wood snapped back his fingers, the digits moving so far in the wrong direction it looked like the nails touched the rear of his hand.

He howled like a rabid wolf, his mouth a perfect O shape.

Hannah reared back for another strike. She swung, but Silas ducked out of the way and tore around the side of the house.

Hannah lunged after him but slipped, falling facedown onto the wet grass.

I let Silas go, skidded to a stop by Hannah. Pulled her to her feet.

"We have to hurry," she said. "He's getting away."

"Go inside and wait for me," I said.

In the same instant, there was a crack of lightning and a boom of thunder. The rain fell harder. Water dripped from Hannah's face. I was wet to the skin.

"I'm not waiting for anybody." She plunged into the thicket that was Boone's side yard.

I followed.

Thorns plucked at my shirt and skin. My feet slid on the mud. Despite all that, a few seconds later I burst free of the vegetation and emerged in the front yard of the old house.

The sky was black, the rain still heavy.

Hannah stood looking at the spot where the Bentley had been.

"Let's go." She headed toward the Prius.

"Where?"

The storm was loud; we had to shout to be heard. At least no tornado sirens were going off.

"We have to find them," she said. "They're part of the cult. They know about my niece."

"But which way did they go?"

She looked down the street in both directions but didn't say anything. She glanced at the house, a bewildered expression on her face.

On the one hand, we were searching for a black Bentley, which would stick out like a Kardashian at an Amish church social, especially in a town as small as Piedra Springs. On the other hand, it was raining heavily, and we didn't know where to begin the search.

"We have to try," she said.

"OK." I nodded. "We'll do a grid search, block by block. Let's get to it."

We both saw the Prius's damaged tires at the same time, the two on the right side, sliced along the sidewall. Not bad work for a man with only one functioning hand. Though maybe Felix chipped in.

Hannah yelled an obscenity and pounded her fists against the hood of the car.

I grabbed her arm, pushed her toward the house. "Go inside. Check on the old man."

"What are you going to do?"

"Find that kid."

"Why can't I come with you?"

"Because I work better alone." I headed off into the rain, wondering why I had turned down her offer of help.

- CHAPTER TWENTY-SEVEN -

I ran down the street, heading east, my pace an easy lope.

Boone's house was in the northwest quadrant of the town.

From what I remembered of the map, there wasn't much to the west—another couple of blocks, then the city limits.

After that there was nothing but West Texas flatlands, a never-ending sheet of earth stretching as far as the mind could imagine, a desolate landscape unbroken until the next tiny town sprang up nearly a hundred miles away, closer to New Mexico than Piedra Springs.

The area to the north was much the same except the nearest town was closer, probably only ninety miles off.

The rain had slackened to a hard, steady drizzle, but the sky was still dark.

The houses got smaller the farther east I went but not by much. This was still the ritzy part of town. The late-model vehicles in the driveways were almost exclusively American made. Pickups and sedans, Fords and Chevys. The occasional Cadillac.

I stopped at each cross street and peered in both directions, much like I had done the day before. Nothing. No cars or people were moving. Even the dogs of the town had taken shelter.

Three blocks later, I jogged past a park lined with live oaks, their trunks as thick as boulders, leaves greasy and slick from the rain.

I stopped at the corner, leaned against one of the trees, tried to catch my breath.

My wife and I had always talked about moving to a smaller city, a better place to raise children than Dallas.

I wondered what our life would have been like in a town like this. Would it have made a difference?

Across the street was a one-story house with fresh flowers in the beds and a Texas flag hanging from a pole mounted by the front door. The home reminded me of where I had lived with my family, a ranch-style house in North Dallas, not far from a high school where my son and I used to toss a football on Saturday mornings in the fall.

A sedan with a roof rack sat in the driveway.

In the front of the home was a large picture window overlooking the street and the park.

A figure appeared in the window. Sheriff Quang Marsh, holding a coffee mug.

So the sedan was a sheriff's department squad car, not a roof-racked civilian vehicle.

Marsh stared outside and took a sip from the cup.

I reflexively shrank back even though I had to be invisible to him because of the dim light and my position against the tree trunk.

A girl appeared by his side. The eight-year-old I'd seen in the softball team photo in his office. They talked for a few moments.

I wanted to break away and continue looking for Molly's son, but I couldn't force myself to move.

Marsh placed a hand on the girl's shoulder and continued to stare outside.

I wondered what he saw that I didn't. There was nothing out here but stormy weather.

The girl disappeared from view. In that instant, I missed my family more than ever, an ache that throbbed deep inside. Rain mixed with tears dripped from my face.

Marsh continued to stare outside, sipping from his mug. After a moment, he raised his arm and pointed east, the direction I'd been headed, as though urging me on.

I blinked several times, wondered if I were imagining the whole thing.

The house was still there. Marsh was not. The light had dimmed, so his cruiser was now nothing more than a mass of shadow.

I ran to the east, hoping I wasn't losing my mind.

- CHAPTER TWENTY-EIGHT -

Two blocks later, I found the Bentley parked in front of a large two-story building made from red brick and limestone.

The building was no longer in use. Plywood covered the windows, and a ragged chain-link fence encircled the entire property. A sign by the front door read PIEDRA SPRINGS HIGH SCHOOL—HOME OF THE FIGHTING BULLDOGS—2A STATE CHAMPS 1993!

I wondered where kids went to class now. Did they have to take a two-hour bus ride every day just to attend school?

There was a hole in the fence by the Bentley, not far from the entrance to the building.

I debated slashing a tire or two with my new knife, but I didn't want to take the time. So I crawled through the gap and jogged to the entry.

The door was open. A sign taped to the glass indicated the building was condemned and a grave danger to anyone who entered.

I stepped inside anyway.

The light outdoors was bright compared to the dimness of the interior.

I was in a long hallway strewn with papers and other trash. Lockers on one side, doors leading to classrooms on the other.

The air smelled stale, like mildew and dust. Other than the patter of rain from the outside, the place was silent and still.

I took a couple of steps and then stopped, one foot poised over the floor.

Water dripped from my shoe onto the dirty tile.

I squinted at the flooring, trying to scan the surface in the low light. After a moment, my eyes adjusted and I could see footprints, wet impressions in the grime. At least two sets, maybe more, the tread from a pair of sneakers distinct from shoes with slick soles.

I followed the prints down the hall until they made a left.

They continued on to a set of double doors marked GYMNASIUM.

The doors were open.

I stepped inside.

The light was better here because there were large windows around the perimeter, about thirty feet up.

What I saw was a gym filled with boxes stacked between five and six feet high, scattered haphazardly about, effectively forming a maze.

I stood in the doorway, letting my senses attune.

My ears picked up heavy breathing at the same instant as an arrow of pain pierced my leg, a sharp blow to the shin just below the knee.

I fell to the ground, tried not to scream. I looked around frantically, searching for the source of the attack.

Felix crouched a couple of feet away in the shadows, holding a baseball bat. He was by the door, leaning against a column of cardboard boxes.

He swung for my head, but I jerked out of reach.

I thought about standing, but the lower half of my leg felt like it was in a blender full of broken glass and carpet tacks. I crawled away as fast as I could, using three of my four limbs. Then I stopped, wondering why Felix hadn't come after me.

I looked back.

He hadn't moved. He was still at the door, hidden by the dim light. He swung the bat at me again even though I was out of range.

That's when I noticed the spear in his side.

A javelin, a piece of athletic equipment.

The Piedra Springs Bulldogs must have had a throwing team at one point—shot put and discus, hammers. Now, the throwing team was gone, as was the high school.

What remained was a spear used in the javelin competition, the shaft of which protruded from Felix's side, the tip embedded in the box he was leaning against.

He swung again with the bat, leaning over to get closer. Evidently this was not a smart move because his eyes went wide as an anguished groan erupted from his throat.

We stared at each other for a moment, both of us in pain.

He took several deep breaths like he was mustering energy for something big. He cupped one hand around his mouth, tried to yell: "Silas!"

His voice was a croak, a shout marred by pain and injury into a ragged whisper.

No response.

The expanse of the gym and the stacks of boxes swallowed the noise.

I crawled toward the end of the spear, keeping out of bat range.

"*Silas.*" Louder this time.

About five feet of javelin protruded from his wounded side. His arm and the bat together equaled roughly the same length.

I reached the end of the spear. My leg throbbed in agony. I tried not to think about how the rest of my day would play out if a bone had been broken.

I ignored the pain. Pointed to the spear. "Who did this to you? The boy?"

Felix glared at me but didn't speak. After a moment, he nodded.

"What's his name?" I said.

No answer. With his free hand, he extended his middle finger in my direction.

I reached up, grabbed the end of the javelin, gave it a little shake.

His face turned white. A mewing sound came from his mouth.

I let go.

He swung at me with the bat, but I was out of range, and he could barely move his arms. The bat banged against the floor.

"What's the boy's name?" I said.

He muttered something, nostrils flaring with each breath.

I placed my palm on the spear, gave it a tiny shove.

Panic in his eyes. He held up a hand. "C-Caleb. Caleb."

"And the girl. Who is she?"

He stared at the ceiling and muttered a string of gibberish, what sounded like Hebrew mixed with nonsensical words.

"Speaking in tongues isn't going to help you," I said.

"Mary," he said. "Blessed and chaste. A chosen one."

"A *chosen one*? What the hell does that mean?"

"She is pure." He glared at me. "Her essence is holy. You wouldn't understand."

"Try me, freako."

"The Lord's bounty." He had a rapturous look on his face, despite his injury. "It has been bestowed upon her. She is a gift to the flock. A multiplier."

I didn't say anything, repulsed by the implication of his words.

"You will never find her." He shook his head. "Because the Lord will smite you down."

Anger bubbled in my gut, cold and sour. My shin felt like it had been dipped in lava.

I gave the javelin a good, hard shake.

He dropped the bat and shuddered, breath coming in shallow gasps. His head lolled to one side and his shoulders slumped.

From somewhere across the room came a man's voice, yelling, "*Stop.*"

I looked around. No one was visible. I tried to stand and succeeded, though everything was wobbly. No broken bones, but I wouldn't be running anytime soon.

I snatched the bat and used it as a cane, limping through the maze of boxes.

"*Caleb!*" Silas's voice echoed across the gym. "I want to help you, son. Talk to me, please."

I headed toward the back of the room, threading my way through the cartons, trying to move as fast and as silently as possible.

"Where is Mary?" Silas's voice was louder, plaintive. "You both need to come home."

The passageway I was following made a sharp turn. The far wall of the gym was a roll-up door, an exit leading to the athletic fields. The door was open. Up ahead I could see the cloudy sky and damp ground of the outside, thirty or forty feet away.

"Everything will be all right," Silas said. "The Apostle will welcome you back."

The voice was closer, just ahead.

I kept limping forward.

The sound of rain grew louder.

I reached the end of the maze.

Sports equipment lay everywhere—footballs and basketballs, helmets, more bats, a half dozen baseball gloves. Another javelin.

Discarded items, stuff no longer needed when a school closed.

Silas McPherson stood in the corner by the open roll-up door and the wall. He was staring at the cartons, holding his injured hand close to his chest.

When he saw me, he shook his head sadly.

I limped toward him, the bat in both hands, cocked back, ready to strike.

"This does not concern you," he said. "You should leave."

I stopped. Shouted: "*Caleb!* If you can hear me, I want you to run away from this place."

Silence.

"I'm a police officer," I shouted. "You'll be safe if you get away from here."

"What do you think the word *safe* means to that boy?" Silas said. "You really think he's going to trust you?"

I didn't say anything, straining to hear movement.

"You are one of the unclean," Silas said. "He's been trained to avoid people like you at all costs."

"He was pretty trusting last night when he was trying to get away from your thugs."

"Last night. What a mistake that was." Silas ambled in my direction. "If only you hadn't interfered. Everything would have been OK."

I moved forward, too. My leg almost gave way, but I kept going, staggering closer.

What was about to happen would be ugly and painful. Silas with four broken fingers, me with a damaged leg. At least I had a bat.

Silas reached into his waistband with his left hand, his movements awkward. He pulled out a pistol.

So much for the advantage of the bat.

"Drop it," he said. "Put your hands on your head."

I didn't move.

"I'm warning you." He aimed at my chest. "I will not hesitate to—"

Thunk.

The baseball came out of nowhere. It hit Silas in the temple with a remarkably loud, hollow sound, and he fell to the ground. Dazed, maybe unconscious, maybe not.

A figure appeared from a passageway in the cardboard boxes.

The boy, Caleb. If he lived through this ordeal, he could probably score a baseball scholarship somewhere. The kid had an arm on him.

He was wearing different clothes, and his left arm had been put in a sling.

"You OK?" I asked.

He didn't respond.

"We need to get out of here," I said. "We'll go to the next town. I know where there's a car we can use."

He darted outside and stopped, skittish like a deer in the woods. He turned and looked at me, rain hitting his head.

"I want to help you," I said. "You and your sister."

We were about ten feet apart. I walked toward him, stopping when he scampered away, keeping out of reach.

"It's OK," I said. "I'm not going to hurt you."

He stared at me, his eyes wide.

"We'll go to a doctor," I said. "Get your arm looked at."

He tensed, shoulders hunched. Then he turned and sprinted away.

I ran after him, forgetting about my leg. I made it about two strides before I fell facedown in the mud, my head thumping against a stone the size of a softball.

A period of time passed, seconds or minutes, it was hard to say.

After a while, I managed to prop myself up with one hand and stare into the distance, but the boy was gone.

- CHAPTER TWENTY-NINE -

Nine Months Ago

The Frisella brothers, the guys who stiffed my father-in-law, Frank, on their bank loan, owned a restaurant by Love Field, a Cajun place stuck between a self-serve car wash and a vape store.

Pirate Red's.

There was a sign on the window that said CLOSED FOR REMODELING, but the front door was unlocked, so I walked in.

The place was small with low ceilings, a bar on one side and a dining area on the other.

A salad bar designed to look like a pirate's schooner divided the two areas. Multicolored Christmas lights were strung from the masts like iridescent riggings. A place for lettuce was amidships, dressings at the stern, croutons and black olives on the bow.

It was midmorning, the day after my meeting with Frank at his office downtown.

I wore my regular clothes—a pair of Wranglers and a khaki shirt, a Stetson, and Roper-style boots. The only difference between this and any other day was that I didn't have a badge pinned to my breast and my pistol was hidden underneath a Carhartt jacket.

The place appeared empty except for a guy with stringy black hair, wearing a tracksuit. He was sitting at a table on the restaurant side, thumbing currency into different piles. A stack of newspapers was on the opposite side of the table.

When he saw me, he put one hand in his lap. With the other he grabbed the business section of the paper and covered the money.

"The Frisellas." I stopped in front of his table. "Where might I find them?"

"What do you think this is, Supercuts?" he said. "Drop-ins *aren't* welcome."

I held up my badge.

He stared at the ID for a moment. His eyes shifted for a quarter second toward a set of double doors at the rear of the dining area. Then he recovered and gave me a hardened stare.

"You got a warrant?" he asked.

"Take your money and get out." I pointed to the front door.

"Who the hell do you think you—"

He stopped talking when I lit the match.

He frowned when I picked up a different section of the newspaper.

His mouth dropped open when I held the flame under the newsprint and tossed the burning paper on top of the pile of money covered by the business section.

He swore and jumped away from the table. Tried to smother the fire with the rest of the newspaper while I headed toward the double doors.

The kitchen was cockroach nirvana, a health inspector's nightmare. Dishes with caked-on food in the sink, a browning head of lettuce on the dirty tile floor, the smell of rancid grease in the air.

The Frisella brothers were fraternal twins who, for some unfathomable reason, had both been named Tommy. One was Tommy Ray, the other Tommy Joe. On the street, the former was called Crazy Tommy because of his drug use and lack of impulse control.

Both Tommys were sitting at a stainless steel worktable.

They were dressed like Colombian smugglers on an episode of *Miami Vice*, identical baby-blue linen sports coats, black silk shirts, and cream-colored jeans. Odd fashion choices for a pair of hillbillies who were as white-bread as bingo night at the VFW hall.

The Tommy on the left looked like he hadn't slept since the last time the Cowboys won a Super Bowl. He had dark circles under his eyes, and his skin was paler than his brother's, the color of spoiled milk, sallow and unhealthy.

He was snorting a line of cocaine from the surface of the table when I walked in.

Next to the coke was a human hand in a plastic freezer sack. Bone and gristle stuck out from the wrist end.

The other Tommy was tapping on a cell. He dropped the phone and pulled a pistol from his waistband.

"Who are you?" He aimed the gun at me. "Didn't you see the Employees Only sign?"

I badged him. "Put down the piece, Tommy Joe. I don't want to have to shoot you and then fill out all the forms."

Crazy Tommy rubbed his nose and growled.

"Who's that belong to?" I pointed to the sack.

"What the hell do you care?" Tommy Joe said. "Did somebody report a missing hand?"

"Just making conversation. Seemed more appropriate than saying, 'Hey, howya doing, what about this weather?'"

"Shoot him," Crazy Tommy said. His voice was ragged.

"That'd be a bad play." I shook my head. "Think about the load of trouble you'd have if you pop a cop."

Crazy Tommy did another line, not caring that a Texas Ranger was watching, while his brother stared at me, a frown of concentration on his face. After a moment, Tommy Joe put down the pistol next to the severed hand.

"See?" I strolled to the gas range on the far wall. "That wasn't so hard."

The range was filthy, covered in dirty utensils and greasy pans. A large stockpot sat on a burner turned to low. The pot was full of what smelled like gumbo.

"So we've made small talk," Tommy Joe said. "How about you tell me who you are and what the hell you want? You're here without backup, which means you don't have a warrant or probable cause."

"You owe the bank a lot of money." I picked up a frying pan. "Did you forget to make the payments on your real-estate loan?"

"That old idiot, Frank?" Tommy Joe shook his head. "He sent a cop to collect?"

Crazy Tommy held the sack with the hand, oblivious to both of us. He stared at the severed limb with a look of satisfaction on his face.

"You tell Frank he's making a big mistake." Tommy Joe's face was a smirk. "Our loan is, whaddayacallit, *nonrecourse*."

I walked back to where the brothers were sitting.

Crazy Tommy put down the sack. Then he bent over and snorted another line. When he looked up, I hit him in the face with the back of the frying pan.

The aluminum surface struck him square on the nose. He fell over onto his back, his head bouncing off the tile floor.

Tommy Joe jumped up. "What the hell?"

"You're running underage girls in your clubs," I said. "Got a steady supply coming in from East Texas."

His eyes were wide, mouth agape.

"Maybe Dallas Vice needs to start paying extra attention to your business."

A moment of silence. Then Tommy Joe smiled. After a few seconds, he laughed.

"Dallas Vice?" he said. "Seriously?"

That should have been a warning that maybe a Texas Ranger who hardly ever operated in Dallas County had no business messing with people and places he didn't understand. But they didn't give out the Ranger badge to men who second-guessed themselves or who were worried by a couple of redneck punks. Also, anger at the position my father-in-law had put me in caused me to be reckless, to ignore the warnings.

I picked up his gun and dropped it in the pot of gumbo. "You need to pay the bank by close of business today."

"How about I pay you now?" Tommy Joe said.

I hesitated for a moment and then nodded.

"Cash. Is that OK?"

I nodded again.

He pointed to the walk-in freezer. "It's in there."

I drew my pistol and knelt on the floor by Crazy Tommy. "You come out with anything other than currency, and I'll shoot your brother in the knee."

Tommy Joe held up one hand. "On the grave of our mother, just the money."

I nodded my approval.

He opened the freezer and stepped inside. Three seconds later, he emerged, carrying a blue duffel bag. He dropped the bag by where I knelt.

"Here's a year's worth of payments," he said. "Three hundred K."

The side of the duffel was marked with the Dallas Police Department logo.

"That should keep Frank happy for a while," he said.

I unzipped the bag, saw the bundles of hundred-dollar bills. I picked it up, slung the strap over my shoulder. It was heavy.

"You still gonna call Vice on me?" Tommy Joe sounded like he was trying not to laugh.

I backed my way toward the door.

"We've been running teenage gash in our clubs for years now," Tommy Joe said. "How do you think we get away with that?"

Crazy Tommy pushed himself off the floor. Blood coated the lower half of his face.

"Keep your head low, Mr. Texas Ranger," Tommy Joe said. "The people that money belongs to are gonna come looking for it."

- CHAPTER THIRTY -

I wiped mud from my face and stared at the tree line on the far side of the athletic field. The abandoned high school was behind me.

Caleb had disappeared, and I wasn't in any condition to run around looking for him.

Every inch of my body felt bad in some way—a shooting pain on one side of my forehead from hitting the rock when I fell, a dull throb below my knee from Felix's blow, a skinned elbow from who-knows-where. Muscles sore from running.

The boy could be anywhere. Blocks in either direction, or on his way to the next county if he'd scored a ride somehow. No hint where his sister might be. Not even a clue if she was still alive.

The rain had stopped and the sky was clear, a faded blue like a pair of old jeans, wisps of clouds in the distance, stretching toward the horizon.

I looked at my watch. It was a little after six. I'd been out for maybe five minutes. I stood and tested my leg. It hurt but didn't buckle. After a moment, I limped back inside the gym.

Silas McPherson was gone. The blow to the head with the baseball hadn't put him out of commission for very long, either.

On the other side of the gym, Felix had disappeared as well. There was a puddle of fresh blood where he'd been. The javelin that had impaled him lay to one side. I wondered if he'd survived having the spear removed.

I hobbled down the same hallway, following the footprints that were now going back the way they'd come. A ragged line of blood drops trailed alongside the prints.

A few minutes later, I emerged from the front door.

The Bentley was no longer parked by the entrance. In its place was a Ford Crown Victoria, dark gray.

The Crown Vic was an older model, at least a decade past coming off the assembly line, but it was in immaculate condition. Freshly washed, not driven in the sudden storm that had just ended.

As I stood on the front steps of the school, the driver's door opened and Hannah Byrne jumped out.

I made my way across the overgrown yard and through the gap in the fence.

"You OK?" She touched my arm.

Her fingers felt good on my skin. It was nice to have somebody give a damn about you, even if it was only in the most cursory fashion.

"Yeah. Why?" I was breathing heavily, the pain in my leg and head throbbing in unison.

"You're limping pretty badly," she said. "And you've got a nice goose egg on your forehead."

I told her what happened. Felix with the spear in his side, encountering Silas McPherson and then Caleb. I didn't tell her about seeing Sheriff Quang Marsh at his home and how he pointed me in the right direction. I wondered if that was real. At this point, I wondered if anything was.

"How did you know to come here?" I asked.

"Boone woke up. He told me to try the school."

That made sense. The Sky of Zion children had been denied a normal existence. A school seemed like someplace they might gravitate toward.

"I think he helps people like them," she said. "You know, to get away."

A one-man underground railroad for runaways from the cult. I wondered if that had anything to do with the dent in his head. I looked at the Ford.

"That's Boone's," she said. "The rental car company is sending somebody from Midland with new tires for the Prius. They won't be here until tomorrow."

"Good," I said. "Let's keep searching for the children."

"You look like you've gone a couple of rounds with Mike Tyson. You really think you're in any condition to go after two kids who don't want to be found?"

A wave of dizziness swept over me. I put a hand on the hood of the car to steady myself.

"He was here. I saw him. We still have a chance."

"But what if Silas found them?" she asked.

I didn't answer.

In the evening light, Hannah looked tired, stress lines etched across her face. I realized she'd been searching for her niece for much longer than I'd been looking for Molly's children—months, maybe years longer.

"What if they're all dead?" she asked.

"We keep going until we know for sure." I limped toward the passenger side of the Ford.

• • •

Instead of continuing the search, Hannah drove to Boone's house over my protests.

Ten minutes later, I was in the kitchen, sitting on an oilskin-covered table while the old veterinarian examined my head. Hannah stood by the sink, tapping on her phone.

"I'm not a horse," I said. "So don't even think about putting me out of my misery."

Boone got some ice from the freezer and filled a plastic sack. "Put that on your noggin."

"Caleb, the boy, he had his arm in a sling," I said. "He was wearing fresh clothes, too."

The old vet pulled the rubber band from his ponytail, tightened his hair, and slid the band back into place. Then he turned on a penlight, flicked the beam across my eyes.

"You took care of him, didn't you?" I said.

"Maybe." He turned off the light. "What's it to you?"

"I've been looking for him. And his sister, since yesterday."

"Maybe they don't want to be found." He held up a finger. "How many do you see?"

I told him one. I didn't mention how fuzzy it was. Then I said, "But they were here, right? Both of them?"

"There're two cots in the cabin out back," Hannah said. "Both looked like they've been slept in."

Boone shot her an angry look. "I don't know either of you from a wet horse turd. Why should I tell you anything about those children?"

"Because we're not Silas McPherson or his weirdo friend, Felix," I said. "We're not part of the Sky of Zion."

"That's not a name you're supposed to mention around here," he said.

"Who told you that?" Hannah asked. "The sheriff?"

"You've probably got a mild concussion." Boone spoke to me, ignoring the question. "I imagine you're seeing things a little fuzzy on the edges and not telling me."

I chose to neither confirm nor deny his statement.

"You should rest for the next few days," he said.

"That's not an option." I paused. "Tell me why Silas McPherson knew to look for those kids here."

"Maybe because I'm the closest thing this town has to a doctor?"

"Do you know where the children are now?" I asked.

He shook his head slowly.

"Would you tell me if you did?"

"That's an asshole question," he said. "Have I mentioned that I never much liked cops?"

I glanced at Hannah but didn't reply.

"Your lady friend, she told me about you." He paused. "I got on the Google and searched you up."

"And what did the Google say about me?"

He put down the penlight. "Take off your trousers."

"Google said that? Really?"

He sighed loudly. "I need to check your leg."

My clothes were filthy from a day of running, fighting, and having a random skinhead die on top of me. They were still damp from the storm. I wanted to take off everything and toss the whole pile into a fire. But what I wanted more was to keep looking for Molly's boy and girl.

"My leg's fine. Nothing's broken."

Boone poked a few places through my pants, manipulated the limb this way and that while I tried not to wince. He nodded like he was satisfied. Then he said, "On the Google, I read about what happened to your family. I'm sorry for your loss."

One of the biggest reasons I'd gone on the road was to be away from people who knew me. I wanted solitude or, failing that, at least the company of strangers, people who didn't know my story and wouldn't say how sorry they were.

"Sorry" doesn't bring back the dead. "Sorry" rips off the scab a little every time it gets mentioned. "Sorry" only helps the person who utters the word; it does nothing for the survivors.

I didn't reply. Fatigue settled on me like a hot, wet overcoat. I didn't feel like I could walk, much less scour the town for Caleb and Mary.

"My boy died in Iraq," Boone said. "Twelve years ago. Losing a child, there's no pain like that in the universe."

Emotion caught in my throat and that stupid word—"Sorry"—slipped from my lips before I could stop it.

Hannah put away her phone. She patted me on the shoulder. Boone opened a cabinet and pulled out a bottle of Advil. Then he filled a glass with water.

"Take a couple of these," he said. "You gonna be hurting pretty bad for the next few hours."

I swallowed two tablets, then drank the entire glass, the only liquid I'd had in a long time. I felt a little better. At least I had another course of action in mind.

I thanked Boone and then said, "Is there a Chinese restaurant in town?"

Hannah arched one eyebrow.

Boone hesitated, a confused look on his face. Then he nodded.

"Can we borrow your car again?" I asked.

- CHAPTER THIRTY-ONE -

The Crown Victoria was parked in Boone's driveway behind the Prius with the damaged tires.

I got in the passenger seat.

Hannah slid behind the steering wheel. "Why are we going to eat Chinese food?"

I stifled a yawn. "If I told you, it would spoil the surprise."

"I've had enough of those for one day." She cranked the ignition.

As soon as she backed out, I fell asleep. The next thing I knew, we were stopping at our motel on the other side of town.

I blinked several times. My eyes felt gritty.

"Why are we here?"

"You smell like a locker room and look like hammered dog crap," she said. "I'm not going to dinner with you until you get cleaned up."

"It's not a date."

"Damn straight it's not." She slid out of the Ford.

I looked at my watch, realized there was enough time. So I got out as well.

Our rooms were three doors apart, two out of a dozen on this side of the motel.

She had parked the Crown Vic toward the front of the building, near the driveway that snaked toward the manager's office. The spot Hannah had chosen offered an easy getaway and was not associated with our rooms. She was getting smarter by the minute.

"What's your cell number?" she said. "I'll text you when I'm ready."

"I don't have one."

She gave me a puzzled look. Her question was unspoken but clear, one I'd heard many times in recent months. *Who on earth doesn't have a cell?*

"Don't have the need for one." I left off the obvious part: there's no one left for me to talk to.

A moment of silence.

"Fifteen minutes, then." She opened her door.

I nodded and did the same.

The Comanche Inn didn't offer maid service, so my room looked exactly as it had when I'd left early that morning.

The bedspread was pulled up, the pillows on top. The towel I'd used was draped over the bathroom door. My bag was in the same spot on the dresser.

I allowed myself to relax, imagining how good a hot shower would feel.

Then I saw my copy of Gibbon's *Decline and Fall of the Roman Empire*.

It was on the nightstand exactly where I'd left it, but the cover was facedown, not faceup like when I'd departed the room.

I grabbed the paperback. The bookmark I'd used the night before, a slip of paper the size of a match, was gone.

They'd lost my place. The bastards.

Several choice swearwords filtered through my head, but I remained silent. I put down the book and sauntered out of the room, trying to be as casual as possible.

Outside, the parking lot looked the same as it had a few moments before. One car, ours. Nobody skulking about.

I limped as fast as I could to Hannah's room and knocked on the door.

Nothing happened.

I knocked again, louder. A moment later, the door opened a crack, held in place by a security chain.

"What?" Hannah stood in the gap, wearing a towel around her torso. "I was getting ready to take a shower."

I held a finger to my lips, motioned for her to let me in.

"Seriously? Now?" She glared at me.

I leaned close, whispered, "They've been in our rooms."

Her eyes went wide. She clutched the towel closer. Then she undid the security chain and opened the door.

I stepped inside and turned on the TV, volume up loud. Then I made my way around the room, eyeing lights, plugs, and appliances.

The clock radio on the nightstand had a slight scratch on the top. I examined the radio more closely.

They'd inserted a video recorder. The lens was barely visible to the left of the time display. The reason I'd spotted it was because an FBI agent had shown me a similar setup about a year before. The equipment was the latest generation, very sophisticated. It was ultracompact, and the radio still kept time and played music.

A T-shirt lay on the bed. I dropped it over the device.

Hannah stood by the dresser and watched me do all this, arms crossed, a fearful expression on her face.

I limped to where she was and leaned close to her ear. "There's a video surveillance system in the radio. A listening device, too, probably."

We weren't touching, but I could feel her stiffen, the breath catch in her throat.

"Get dressed; pack your stuff. Meet me outside in two minutes."

She nodded.

I left, headed back to my room. There, I packed up my stuff as quickly as possible. If someone was watching in real time, hopefully he or she would think I was leaving town.

Hannah was by my door when I stepped out of the room, wearing the same clothes as earlier in the day. She had a backpack and purse over one shoulder and a wheeled carry-on in hand.

The parking lot was still empty except for the Crown Vic. Our rooms were at the back of the motel, out of view of the front desk.

"Follow me." I headed to the last room, the farthest from Main Street and the office.

The door was locked.

I pulled a Leatherman tool from my bag. "Got a hair pin?"

No answer.

"Actually, I need two."

She rummaged through her purse and came up with a handful of pins. I selected a pair and went to work, using the largest one as a tensioning bar held by the pliers on the Leatherman, the smaller one as a pick.

"This is actually going to work?" she said.

"It's a simple lock, pin, and tumbler. The dead bolt's not engaged because the room's unoccupied."

Three minutes later, we were inside.

The room was what passed for a suite at the Comanche Inn, a sitting area to one side, a king-size bed on the other. The decor was from the sixties, shag carpet and floral patterns.

I scanned the room for devices. There wasn't a TV or a radio anywhere to be seen.

"Looks clean," I said.

"How do you know for sure?"

"I don't."

Hannah was silent for a moment. Then: "They watched me undress."

I nodded but didn't speak.

The sense of violation was real; I felt it, too. Even though Piedra Springs was dying, this was a pleasant little town. Silas and Felix, the murdered woman named Molly, the starving apostates—none of these people meshed with what this place should be.

"You go first." I sat in an easy chair by the front door.

Hannah walked to the bathroom. Halfway there, she stopped and turned around. "Everything that happened today . ... thanks for looking out for me."

I shrugged, not sure how to respond. I hadn't had many real conversations lately.

"I'm not used to people doing that."

"A little kindness keeps everybody on an even keel," I said.

The phrase was one my father used to say. I didn't tell her that.

She nodded and smiled, a shy expression on her face. Then she disappeared into the bathroom. Ten minutes later, she came out, damp from the shower, wearing fresh clothes, a pair of jeans and a peach-colored blouse.

Ten minutes after that, I emerged from the bathroom, too, wearing a clean T-shirt and Levi's, my hair wet but combed.

Hannah stood by the window, peering through the blinds. She turned and looked at me.

"The guys in the gray pickup," she said. "They're here."

- CHAPTER THIRTY-TWO -

I peeked between the blinds of the room we'd commandeered.

An extended-cab gray Chevrolet pickup was parked by the unit where I was registered.

Mr. Goatee, the man who killed Chigger, stood by the front of the truck, his partner next to him. They wore the same hats, the Stetsons with the Tom Mix creases.

The guy with the goatee walked to the back of the truck. He reached into the bed and pulled out a black tube about six inches in diameter and three feet long. The tube had handles at the midpoint and at one end. By the way he hefted it, you could tell the tube weighed a lot.

"What is that?" Hannah asked.

"A battering ram."

The other guy removed a short-barreled shotgun from the cab of the truck. He jacked a round into the chamber and nodded to his partner.

Mr. Goatee approached my room from the side. Because of the angle, I couldn't see what happened next. But I could hear it.

WHUMP.

The battering ram struck the door, probably just above the lock.

Footsteps, the scrape of shoe leather on concrete as the two men moved along the sidewalk outside the room.

Silence as they entered.

A few seconds later, they reappeared. They stood in the parking lot for a moment and talked. Then they repeated their break-in routine on Hannah's door.

While they were in her room, I made sure all the lights in the suite were off. I pointed to a spot in the corner, told Hannah to crouch there.

She complied.

I peered out the window.

The two men were finished with Hannah's room. They stood by their pickup and looked in either direction, talking with each other.

After a few minutes, they got in the pickup. The vehicle backed out of the spot by my room, turned, headed toward Main Street. It stopped by our borrowed Crown Victoria, idling there for a few seconds. Then it left.

I let the blinds drop. "They're gone."

Hannah didn't move.

I pulled her up.

She hugged herself like the room was cold, teeth chattering.

"It's OK," I said. "We're safe."

She stared at my eyes but didn't speak.

"Take deep breaths." I held her hand. "Everything's going to be all right."

She drew in a big lungful of air, let it out slowly.

"Let's get out of here," I said. "Before they come back."

• • •

For whatever reason, most little towns in Texas have a Chinese restaurant, usually run by first- or second-generation Chinese Americans.

Maybe this was because small towns seemed like good locations for immigrants to establish their beachhead on the American dream. Maybe it was because there were a lot of Chinese on the run from something back home, and they figured dinky little towns were good places to hide out. Maybe they were laundering money for the triads or smuggling rhinoceros horns.

Who's to say?

The Chinese restaurant in Piedra Springs was named Mr. Wong's.

It was located in an old Pizza Hut building on the outskirts of town, between a used-car lot that was out of business and a convenience store called Smitty's QuickPak. The latter had an illuminated marquee sign in front that read PLAY THE LOTTO HERE! and WIC CARDS ACCEPTED!

Hannah parked between a Cadillac and a Ford pickup. The Ford was hitched to a trailer full of welding equipment. The lot was about a third full, maybe a dozen vehicles, including a three-quarter-ton black Suburban parked across from us, nose out.

I recognized the Suburban, realized our timing had worked.

If you've been part of an organization long enough—one as small as the Texas Rangers, anyway—you'll pick up on your colleagues' quirks and idiosyncrasies.

Such as the Ranger in South Texas who was a vegetarian. Or the guy in the Panhandle who couldn't go more than a week without finding a poker game.

Or the fact that Aloysius Throckmorton always ate Chinese food on his first night in any town.

Hannah and I stepped inside Mr. Wong's. Beads hung from the ceiling and formed an entryway, directing traffic to a hostess stand where an Asian woman in her forties stood.

"We're meeting somebody." I breezed past her before she could speak. Hannah followed.

The interior was dimly lit, decorated with silk lanterns, purple holiday lights, and an acrylic painting of Bruce Lee on one wall.

Throckmorton was in a booth in the corner, sitting next to a Latina woman in her forties with bleached blonde hair and lipstick as red as rubies.

Another quirk about my former colleague—despite a wife back home in Mesquite, Texas, he had a thing for Mexican women, the trashier the better.

He looked up as I approached. His jaw dropped open.

I directed Hannah to the opposite side of the booth. I slid in after her.

"What the shit are you doing here?" Throckmorton said.

"May we join you?" I asked.

"No. You most certainly may not." He looked at Hannah. "Who are you?"

"I'm a reporter." With her phone, she took a picture of him and the woman. "That just went to my Twitter feed."

He frowned. "Your twit-what?"

"No peectures." The Latina shook her head and looked at Throckmorton. *"Si mi marido me ve, estoy en un gran problema."* If my husband sees that, I'll be in big trouble.

He elbowed the woman, pointed to the door. "Wait in the car . . . *Esperar en el coche.*"

She jabbered at him in Spanish and gestured to her plate of General Tso's chicken.

Throckmorton sighed and indicated a table across the room. The woman grumbled but picked up her food and moved.

A waiter came over and asked if everything was OK. Before Throckmorton could speak, I told him that Hannah and I would like two orders of beef with snow peas, egg rolls to start, hold the MSG.

When the waiter left, Throckmorton glared at me. "I'm gonna kick your ass so hard, you'll be shitting out of your mouth for a month."

"The Sky of Zion," I said. "They have a compound south of town. What do you know about them?"

He didn't reply, a quizzical expression on his face.

"They're a religious cult," I said. "And I think they're involved with the two murders."

Throckmorton was a bully and an asshole, but he was also a good cop, the three characteristics not always mutually exclusive. He tried to enforce the law to the best of his abilities, working to see that justice was done, just so long as that didn't interfere with a plate of good Chinese food and getting a little strange on the side.

"You're the suspect in those killings." He took a sip of iced tea. "And you lay the blame on a God Squad that keeps to themselves and doesn't bother anybody?"

"How do you know they keep to themselves and don't bother anybody?" I asked.

His lips tightened.

After a moment, he said, "It's awful convenient, is all I mean."

"Does that mean you know who they are?" Hannah asked.

"I don't talk to reporters." Throckmorton squinted at me. "What happened to your head?"

"I fell down."

"This town ain't been good for you, has it?" he said. "You shoulda stayed on the bus. The road's only your friend so long as you keep moving."

Wisdom comes from the strangest of places, like a philandering Texas Ranger in a Chinese restaurant a hundred miles past the exit for the middle of nowhere. Bubba Confucius.

"I think the woman who was killed last night was part of the Sky of Zion," I said. "I think she was trying to get away."

"So?"

"So investigate," Hannah said.

Throckmorton shot her a look. "Funny how you keep talking. It's almost like you think I'm listening."

"Quit being an asshat," I said. "It's worth a trip out to the compound, and you know it."

Throckmorton held up three fingers and folded them down, one by one. "*Número uno*, the dead woman's got no ID. Two, her prints aren't on file anywhere. And three, there're no witnesses or real suspects, as much as I'd like to nail the suspect part on you."

"What about Chigger, then?" I said.

"And the imaginary men in the gray truck?" He arched an eyebrow.

"They're not imaginary." Hannah related what had happened at the motel.

Throckmorton didn't interrupt. When she was finished, he drummed his fingers on the table and stared at the painting of Bruce Lee.

"There's more." I told him about the neighborhood of apostates, gave him a brief rundown of my encounters with Silas McPherson and his stubby friend, Felix. I held off on the part at the high school for the moment.

When I was finished, I said, "The woman who died, she was dressed like a member of that organization."

He turned away from Bruce Lee. "So this guy in the Bentley, he's looking for the children, too?"

Hannah nodded. "Isn't that worth a little shoe leather on your part?"

Throckmorton ignored her and focused his attention on me.

"The woman in the alley is one of those cases that ain't never gonna be solved." He paused. "You hear what I'm saying?"

I didn't reply. There were certain situations where it just didn't make sense to keep pouring good resources after bad. Example: when the crime scene included an unidentified murder victim and no leads.

"But I'm giving you new information," I said. "Silas and the Sky of Zion. This is something you can use, an angle to pursue."

He was silent, and I wondered how new my information really was.

"You looked around this town?" he asked. "Seen how bad things are?"

I didn't respond.

"These Zion people, they seem to have a lot of money and property," he said. "Hard to get much traction against somebody who owns half the town."

Hannah opened her backpack, pulled out a sheaf of papers. "Actually, it's not quite half yet, at least according to the appraisal district."

"What are you talking about?" Throckmorton said.

"The amount of the town they own." She spread out the papers.

"I was speaking metaphorically," he said.

"I wasn't." She pointed to the papers.

Throckmorton and I scanned the documents, ownership records sorted by location. Home after home after home, all with the same owner—Piedra Springs Housing Corporation, LLC, mailing address a street in Midland. Also, several blocks of downtown, including the bar where I'd stopped the night before, were owned by the same entity.

"I stopped counting at three hundred," she said. "That's roughly a third of the homes in the city."

"Did you look up the address in Midland?" I asked. "This housing corporation?"

She nodded, gave me her phone.

The browser was open to the Midland County Appraisal District's website, the search results for the address of the Piedra Springs Housing Corporation.

The owner was ZL Enterprises, the same entity associated with the phone number on Silas McPherson's business card. That meant a third of the town appeared to be connected to the enigmatic man in the Bentley, if not owned outright.

Throckmorton tapped the papers. "Are all these houses occupied?"

Hannah shrugged. "I don't know."

"If they are," Throckmorton said, "then that's a pretty big block of voters."

No wonder Sheriff Marsh was running scared. He was on the verge of losing his job unless he played ball with the dominant power in the county.

We were all silent for a moment. The waiter brought our egg rolls. I took a bite and then pushed away the plate. I was famished, but the food instantly soured my stomach.

"I saw the boy. His name is Caleb." I related briefly what had happened at the abandoned high school. "His sister's name is Mary."

Throckmorton stared at me, a vaguely sad look in his eyes. I could only imagine what he was thinking—the guy who'd lost his kids was now seeing imaginary children.

An image of Sheriff Quang Marsh in the front window of his house flashed in my mind. Again I wondered if I was losing touch with reality. I touched the bump on my head. The pain was real.

"I saw the boy, too," Hannah said. "He was running from Felix."

"That's the fellow who got stabbed by a spear?" Throckmorton asked. "But somehow managed to get away?"

Neither Hannah nor I spoke.

Throckmorton pulled out his phone and typed a text, grumbling as he did so. "Fine. I'll send a trooper over to the high school."

I felt a moment of satisfaction. He was interested enough to at least make the most cursory of efforts to follow the leads we had presented him.

"I want you to run a name for me," I said.

"Let me guess. Silas McPherson. The guy in the Bentley."

I nodded. Ate another bite of my egg roll. It tasted like sawdust.

"You're bound and determined to swat this hornet's nest, aren't you?" Throckmorton said.

I shrugged.

He sighed. "What else do you have on this guy?"

I relayed a description and an estimate of Silas's age.

He tapped out a message.

The waiter brought our food as the Latina wandered back to the table, finished with her meal. Throckmorton told her to go wait in his Suburban.

I forced myself to eat, needing the fuel. Hannah and I were halfway finished with our food when Throckmorton's phone dinged.

"Huh." He read the screen, a thoughtful expression on his face.

I looked up. "Huh, what?"

"Silas McPherson is clean. In fact, he's so clean, he doesn't even exist."

- CHAPTER THIRTY-THREE -

Throckmorton stuck me with the tab.

I paid, put down a good tip. Then Hannah and I left the restaurant.

The sky was deep into dusk, a pale-yellow horizon streaked with clouds the color of eggplant. The air smelled like dust and hot asphalt mixed with hay and livestock, the latter from a cattle trailer parked near the exit of the parking lot.

I stared at the clouds and wondered what the divine message was for this evening. Overcast with a chance of brimstone? Across the parking lot, Throckmorton stood by his Suburban, silhouetted against the western sky, a mythic figure in a cowboy hat and khaki shirt.

A mythic figure who was talking to himself.

After a moment, I realized he was using an earpiece hooked up to his phone. He ended the call and motioned me over.

Hannah and I approached.

"What do you know about Chigger?" he asked.

"Not much," I said. "Other than he was a skinhead loser."

"Apparently he had a flag in his jacket. Made the feds all hot and bothered when they heard he got popped."

"Yeah?"

"He was some kinda tech guy. Did contract work for a crew on the East Coast."

"A Russian crew?" Hannah said.

Throckmorton stared at her for a moment and then nodded. "He screwed 'em over somehow, which is a bad thing to do if you want to keep on breathing."

"The guy who shot Chigger wasn't Russian," I said. "He was just at our motel, knocking in doors. He's part of the same group that was after the woman."

"The guys in the hats?"

I nodded.

"And they're part of this Sky of Zion thing? You're sure?"

I nodded again.

He rubbed his eyes, tired-looking all of a sudden. "You know what religion makes up the largest percentage of FBI agents?"

I looked at Hannah. She shook her head.

"Mormons." He put away his phone. "Do you know why?"

Neither of us replied.

"Because they're incorruptible," he said. "They don't booze it up or gamble or whore around. They drink fruit juice and go to church a lot."

"What's your point?" I asked.

Hannah spoke before he could answer. "They used to be considered a cult."

Throckmorton touched his nose with his index finger. "Score a point for the lady reporter."

"They were considered America's first domestic terrorists," Hannah said. "And now look at them."

Throckmorton turned to me. "I don't suppose there's any possibility you could just get on a bus tomorrow and head to Vegas or something?"

"Not a chance in hell," I said.

"Considering how much of the town they own," he said, "these Zion people obviously have a lot of money, too. That means they probably have friends in Austin. Legislators, lobbyists, you know the drill."

I nodded. "Tell me about the Russians Chigger was contracting for."

"Looks like they were working some kind of money-laundering scam," he said. "Wiring a lot of cash this way and that."

Hannah glanced at me but didn't speak.

"If the feds are on it, that means there's been a breach," he said. "Something ruptured along the pipeline, raised a flag somehow."

I remembered my first sighting of Silas McPherson. The big Bentley parking in front of the bank on Main Street.

"What if the Russians and Silas McPherson are running money through Piedra Springs?" I said. "Chigger screwed up somehow, and the Russians got Silas to clean up their mess."

"That's a great theory," he said. "Except for one thing. Why would anybody be funneling money through Piedra Springs? A ten-dollar bill blows across Main Street and half the town gets a boner."

I started to answer him but had no ready reply. He was right. Any money coming through this place would raise eyebrows to the moon and back.

The woman rapped on the window of the Suburban. She said something that was hard to understand because of the glass. Her message was clear, though: she was ready to leave Mr. Wong's.

"I got to git," Throckmorton said.

"Who's president of the local bank?" I asked.

"Do I look like the chamber of commerce?" He headed toward the driver's side of the Suburban. "Get on the bus in the morning."

He looked at Hannah. "You, too. Go back to wherever you came from."

"Why did you tell us about Chigger and the Russians if you wanted us to leave?" I asked.

"Because I'm a nice guy?" He opened his door. "I see either of you again, I'm gonna arrest you. Just because."

We watched his SUV speed down the road as night descended.

- CHAPTER THIRTY-FOUR -

I drove this time, Hannah in the passenger seat.

We headed down Main Street, the sky above an inky black swathed in stars. The image reminded me of a half-forgotten Sunday school lesson. Yahweh's promise to Abraham, descendants too numerous to count, like grains of sand.

I wondered how many people were at the Sky of Zion compound.

The map on the Internet indicated the prison site was pretty big, a substantial sliver of what was one of the larger counties in the state. How many acres would that be? Ten thousand? Twenty? More than that?

A gray pickup was parked in front of Earl's Restaurant. A county squad car sat a couple of spaces over. In the front window, I could see Sheriff Quang Marsh in the same booth as last night. He was alone, drinking coffee. No sign of anybody wearing the Stetsons with the unique crease. That didn't mean they weren't there.

A lot of cars were parked in front of Jimmy and Dale's, more than at the restaurant. The woman's death less than twenty-four hours ago clearly had no impact on tonight's business.

Our luggage was in the trunk. After seeing the two men at the Comanche Inn, we decided that we wouldn't stay there anymore. I figured to ask Boone to put us up for the night. If that didn't work, I'd park somewhere out of the way and we'd sleep in the car.

"Why don't we just keep driving?" Hannah said. "By dawn we could probably be in New Mexico, away from all this."

"Is that what you really want to do?"

She was silent as the dreariness of the town passed by. She shook her head.

"What's your take on Silas?" I asked. "What's his angle in all this?"

"His angle?"

"Does he really believe all that stuff about the Supreme Apostle and the thirteenth tribe of Israel?"

"Of course he does," she said. "He has to. Otherwise why would he be living on the outskirts of nowhere?"

"So he's condoning murder? Assuming his people are responsible for Molly's death."

She nodded.

"How does that work in terms of their theology?" I asked. "Ten Commandments–wise, if nothing else."

"The ends justify the means. You ever hear of Osama bin Laden?"

I didn't reply.

She rubbed the side of her face like she was trying to decide on the right words. Then: "Think of the Sky of Zion as a life-form, a living organism."

"OK." I nodded.

"What is any organism's main goal?"

I pondered the question for a moment. "To survive."

"Exactly. By whatever means necessary."

I turned right on a street a couple of blocks past the bank and headed north. "So what are the means? What are they doing out there?"

She shook her head and shrugged, and a few minutes later, I parked in the garage at the rear of Boone's property.

We grabbed our bags and walked through the backyard.

A full moon hung overhead. The air was cool, smelling of honeysuckle and damp earth.

Suzy sat on the back steps, looking like she was waiting for us.

"Hey." She crossed her arms.

"Hey yourself," I said.

"Who's she?" Suzy pointed at Hannah, a sullen tone in her voice.

I introduced them and said, "Where's Boone?"

"Inside." Suzy stood. She opened the screen door and motioned me in.

I entered. As soon as I crossed the threshold, she let the door slam shut on Hannah and stalked off down the hallway.

Hannah opened the door and stepped into the kitchen. "Nice girl. Friend of yours?"

"She has trouble expressing herself in healthy ways," I said.

We found Boone in the library, staring out the window at the darkness.

He glanced up. "Figured you'd be back."

"We need a place to stay," I said. "The Comanche Inn is getting a little crowded."

"Boys from the compound?"

I nodded.

"Zealots with guns." He shook his head. "Bad combination."

"Will they look for us here?" I didn't want to bring danger to the old man's home.

He didn't answer. He returned to staring out the window, the very same window from which Hannah had seen Caleb, a runaway from the Sky of Zion compound, while I'd been talking to Silas McPherson, a member of the Sky of Zion leadership structure.

A moment passed as I pondered the coincidence of two people from the same organization being at this particular house at
the same time, as well as Hannah's earlier comment wondering if
Boone was somehow involved in helping members get away from
the compound.

"You help them escape, don't you?" I asked.

He looked away from the window but didn't say anything.

"Molly was supposed to be meeting someone," I said. "Was that
you?"

Another period of silence. Then: "All she had to do was call when
she got close to town," he said. "But I think she didn't know how to
use the cell phone we left her. The ones raised out there struggle with
technology."

"How many have you helped get away?" I asked.

"What's it matter?" he asked. "You want to give me a medal or
something?"

I didn't reply.

"This used to be a nice part of the world before they got here." He
shook his head. "Good folks lived here."

"Have they tried to stop you?" I asked.

"What's it to you, son?" He rubbed the old injury on his head. "You
just show up in town one day and you think you can fix everything?"

Hannah patted his arm, but he pushed away her hand.

"Suzy's in the room at the head of the stairs, next to mine." He
headed to the door. "Plenty of other places in this house to lay your
head."

"Have you thought about leaving?" I asked.

"Piedra Springs?" He snorted. "This is my home. Nobody's running
me out."

• • •

Boone was upstairs, his snores filtering all the way to the library where Hannah stood by the desk, leafing through the ledger that Silas McPherson had been examining. She handed it to me.

The ledger was really a checkbook, a binder with three checks on each page. The section she was holding had just stubs, the checks having been torn off and given to the payees.

"Look at the names." She pointed to the first stub.

Joshua Johnson, one hundred dollars, written two days before.

"That's my brother-in-law," she said.

I scanned several more pages. All were for the same amount, made out to individuals.

"I think he's funding the apostates," she said.

"I thought they wouldn't take anything from unbelievers."

"Maybe it's just for the children," she said. "Maybe they trust him, and they take his money so their kids won't starve."

"So he helps some people escape and he gives others money to survive." I handed her the checkbook. "No wonder he's on Silas's shit list."

Hannah flipped through a few more pages. Then she put down the book and left the room, eyes welling with tears.

I waited a few moments and went to look for her.

She was on the front porch in one of the swings, staring at the moon.

"You OK?" I sat beside her.

"Why do people do this to themselves?" Her voice was quiet, choked with emotion. "What was so bad in my sister's life that she took up with these people?"

I shrugged, not having a good answer. Why did anyone do anything? People were complicated.

"You never asked about why I'm on leave from the paper," she said.

"What business is it of mine?"

She didn't say anything.

"What's past is past," I said. "Where I come from, you're judged by what you are, not by what you used to be."

The burden of your history is something you can never get away from, but you shouldn't let it color your future. Another saying of my father's, the history prof.

"That's quite a place you're from," she said.

I remembered moonlit nights like this one, sitting in the backyard with my wife and a bottle of wine, our whole lives in front of us. I wiped the tears from my eyes.

After a moment, Hannah took my hand, and we continued to stare at the night sky.

- CHAPTER THIRTY-FIVE -

I made sure all the doors and windows were locked. Then I found a guest room upstairs at the end of the hall.

The room had a four-poster bed with a mattress that dipped toward the middle, a moth-eaten rug, and faded wallpaper patterned with English gentlemen hunting foxes.

I tossed my bag on the dresser and went next door, where I discovered Hannah in the middle of a similar room, examining her surroundings, suitcase still in hand. Her face was haggard, bags under her eyes, skin pale. I imagined that I looked the same. It had been a rough day for both of us.

"Does your phone have service?" I asked.

She pulled her cell from her pocket and handed me the device.

"Thought you didn't have anybody to call," she said.

"I don't. Be right back." I returned to my room and sat on the bed.

Not much signal was showing on the borrowed phone, but I didn't plan on downloading the 3-D version of *Avatar*.

I opened a browser, typed in the web address for the Federal Bureau of Prisons, inmate lookup.

This was something I did every week or so, whenever I had access to the Internet.

I entered my father-in-law's name. Clicked "Search."

A moment later, his prisoner number appeared next to his location, a low-security facility in Beaumont, Texas. Not like he was going anywhere, but seeing the information gave me a certain level of satisfaction. The bastard was incarcerated, where he belonged. He wouldn't be released until his sixty-ninth birthday, five years from now. Upon his release from the federal penitentiary, he would begin serving a sentence in Huntsville for a different set of crimes.

I smiled, feeling just the tiniest bit better.

Hannah appeared in the doorway. "What are you so happy about?"

"A guy I know who's in prison."

"Did you put him there?"

I hesitated, unsure of how to answer. "It's my father-in-law." I got off the bed, handed the phone back to her. "So why are you on leave from the paper?"

She stepped inside and looked around. There was a sofa against one wall, opposite the door to the bathroom.

"Do you mind if I sleep there?" She pointed to the sofa.

"You can have the bed."

She opened the closet, found a blanket and a pillow. Plopped both on the sofa and then sat down.

"I wanted to write a story about the Sky of Zion," she said. "A long-form piece. The perspective of a family member who's watched a loved one get sucked into the cult."

"What happened?"

"My editor and I, well, we disagreed on the direction of the article."

"What direction would that be?"

"She thought I was, how should I put it, losing my objectivity."

"Did you have a breakdown in the newsroom?"

"I suppose so," she said. "If by breakdown, you mean did I punch the bitch in the face?"

I chuckled.

"I'm not a violent person," she said.

"Me neither. Unless somebody forces my hand."

We didn't speak for a period of time, comfortable in the silence, enjoying each other's company.

"I've been thinking about Silas," she said. "About how he had so much information on me."

"My guess is he keeps tabs on all the members of the church. Friends, family, known associates. Likely weaknesses. Wardens do the same with their inmates."

I thought about my father-in-law. He didn't have many friends or family left. A brother in Amarillo. My wife's sister, married to a doctor in Portland. And me.

She said, "I think I could be violent with Silas."

The room filled with a soft hum followed by the pleasant rush of cool air as the central air-conditioning turned on.

"Me, too."

She yawned. "You ready to go to sleep?"

I nodded, fatigued to the core, unaware up to this point in my life that it was possible to be this tired and still be functional.

She disappeared into the bathroom with her bag. A few minutes later she emerged wearing an oversize T-shirt that reached to midthigh.

We stared at each other, awkwardness overcoming our exhaustion for the moment.

She said, "You're not some weirdo who sleeps in the nude, are you?"

I shook my head.

"My last boyfriend did that, said he was allowing his chi to flow freely over his skin."

"Last boyfriend? As in ex?"

She nodded. "He didn't understand why I punched my editor. Among other things."

I went into the bathroom. Brushed my teeth. Stripped down to my boxers and a T-shirt. When I came out, Hannah was in the bed with the covers pulled up to her neck, facing the far wall.

"Turns out I don't want to sleep on the couch," she said. "And I don't want to sleep alone in the other room."

I shrugged. "Like I said, I'm fine on the couch."

"Get in," she said. "I'll stay on my side."

That gave me pause, but I turned out the lights and slid under the covers. This was the first time I'd shared a bed with anyone since my wife had died. It felt wrong and right at the same time.

We were back to back.

"You married?" she asked.

I didn't say anything. In my mind, I saw the curve of my wife's hip, the lines around her eyes when she laughed.

The grief came in waves. Sometimes it was just a few inches of water lapping on the shores of my mind, other times a tsunami. Tonight was somewhere in the middle. Rough seas, choppy but manageable.

"Girlfriend?"

I didn't speak. A heaviness that was more than fatigue settled on my chest.

"You asleep already?" Hannah asked.

"Sorry, I was thinking about something else. I don't have either. My wife, she, uh, died."

A moment passed.

"You want to tell me about it?" Hannah said.

I closed my eyes, praying for a dreamless night. "No."

The AC turned off, and the room was completely silent.

"Good night, Arlo." She reached across the bed and patted my arm. Her touch was soft and comforting, and soon I fell asleep.

• • •

My wife came to me in my dreams, as I knew she would.

The last time we made love, a crisp fall night that might as well have been yesterday, the details were so clear in my mind.

The kids were asleep. The house was quiet. Moonlight streamed through our bedroom window. She clutched my back, pulled me deeper. Her breath came in shallow gasps, a strand of hair streaked across her face.

The tingling began in the pit of my stomach.

I tried to hold back, tried to wait for her.

The tingling grew stronger, and I realized it was not the feeling of sex.

It was fear.

- CHAPTER THIRTY-SIX -

Nine Months Ago

The diner was in East Dallas, the kind of place where the busboys carry blackjacks and the cook learned his trade in prison.

I ate there at least once a week, occasionally meeting with low-level informants who knew to find me there, people looking to drop a dime on someone who had screwed them over on a drug deal or some other transaction in the underworld economy.

The diner was sandwiched between a strip club and a store where you sold blood for cash, in a neighborhood only slightly less charming than a bail bondsman's waiting room.

The woman sitting across from me was named Chloe. She was a lieutenant with the Dallas Police Department, the vice squad, a third-generation cop. Her father had been one of the officers who'd helped arrest Lee Oswald at the Texas Theater that November afternoon in 1963. Her grandfather, a deputy sheriff back in the 1930s, had been a grand wizard of the Ku Klux Klan.

It was lunchtime.

I had been in a booth by myself, eating a hamburger, when Chloe slid across from me, uninvited.

She was in uniform. Her hair was pulled back in a bun, which accentuated the angles of her face, the jutting jaw and long, thin nose, the wide cheekbones. Her eyes were the color of concrete, cold and hard, and never seemed to blink.

I was on duty, badge pinned to my breast.

"You must be Arlo Baines." She introduced herself. "Look at you in your starched shirt and your cowboy hat. Aren't you a picture?"

Before I could reply, a half dozen other officers sat down at the tables around us.

Some were in uniform. Others wore tactical garb—utility pants, combat boots, SWAT T-shirts. They were all big men, stocky, more than six feet tall, no doubt chosen for their ability to intimidate.

The tables where they sat were occupied with other patrons, but that didn't seem to matter. On any given day, half the customers at this particular diner were either just out of jail or had outstanding warrants they were dodging. The civilians got up and left, meals unfinished, coffee still steaming in their cups.

After a few moments, no one was in the dining room but me and a bunch of cops.

"My first husband wanted to be a Texas Ranger," Chloe said. "But he gave me gonorrhea."

"What's one got to do with the other?" I asked.

She glared at me with her unblinking eyes. "You think it's OK for a disease-ridden piece of shit to be a Ranger?"

I didn't reply. I looked at the other cops. They were all staring at me with deadpan expressions.

"He quit the DPS not long after I divorced him," she said. "Everybody decided that was in his best interest. Last I heard he was selling used cars in Lufkin."

"What's with all the muscle?" I pointed to the other officers.

"I like strong men around me." She pulled a pack of Capri Ultra Lights from her pocket. "Are you strong, Arlo?"

I took another bite of my burger. Chewed. Swallowed. Drank some iced tea. Thought about finishing the burger, but I was getting full. So I pushed away the plate.

When it was obvious that I was done with my meal, Chloe lit a cigarette. Smoking was illegal in Dallas restaurants, but I didn't think the manager was going to come over and complain.

"Nice talking to you." I started to slide from the booth.

"If I were you, I wouldn't go just yet." She tapped some ash onto my plate.

I stopped. "Are you threatening me, Chloe?"

No good deed goes unpunished, the favor I'd performed for my father-in-law being a prime example. I should have impressed upon the Frisella brothers a little more forcefully the need to not discuss our business together.

"Not at all," she said. "I'm just giving you some advice."

"I don't need advice from Dallas PD." I stood, headed toward the exit.

The other cops didn't try to stop me. I'd gotten about ten feet away when Chloe spoke again.

"Dr. Sanders," she said. "A three-thirty appointment, right?"

My blood felt like it had stopped flowing. My skin turned to ice.

I turned around. "What did you say?"

My voice was low and husky. Sounds were muted, my vision tunneled.

"That's your son's orthodontist. Dr. Sanders. His next appointment is tomorrow afternoon, right?"

"You fucking bitch." I tried to control the shaking of my limbs.

"Your daughter's got ballet at four fifteen, so your wife, she's gonna be spread thin, running all over town."

I reached for my pistol, but two officers from the nearest table had been waiting for that. One had his gun out already. He aimed at my face. The other took my weapon from the holster. Then he removed the backup piece in my hip pocket, the knife from my belt.

Chloe said, "Sit back down, Arlo. We're not finished yet."

I reached for my cell phone, the last weapon I had. One of the officers grabbed that, too. He took the phone and my guns and my knife and put everything on a table across the room, a long thirty feet away.

Another officer pushed me back to the booth, forced me to sit. I resisted the urge to lash out at the man. He had too many allies, and I was unarmed. The best course of action, the only one, was to bide my time.

She waved away the other cops. They retreated to the front of the diner, out of earshot.

"The duffel bag you got from the Frisella brothers," she said. "I need it back."

"Do you have any idea what it's gonna be like when every single Texas Ranger in the state comes after you?"

"Shut your piehole, Arlo, and listen to me."

I stared at her face, imagining those gray eyes empty and dead.

"The contents of that bag weren't theirs to give," she said. "Or yours to take."

I didn't reply.

"If you hand over the bag, then nobody's gonna hurt your family." She lit another cigarette. "That's deal point number one."

I weighed the odds of reaching across the table and strangling her before the other officers stopped me.

"Deal point number two," she said. "If, after you give me the bag, you come looking for any sort of payback, you need to get it through your head that I will be unable to guarantee the safety of your wife and kids."

I flexed my fingers, tensed my legs.

"Do you understand what I'm saying?"

My breathing was shallow and rapid. I couldn't reply if I wanted to.

One of the cops moved a little closer, still out of hearing range. He pulled a Taser from his belt and held it by his side.

Chloe leaned across the table. "Say that you understand, Arlo. Say, *I understand.*"

My stomach churned, bile in my throat. After a moment, I whispered, "I understand."

"Whew." She leaned back. "Glad we got that over with."

I felt like I'd run a marathon. My heart pounded. My skin was sweaty.

"Now let's work out the details," she said. "And those are really simple, so I don't expect we'll have much trouble. Ready? You give me the fucking bag of money."

I took several deep breaths, willed myself to remain calm. The details were going to be harder than she expected.

"I don't have the bag," I said.

She stared at me, head cocked.

"The money is in the bank. It's not mine to give back anymore."

"Oh, fuck a duck." She massaged her temple. "My partners are not going to be happy to hear that."

"The Frisellas owed that money for a real-estate loan. They settled a debt."

She rolled her eyes. "The Frisella boys are hemorrhoids with bad suits. What they owe to some bank is immaterial to this situation."

She pulled out a phone and sent a text. The phone dinged in reply. She texted back, and a period of time passed. Probably only a couple of minutes, but it felt like hours. Chloe drummed her fingers on the tabletop. She lit another cigarette, took two puffs, and stubbed it out.

The phone rang. She answered. A one-sided conversation ensued. She listened a lot, occasionally saying "yes" or "uh-huh."

The called ended, and she turned her attention back to me.

"Five o'clock today. That's when we need the money."

"I told you. I don't have it."

"You won't have any trouble finding the drop-off location," she said. "It's your house."

My heart started pounding again.

"Don't do anything stupid, Arlo. We're there already, keeping your family company."

- CHAPTER THIRTY-SEVEN -

I awoke in darkness, drenched in sweat. I reached for Chloe's throat, but my limbs were paralyzed.

An unfamiliar hand stroked my face. Arms I didn't know cradled me.

A woman's voice spoke in a soothing tone. "Shh. It's OK."

I sat upright.

Hannah was next to me in the bed. "You had a bad dream."

I looked around the room. Boone's house. Piedra Springs.

"Who's Chloe?" she asked.

"Wh-what?"

"You were thrashing around, mumbling that name."

"She's a . . ." I couldn't find the words.

Air caught in my chest, not going in or out. A metallic taste filled my mouth.

"It's OK," Hannah said. "Relax."

I concentrated on breathing, big, slow lungfuls.

"Is Chloe your—"

"No, no. That's not my wife." I paused. "Chloe is . . . she's dead now, too."

Hannah didn't say anything.

I got out of bed, stumbled to the bathroom. I drank a glass of water, then slid back under the covers.

"Are you OK?" she asked.

"I haven't been OK in a long time."

We were silent for a moment.

"Me neither." She fluffed her pillow. "Let's go back to sleep."

I closed my eyes, and fatigue overtook me. Soon I drifted off.

• • •

Hannah and I woke the next day when the sun streamed through the bedroom window.

Though we hadn't been physically intimate, there was an awkwardness between us like lovers after a first encounter. Hannah slid from the bed, pulling her T-shirt down on her legs. She grabbed her suitcase and disappeared into the room next door.

Twenty minutes later we met downstairs, cleaned up, ready to start the day.

Boone was in the kitchen, cooking bacon. A Mr. Coffee percolated on the countertop, nearly finished brewing a full pot. There was no sign of Suzy.

"Y'all want breakfast?" he asked.

Hannah shook her head at the same time as I said, "Yes."

Boone chuckled.

"We've got a long day," I said. "We need to fuel up."

Hannah acquiesced as Boone whipped some eggs into a mixing bowl. The old man seemed contented, puttering around in the kitchen. His hair wasn't in a ponytail, the gray locks dangling around his shoulders. I wondered how long it had been since he'd cooked breakfast for more than one person.

"While we eat," I said, "you can tell us about the banker in town."

He removed the bacon from the pan. "Why do you want to talk to him? He's like an impacted bowel but without the pleasant memories."

Hannah poured three cups of coffee. "Bankers make good sources. They know a lot about what's going on."

"They also crack easily," I said. "If you know how to break them."

• • •

Boone let me borrow his car again. He walked us out to the garage after we'd eaten.

"Those kids aren't in town anymore," he said.

"How do you know?" I asked. "I thought you were supposed to get them to safety."

"That's making the assumption they still want to get away."

"What do you mean?"

"Their mama's dead, and they're all alone," Hannah said. "Odds are they went home."

"The compound." I sighed.

Boone nodded.

"Think about it," Hannah said. "That's the only world they've ever known."

"Back to what's familiar," Boone said. "They were talking about doing that the night before last."

"And you're just now telling me?" I tried not to sound angry.

"What difference would it make?" he said. "Not like you can just waltz in and find them."

No one spoke.

"You're not thinking about actually going there, are you?" Boone asked.

Silence. Hannah and I looked at each other.

"Go talk to the banker or whatever makes you feel good. Then leave town."

"We'll try to get your car back in one piece." I headed to the driver's side.

• • •

Before we talked to the banker, I decided to get a gun.

It was a little after nine in the morning when I parked in the lot between the feed store and the bar, the place where Molly's body had been discovered. Both businesses were closed, and the crime scene tape was gone.

At the rear of the bar was a large dumpster that reached halfway up the wall.

I hopped on the dumpster and then pulled myself onto the roof. The movement sent a spike of pain through my knee, like an ice pick on the inside trying to poke out. As soon as the pain appeared, it just as quickly vanished. I walked around the rooftop for a moment, working out the kinks and various aches from yesterday.

The pistols I'd taken off the guards the night before last were where I had tossed them. In the middle of the roof, both lying by an empty wine bottle and a faded running shoe.

The guns were Glock 9mms, a workhorse of a pistol, pretty much indestructible. I picked one at random and fieldstripped the other, dropping the frame in the dumpster and leaving the barrel on the roof.

The magazine of the one I kept was full, one round in the chamber. Eighteen bullets total.

I slid the pistol in the waistband of my jeans behind my hip and covered the grip with my T-shirt. Then I climbed down and got back in the Crown Victoria.

When the door shut, Hannah asked, "Did you get one for me, too?"

"No." I started the car. "You see anything that needs shooting, you let me know, and I'll take care of it."

• • •

Turns out Boone didn't live in the biggest house in Piedra Springs. The president of the First State Bank did, a two-story colonial on the northern fringes of town.

Where Boone's place was run-down, the banker's home was immaculate. White columns gleamed in the morning sun, stark against the deep green of the lawn and the spray of color in the flower beds.

A late-model Chevrolet Malibu was parked across the street, the only vehicle not in a driveway. The Malibu faced east and had a tiny sticker on the front window that looked like it could have been a bar code for a rental-car company.

A man in his thirties with close-cropped blond hair sat in the driver's seat. He watched us go by, craning his neck as we passed.

At the end of the block, I turned right and headed north, intending to circle back around.

But there was nowhere to circle back. The street morphed into a state highway a hundred yards later as the city limit sign appeared. Ahead of us lay the open range of West Texas.

I pulled onto the shoulder. "The guy in the Malibu. What'd you make of him?"

Hannah stared into the distance. "Seemed like he didn't belong."

I nodded.

"He looked like a cop," she said. "Maybe a federal agent?"

"Maybe." I got out of the car, popped open the trunk.

Boone struck me as a resourceful fellow, so it came as no surprise that the rear of the old Crown Victoria was filled with all sorts of useful stuff. Tire irons and towropes, a can of WD-40, duct tape. A tool kit with enough tools to rebuild the engine on a '56 Dodge.

I debated my choices and selected two items—the duct tape and the WD-40—and got back in the car.

I made a U-turn and drove back the way we came, heading in the direction the Chevy was pointed. I slowed and parked behind the car. The man with the blond hair was facing away from us.

"Wait here." I grabbed a map of Texas from the glove compartment.

"What are you planning to do? Direction him to death?"

I ignored her attempt at humor and hid the WD-40 in the folds of the map. Then I got out of our car, map in one hand, duct tape in the other.

I left the tape on the hood of the Crown Victoria as the driver's door of the Malibu opened and the blond man got out. He strode toward me.

We met between the two vehicles.

It was pretty obvious he wasn't a cop or a federal agent.

He wore a pair of baggy jeans and an untucked knit shirt emblazoned with an oversize logo of a polo player. His biceps were like hams, straining the material of his shirt. Tattoos covered his forearms and hands, religious figures and Cyrillic writing.

Anybody in law enforcement would recognize him for what he was—a Russian mobster, part of the ethnic group who had wrested control of most organized crime from the Italian mafia.

"Excuse me." I smiled, tried to look harmless. "Do you know where Earl's Family Restaurant is?"

"What you talking 'bout?" He had a thick Russian accent. "Who is Earl?"

"They're supposed to have good enchiladas." I paused. "Do you like Mexican food?"

He stared at me, no doubt trying to figure out why a guy who smelled like a cop was treating him like a restaurant app.

I took a quick look around. The street was empty. I let the map flutter away, and I sprayed him in the face with WD-40.

He screamed, pressed his hands to his eyes.

I kneed him in the crotch, slammed his head against the side of the Malibu.

He fell to the ground.

Before he could recover, I grabbed the duct tape and bound his feet and hands, slapped a strip across his mouth. Then I searched him.

In his hip pocket I found a wallet containing a New Jersey driver's license in the name of Vasily Bazanov. A pay-as-you-go smartphone was in his front pocket. No guns or weapons, not even a penknife, meaning he'd flown in with a carry-on only and had not made the effort to procure weapons.

I tossed the wallet on the floor of the front seat but stuck the phone in my pocket. I grabbed the keys from the ignition, put those next to the phone. Then I wrestled him into the back of the Malibu, leaving him on the floorboard.

He blinked away WD-40 and glared at me with red, watery eyes as I shut the door. The front windows were open. He'd be OK for an hour or so. Hopefully.

Hannah stood by the Crown Victoria.

"I found one of your Russians," I said. "Let's see if we can scare up another one."

- CHAPTER THIRTY-EIGHT -

We strode up the sidewalk to the entrance of the home.

On the stoop was a doormat adorned with a pair of ducks. Under the ducks were the words *Welcome to the Stodghills*.

The front door was ajar.

I stepped inside, Hannah right behind me.

The foyer was garish—white marble floors, green and pink flocked wallpaper, an alabaster statue of a wood nymph playing the flute. The air smelled like lemon furniture polish.

Hannah and I headed down the hallway toward the rear of the house.

A large kitchen and family room overlooked a pool.

This part of the home was decorated in early Paula Deen, lots of chintz and ceramic farm animals. The pool area continued the wood nymph theme with several marble statues of half-naked mythological figures cavorting about.

Two people were outside.

A man in a maroon tracksuit, kneeling by the water.

And a second guy who had his head under the water, courtesy of Maroon Tracksuit, who was pressing down on his neck.

I opened the back door and approached the two men.

Maroon Tracksuit watched me get closer, an unconcerned look on his face. He was in his forties, stocky like a wrestler. His head was shaved. A tattoo of an eagle with its talons extended adorned his neck. Under the eagle was Cyrillic lettering.

After a few seconds, he let go of the man whose head was underwater.

The second guy jerked up, gasping for air. He looked to be in his forties, too, but he wore different clothes, a pair of khakis and a white oxford cloth shirt.

Even though I already knew the answer, I asked anyway: "Which one of you is Stodghill?"

Maroon Tracksuit nodded toward the gasping man. Then he said, "Who are you?"

"My name is Arlo. And who might you be?"

"You can call me Boris." His accent was as thick as that of the guy in the Malibu.

I looked at Hannah. "Another one. What are the odds?"

"It's like John," she said.

I turned my attention back to the Russian. "Before you drown Stodghill, could I talk to him for a minute?"

Boris sighed. He looked tired, like he'd had a long flight and all he wanted to do was take care of the business at hand and then go home. He pulled out a cell, punched in a number.

The phone in my pocket rang.

Boris quit looking tired. He looked confused. Then wary.

This was probably supposed to be a simple assignment, to deliver a message, hence his partner's lack of weapons. Now, the situation appeared to be getting complicated.

I pulled the phone from my pocket but didn't answer. "Vasily is unavailable to take a call at the moment."

Stodghill curled into a fetal position.

Boris stood, curious but not fearful.

I tossed the phone into the pool.

Boris crossed his arms. "What you want, Mr. Arlo?"

I looked at Hannah. She said, "Are you from Brighton Beach?"

No answer.

"I'll take that as a yes," she said. "Which means you're part of the Zharkov crew."

Boris looked at me. "Why you let woman do your talking?"

I shrugged. "I'm secure in my masculinity. What can I say?"

"This is important meeting." Boris nudged the banker with his foot. "You go away now, yes? Come back later."

"Sorry, no can do." I shook my head. "I need to talk to Stodghill, and I guess to you, too, about the Sky of Zion compound."

A pronounced silence from both men.

Boris stared at me, eyes narrowing into slits. Stodghill quit groaning, a new fear in his eyes, one that didn't have anything to do with getting drowned by a Russian thug.

"You look like *politsiya*." Boris nudged the banker with his foot again. "Hey, Stodghill. *Politsiya* is here."

Stodghill sat up. His face was pale, eyes wide with fear.

"I'm not a cop," I said. "That means I don't have to follow cop rules."

"This is good." The Russian nodded. "*Politsiya* bad for business."

"I'm looking for some kids who ran away from the compound." I described the two children. "Caleb and Mary, those're their names."

"These children, they are yours?" he asked.

"No. But I want to find them anyway."

He frowned. "I not understand."

"Let's circle back to the children in a minute," Hannah said. "Tell us about the scam."

"Scam?" Boris said. "No scam. Business only. And business is private."

"We know you're running money through the local bank, using their network," Hannah said. "And the money is connected to the Sky of Z—"

"No, no, no." Stodghill's face got paler, if that were possible. He looked at Boris, whispered, "They know about the network."

"Shut up," Boris said. "They know nothing."

Stodghill groaned and crawled toward the house.

I shot Hannah a look. "Tell us how to get onto the compound."

Boris grinned. "You have army?"

I didn't answer.

"You need army for to go to compound," Boris said. "Many guards there."

The banker was halfway to the door, still on his hands and knees.

"What if I neutralize Silas?" I asked. "Will that make the guards easier to handle?"

Boris nodded. "You make Silas go away, you give Boris much happiness. Silas end business arrangement with Boris and make deal with competitors. That's why Boris having meeting with Stodghill."

We all looked toward the house. The banker had reached the door. He glanced at us and disappeared inside. I wondered why Boris wasn't going after him but realized there was little danger. What was Stodghill going to do, call the police?

The Russians had been laundering money for the church. Money was flowing through Stodghill's bank, illegal money, facilitated by Boris's crew, heading to the Sky of Zion. Or maybe it was the other way around.

The direction didn't really matter at this point. What did matter was that for whatever reason, Silas had switched vendors and Boris's people were angry. Boris couldn't get to Silas because he was at the compound. But he could lean on the banker.

That left one question: What was the money for?

"Tell me about the network," I said.

"Boris tell you any more, he must kill you."

Hannah took over. "They're running a server farm."

Boris wagged his finger at her. "Lady should be careful, talking so much."

A server farm, essentially anything from a roomful to a small city's worth of computers, made sense.

"The compound is a religious facility, protected by the First Amendment." She looked at me. "Their servers are probably hosting gambling sites or portals to the dark web."

The dark web was a little-understood corridor off the information superhighway, a place to buy and sell a variety of illegal goods—drugs and weapons, stolen antiquities, the odd lot of plutonium.

The Sky of Zion servers weren't completely out of reach, but the constitutional protections guaranteeing freedom of religion made it difficult for law enforcement to access them.

Boris took off the jacket of his running suit. Underneath he wore a wife-beater T-shirt. His arms were covered in tattoos. He lumbered over to a statue of the Venus de Milo. From behind the statue, he pulled a machete.

I took a step back. "What are you going to do with that?"

"Stupid banker man. We had business arrangement. Now, Boris must cut off finger to teach lesson."

"Is that really necessary?" I asked. "Couldn't you just ruin him socially?"

"You telling Boris how to do his job?" He cocked his head. "You and Boris still must discuss the Vasily situation. Perhaps Boris cut off your finger, yes?"

I pulled out the Glock, kept it pointed to the ground. "Perhaps not."

Boris eyed the pistol.

Hannah looked like she was about to say something, but she stopped when Stodghill came back outside carrying a shotgun.

I grabbed her arm, pulled her out of the line of fire.

"Why does everybody have gun but Boris?" The Russian sighed. "Stupid NRA."

The banker advanced toward the thug.

Boris rolled his eyes. "Don't be acting like idiot, Stodghill. Put gun down."

The banker raised his weapon.

"You be in shit pile of trouble," Boris said, "if you trigger pull—"

BOOM.

The blast sounded like a cannon, bouncing off the water and the exterior walls of the house.

Boris's head disappeared.

One second it was there. The next it was gone as chunks of skull and brain matter scattered about.

The Russian's headless corpse fell backward into the pool. A red stain fanned out across the clear water. Hannah gasped and clutched my arm.

Stodghill turned the weapon toward us. His face was contorted, teeth bared, a smile of rage.

I moved Hannah behind me, raised the Glock. "Put down the weapon. We're not going to hurt you."

He moved a step closer.

"We'll leave," I said. "You'll never see us again."

He took several deep breaths. His fingers on the forend of the shotgun grew white. Then he blinked like he'd just woken up from a bad dream. He lowered the gun. After a moment, he dropped it on the pool deck.

The expression on his face was one of bewilderment. A nonviolent man had just committed the most violent of acts.

"Wh-what have I done?" he asked.

"You killed a man." I stuck the Glock back in my waistband. "He probably deserved it, but that's still a heavy load."

The banker shook his head, breathing heavily.

In that instant, he reminded me of my father-in-law in the aftermath of the attack. Men accustomed to barricading themselves behind their desks, fighting their battles via lawyers, forced to confront the primal nature of life and death.

"My wife is in San Antonio," he said. "She's going to be home tomorrow."

He enunciated each syllable precisely, like this information was dreadfully important.

"She's going to be pissed about the pool," I said. "Among other things."

"I didn't want to kill him." He covered his mouth like he was going to be sick.

"But you did." I sighed. "You got in bed with the wrong people."

"They told me no one would find out." He sat down in a chair. "The bank's had a rough couple of years. We needed the money."

Everything came down to dollars and cents. I remembered my father-in-law's office, the view of downtown Dallas. The lengths he went to in order to survive.

"Tell me about the money," I said. "What was it for?"

He stared at me with a mournful expression on his face. "They were selling . . . things."

"Things?"

"The money they got, they needed it to be untraceable."

"What were they selling?" I asked.

"I never knew. Never wanted to, really." He paused. "My grandfather started the bank in 1947. I couldn't let it end on my watch."

I felt sorry for him, and I hated myself for that.

Hannah's teeth chattered, her skin pale.

"Do you have a passport?" I asked.

"What?" He stared at me, confused.

"A passport. Do you have one?"

He nodded.

"The Midland airport is about three hours away. If you leave now, you'll have a good head start."

"But this is my home," he said.

I looked at the body in the pool. "Not anymore."

- CHAPTER THIRTY-NINE -

Nine Months Ago

I sped out of the parking lot of the diner in East Dallas, gravel churning under the tires of my pickup, my heart racing.

In the rearview mirror, I could see Chloe standing in the doorway of the restaurant, her uniform dark against the shadows. It looked like she was making a call, but with the way the light played, it was hard to tell.

The sun was hot and bright overhead. The world around me looked brittle, ready to break.

Images of my wife and children played in my head like a movie reel about to jump its sprockets.

Breakfast that morning. My daughter playing with her dolls, the boy eating cereal. My wife making a grocery list.

Innocents, caught in the cross fire of something beyond the bell curve of their experience. All because of Frank's greed.

I blew through a stop sign and placed a flashing red-and-blue light on the dash.

My home was on the other side of town, the northwest quadrant of the city, a twenty-minute drive with no traffic. The quickest route was to loop through the central part of town, head north on the Dallas North Tollway.

The highway leading to downtown was a few blocks away. My skin felt clammy from fear, mouth dry.

I dialed Frank's cell as I drove. He answered after the first ring.

"You need to give back the money," I said.

A car honked as I sped through another intersection.

"That's not possible." He lowered his voice. "The FDIC regulators are here now."

"I don't give a damn about the regulators," I said. "They have my family."

Silence.

"They have your daughter," I said. "And your grandchildren."

A sharp intake of air from the other end.

"If you don't hand over the money," I said, "they're going to kill them."

He gasped. A few seconds passed, but he didn't respond.

"Did you hear me, you miserable piece of shit?" I was yelling into the phone now. "They're going to *kill* them."

Voices in the background.

"I heard you," Frank said. "Let me think. I don't know what—"

Men talking on the other end. Giving orders. Other men responding, an argument of some sort. A woman's voice cut through the babble, Frank's assistant, plaintive-sounding, asking for everybody to be calm.

I got on the highway that led to downtown, speeding toward home, weaving in and out of traffic.

"Arlo. Listen to me." My father-in-law's voice was low and serious. "I can't get to the cash right now. You have to believe me. I would if I could."

"You're a banker, Frank. Walk into the damn vault and get out three hundred thousand dollars. It's as simple as that."

"You don't understand. We've got a situation here—"

Sounds of a scuffle. One man's voice raising above the others, saying words I often used during the course of my job.

Put your hands behind your head.

Several seconds passed. Then another voice came on the line. Gruff, hard-sounding.

"Who is this?"

"Arlo Baines," I said. "I'm a Texas Ranger. Put Frank back on."

The voice chuckled. "Frank's in custody right now. He's not taking any calls unless they're from his lawyer."

The line went dead as the Dallas skyline loomed in front of me.

I jerked the wheel, slung the truck onto the shoulder, passing a long line of traffic in the main lanes. At the same time I dialed the general number for the northwest substation of the Dallas Police Department.

I asked for a lieutenant I knew, a friend.

He came on the line, and I told him there was a case I was working on that might be putting my family in danger. I didn't elaborate or bother to explain that the danger came from fellow officers, members of his own department. I figured if there were enough friendly blue uniforms on the premises, I could at least buy some time.

He readily agreed to send several patrol units to my home. He said the closest one was less than two minutes away, and he'd call as soon as he could to let me know what was going on. Then he hung up.

I pushed my speed to ninety, heading north on the tollway, the highway that split the city in two.

The lieutenant called back three minutes later, told me to pull over.

"Why," I said.

"Please, just do what I'm asking."

I exited at Lovers Lane and stopped at a service station. The pit of my stomach felt like it was filled with broken glass.

"Where are you?" the lieutenant asked.

I told him.

He said, "What's the case you're working on?"

"You want to get into that *now*?" I tried to keep my voice calm. "Just tell me what you found. Tell me they're OK."

Silence.

"Please." I felt the emotion crawl up my throat, hot and foul tasting. "Say they're OK."

"What in the hell did you get yourself into, Arlo?"

I didn't reply. My vision tunneled.

"A squad car's on the way to get you," he said. "You shouldn't be driving."

"My family. What's going on at my house?"

"I'm sorry, Arlo." He paused. "I am so sorry."

- CHAPTER FORTY -

We left the banker in his backyard in Piedra Springs, along with the headless Russian. We were halfway across the front yard, walking briskly, when the muffled boom of a shotgun sounded.

Hannah looked at me, startled.

"We'd better hurry." I jogged the rest of the way to the Crown Victoria.

The Ford was still behind the rental Malibu. I glanced in the back of the Chevy, saw the second hood was still there.

We hopped into the Crown Victoria as a man walked out of the house across the street. He held a newspaper in one hand, a napkin in the other, like he'd been having breakfast when he'd heard the second gunshot and decided maybe he should see what was going on.

I slipped the transmission into drive and pulled away from the curb.

In the rearview mirror, I could see him stare at us as we drove away.

"What do we do?" Hannah paused. "We should call the police . . . shouldn't we?"

"They'll be here soon enough." I turned at the first cross street, heading toward the center of town.

She buckled her seat belt. "We should've taken the gun with us."

I slowed for an intersection. "Bet he had more than one weapon in that house."

We were both silent.

"You ever see anybody get killed before?" she asked.

I hesitated and then nodded, thinking about my father-in-law and his revolver, Chloe and her two partners, crooked vice cops in too deep with a crew out of Laredo. A sudden wave of sadness swept over me, the wastefulness of it all, the lives lost, smiling faces I would never see again.

"Where are we going?" she asked.

"Where do you think?"

She didn't answer.

"You want to quit now?" I said. "Go back to New York?"

"No." Her voice was forceful.

We stopped at Main Street as a squad car turned in front of us, heading the way we'd come, lights flashing.

There was only one southbound road out of town, a county highway just past the courthouse. I headed that way.

A Greyhound was idling in front of the bus depot. I wondered where it was going. I imagined myself onboard, no particular destination in mind, the humming of tires on asphalt as soothing as a tranquilizer.

I turned onto the road leading south.

When we passed the city limit sign, I sped up to eighty.

The road was flat and straight, devoid of traffic, bordered on either side by barbed wire and a rocky terrain that was empty of structures except for the occasional windmill or abandoned farmhouse.

"How far?" Hannah asked.

"Maybe twenty miles." I remembered the map from yesterday. "This road ends at a T intersection. From there, we go west for another ten miles or so."

We were both silent for a period of time. The land became more broken, outcroppings of limestone forming gullies and cliffs. The sky was cloudless, and the gauge on the Ford indicated an outside temperature of ninety degrees. It was not yet ten in the morning.

"Do you remember that old John Wayne movie *The Searchers?*" she asked.

I nodded. "He was looking for his niece. She'd been kidnapped by the Indians."

"You remember the ending?"

I didn't reply, maneuvering around an empty cattle truck that was going about half our speed, the only other vehicle we'd seen in the last ten minutes.

"When he found the girl," Hannah said, "she didn't want to come home."

I sped up until the Ford began to shimmy. I eased off the gas until we were going a little less than a hundred.

"She was more Indian than white." Hannah paused. "What if my niece is the same way?"

I started to answer, to say something like *we'll figure out how to cross that bridge if we come to it* or *let's don't borrow trouble.* But the words died on my lips as we crested a small hill and saw the line of pickup trucks.

They were all gray, what looked like Chevy extended cabs. Eight, maybe ten of them, heading north. Right toward us.

- CHAPTER FORTY-ONE -

The pickups sped past, the drivers paying the Crown Victoria no mind.

Two men were in each vehicle. They wore identical hats, the crown higher in the rear than in the front.

"How many did you count?" Hannah asked.

"Nine trucks. Eighteen soldiers."

"Soldiers? Is that how you think of them?"

I didn't reply. The answer was obvious. They were infantrymen. The cult's military wing.

She looked out the rear window. "Wonder where they're going?"

"Maybe they're making a doughnut run."

"That's a lot of doughnuts."

We were silent for a half mile.

"How many people are going to be there?" I asked. "At the compound?"

"This is the biggest cluster of them," she said. "The home of the Supreme Apostle and all."

A highway sign appeared: THIS ROAD MAINTAINED BY THE SKY OF ZION—SYNOD 293.

"A synod is a subdivision in the organization." She answered the question I hadn't asked yet.

"Like a chapter?"

She nodded. "Their website says they've got more than seven hundred of them."

On one side of the road, a pair of cows stood by a stock tank, tails swatting at flies.

"The main synod used to be in Arkansas," she said. "Then it moved to Missouri in the seventies."

"And now it's here?" I asked.

She nodded. "They keep searching for the promised land."

"Not a lot of milk and honey around these parts." I paused. "Where are the rest of them?"

"Mostly in the Midwest. Kansas, Nebraska, a whole string in Oklahoma. There're a few on the East Coast and one in Los Angeles."

Two buzzards were hunched over something in the road up ahead. As we got close, they flew away, one of the birds dragging what looked like the entrails of a dead animal in its beak.

Hannah continued. "A branch of the organization operates in Mexico, too, outside of Chihuahua. Beyond that, the details get sketchy, probably by design." She paused. "Like I said, the largest number of synods is here. Probably three hundred."

"So how many people is that?" I looked in the rearview mirror. The buzzards had returned.

"Each synod has twelve elders," she said. "Each elder has eleven church members under him."

"A hundred and forty-four," I said. "Times three hundred."

"That's more than forty-one thousand people," she said. "If each synod has a full roster."

I swore under my breath, and we were silent for a half mile or so.

The terrain changed. The limestone outcroppings were bigger, the land more broken. In the distance, a series of mesas became visible, long plateaus stark against the southern sky.

"They're not growing food for that many people around here," I said. "And there's only one grocery store in town, a Brookshire's off Main."

Hannah nodded. "Their numbers are like their beliefs. Bullshit."

"So how many do you think there really are at the compound?"

"Does it matter?" she said. "Since there's only the two of us?"

Up ahead, the end of the road came into view. I slowed.

The north-south highway out of Piedra Springs stopped where a state highway ran to the east and west. At the intersection, facing us, was an old gas station. The pumps were gone, but the canopy and the building itself remained.

A large sign in front of the canopy read SKY OF ZION INFORMATION CENTER. The sign was next to a flagpole with an American flag flying at half-mast.

A single gray pickup was parked in front of the station next to a four-wheeler. Off to one side was a navy-blue panel van.

I slowed, turned into the parking area.

Hannah pressed her hand against the dash. "Are you nuts?"

"No sense waltzing in cold." I stopped by the van. "Besides, you think all forty thousand know about us?"

"You mind if I stay in the car?"

"Suit yourself." I got out of the Ford.

A moment later, Hannah exited her side, muttering.

The air was hot and smelled of sage and the fading chemical aroma associated with an abandoned service station—oil, stale gasoline, old rubber.

On the door was a sign that read OPEN—ALL ARE WELCOME.

"I wonder if they really mean that," Hannah said.

"We're about to find out."

- CHAPTER FORTY-TWO -

Hannah and I entered the Sky of Zion Information Center, really just an old service station.

The interior had been refurbished into something that looked like a moderately successful insurance agency, the State Farm office in Des Moines, say. Wood paneling, utilitarian carpet, a cheap particleboard desk designed to look expensive.

A woman sat behind the desk. She was in her forties and wore a long-sleeve dress, the fabric a peach-colored gingham, pale like it had been washed too many times.

Her eyes were red and teary. A nameplate on the desk read SISTER JANE.

"Hello." I smiled.

"By the Lord's grace, welcome." She dabbed her eyes. "Are you here for the funeral?"

Hannah and I looked at each other.

"We were just passing through," I said.

"Please excuse my appearance." She touched her hair. "We are in a period of mourning."

"Oh dear," Hannah said. "Who passed?"

"Brother Felix. He died in the night."

"Brother Felix?" I tried to keep my tone even.

"Part of the first family," she said. "Descended from the Great One himself."

"What a shame." Hannah glanced at me. "So sorry for your loss."

"Would you like some literature about our organization?" Sister Jane held up a brochure.

Before I could take the offered item, a door at the rear of the room opened, and three men entered.

The first was in his fifties. He wore a pair of jeans, a pearl-button white shirt, and a Stetson with the crown higher in the rear than in the front.

The other two men were younger and clearly not part of the Sky of Zion.

One was in his thirties, good-looking like a bit player on a soap opera. He wore a pair of khakis and an expensive-looking knit polo shirt. His hair was coiffed to perfection, slicked back with so much gel it was probably bulletproof.

The guy behind him carried a professional-grade video camera. He was in his twenties. He wore cargo shorts and a faded T-shirt. Nothing about him was coiffed.

The guy in his fifties introduced himself as Brother Ted, Synod Number 63, the chapter tasked with manning the information center. He was all smiles and charm, like a salesman, which he was, in a manner of speaking.

The other two were from England, a BBC team doing a story on the Sky of Zion. The one in the knit shirt, the on-camera pretty boy, was named Ian.

Ian and his video guy were supposed to be touring the compound, but the funeral had thrown a kink into their plans. Apparently, the death of someone from the first family caused quite a disruption in the daily routine of the church members.

Ian asked if it was OK if he filmed us.

Before Hannah could reply, I told him yes, of course, and the camera guy trained his lens on our faces. Ian did a brief intro, something about wandering pilgrims on the plains of the American West, where once the buffalo and Native Americans roamed in perfect harmony.

Brother Ted ignored Hannah, looked at me. "Are you familiar with the Sky of Zion?"

"A little. I'm not sure where to start."

"How about telling me why you stopped by, friend?" He smiled warmly.

"My wife and I"—I put my arm around Hannah—"we're, uh, looking for something."

"You feel lost?"

"Yes." I nodded. "Lost and searching."

"What are you searching for, friend?" Brother Ted clasped his hands in front of his waist. His demeanor was that of an undertaker trying to sell a casket, solicitous and somber, empathetic, yet eager to make his quota for the month.

A moment passed. Then I said, "Hope, I suppose."

Brother Ted beamed. "You've come to the right place. The Apostle promises hope for all who have faith."

"There's so little of that in this world," I said. "And I want to believe."

Ian nodded approvingly. "This is dynamite, mate. Keep talking."

I smiled sheepishly.

"I'd love to give you a tour of the compound and explain who we are," Brother Ted said. "But we have a funeral in a little while."

"Brother Felix, yes," Hannah said. "We were sorry to hear the news."

"He was a great man." Ted nodded. "Spirit-filled. Part of the ruling council."

"Perhaps we could pay our respects to Brother Felix?" I said. "And see some of the compound, too?"

Silence.

"Is the funeral open so anyone could attend?" Hannah asked.

Ian's eyes grew wide. "A bloody good idea."

"Yes, yes." Ted nodded thoughtfully. "That is a good idea."

"You want to ride with us in the van?" Ian said. "We could talk some more. Get a little background footage."

"I'd rather if we took our car." Hannah touched her stomach. "I've been feeling a little ill today."

I frowned. "Are you OK, honey?"

With the appearance of Ted, Sister Jane had effectively disappeared into the background, a doormat looking for a floor upon which to be unobtrusive. Now she came around from behind the desk.

"Just a little nauseous," Hannah said.

Sister Jane touched her chin with a finger. "Forgive my intrusion, but are you with child?"

Brother Ted shook his head. "Where are your manners, woman?"

Hannah smiled deeply, grasped my hand. "Eight weeks. We've been trying for so long."

"Oh, how wonderful," Jane said. "Children are a blessing from God. The Apostle's bounty."

I followed Hannah's lead. "That's why we came this way. We're looking for somewhere to raise a family. Safe. Full of good values."

"The city is a bad place for children." Brother Ted shook his head. "The little ones who live at the compound are much happier."

"Really?" I said.

Sister Jane nodded. "It's a fact. The ruling council did a study."

I looked at Hannah and smiled. She smiled back.

Brother Ted told us the funeral started shortly and that he'd need to make a call to get approval for us to join Ian and his camera guy. He picked up an old-style rotary phone from the desk, dialed a number. Then he looked at me and said, "I'm sorry, friend. I didn't catch your names."

I introduced Hannah and myself using the names of my wife's parents, Frank and Beth Cartwright.

He relayed the information to whoever was on the other line, listened for a moment, and then hung up.

"We're all set," he said. "You and Ian can follow me in."

- CHAPTER FORTY-THREE -

Nine Months Ago

Frank Cartwright made bail at seven that night.

The crime scene investigators were still at my house, processing the evidence surrounding the murders of my wife and two children.

There was a lot of evidence.

A rear door that had been kicked in. Blood splatters. Smashed dishes, upturned table.

Empty bullet casings, later determined to be Remington .40-caliber ammunition fired through the barrel of a Sig Sauer P229. The pistol was a DPD-issued firearm reported destroyed in a house fire months before.

Muddy footprints in the kitchen and on the back patio. The impressions were from two different men's shoes, a size ten and a size twelve. Both soles had heavy lugs, later analysis revealing the prints had been made by the same brand of tactical boots, a style favored by police officers.

In the alley, investigators found a cluster of cigarette butts, Marlboros and Salems.

DNA from the Marlboros would later be traced to a vice cop named Boulay. Another vice officer, a guy named Keating, had smoked the Salems.

In the months after the murders of my family, internal affairs investigators would learn that the three officers—Chloe, Keating, and Boulay—had been working for an offshoot of the cartel that controlled Laredo, shuttling product in and out of Dallas, mostly cocaine. The $300,000 that had been in the Frisellas' freezer didn't belong to the three vice cops. The cash was the cartel's property, which helped explain the fervor with which everyone pursued the money's return.

Neither internal affairs nor the homicide investigators could determine what caused the killers to snap and murder my family before Chloe's five p.m. deadline. Not that the investigators knew about the deadline—I never told anyone about my meeting with her or the money I'd taken from the Frisellas.

There was cocaine residue on the kitchen table, extremely pure and uncut, and the most prevalent theory, one to which I subscribed, was that the killers suffered from a drug-induced psychosis, which led them to kill instead of waiting for Chloe's go-ahead.

I was at the northwest substation while the crime scene techs processed the evidence and the homicide investigators filled out the paperwork.

My lieutenant friend sat with me in his office. He offered coffee at first, which I declined. Then he pulled out a bottle of Cutty Sark and asked if I wanted a shot.

I accepted the booze. The whiskey burned all the way down but did nothing to ease the coldness growing deep inside me. The lieutenant poured me another round. I took a sip and then tossed the rest into a potted plant when he wasn't looking.

Officers came and went, offering their condolences and support. My superior, a captain named Rhodes, arrived and told me that all the resources of the Texas Rangers would be behind this investigation, and whoever was responsible would be caught.

Rhodes grabbed my shoulder, looked me in the eye. "We're gonna catch these bastards, Arlo. They'll get the needle. I promise you that."

I nodded like I believed in his outcome.

It was dinnertime. A sergeant asked if I wanted something to eat. I declined, but the lieutenant told him to bring me a hamburger anyway.

A chaplain came and sat with me for a while, asking if we could pray together. I said OK, and he held my hand while looking toward the ceiling and rambling on about a better life and how revenge belongs to the Almighty.

I thanked him and went to the men's room and sat in a stall, just to be alone.

There, I pulled out my phone and sent several text messages. Then I made a couple of calls.

After that, the tears came, and I was powerless to stop them. Big, heaving sobs erupted from my chest, anguish for the loss of all that was good in my life and a deep, pervasive grief over things that would never be the same.

After a few minutes, I got myself together.

The men's room was still empty.

I logged on to a car service and ordered a ride to the gas station where my pickup was located.

The door to the men's room opened. Captain Rhodes said, "You OK, Arlo?"

"Fine, sir. I'll be out in a second."

"Take your time, son."

The door shut.

I waited a moment and then exited the bathroom.

Outside, there was a hallway. To the left was the lieutenant's office. To the right was an exit to the parking lot.

I headed right.

Three minutes later, I was in the back of a Chrysler 300.

"Where you headed?" The driver pulled onto Harry Hines Boulevard.

"I'm going to pick up my father-in-law," I said, and gave him the address of where I'd left my truck. "We have an appointment later."

- CHAPTER FORTY-FOUR -

Hannah Byrne and I headed west on the desolate highway, our vehicle in the middle between Brother Ted, in the lead in his gray pickup, and the van with Ian and the camera guy. Sister Jane had stayed at the information center in case any other wayward souls dropped by.

"Who are Frank and Beth?" Hannah asked.

"No one important."

The sun was high overhead. Heat waves shimmered off the asphalt.

"I'm not really pregnant," she said.

"Yeah, I figured."

The mesas we saw earlier grew closer. After a couple of miles, we came upon a crudely painted sign, whitewashed plywood with jagged red lettering: SKY OF ZION—SINNERS REPENT!

A few hundred yards later, the first cluster of homes appeared, the only signs of human habitation we'd seen since leaving the welcome center. Four double-wide trailers, also painted stark white, lined up in a row, side by side. A clothesline, laundry whipping in the wind, sat next to an empty cattle pen at the rear of the homes.

"According to the map, the compound is on the south side of the road," Hannah said. "The trailers are on the north. That means they probably own the land all around here."

Another mile zoomed by, and we passed a second group of trailers. Several four-wheelers were parked in front of one of the double-wides.

"You think they get enough cash from a server farm for the Russian mob to buy this much land?" she said. "Not to mention an entire prison."

We crested a hill, and the old prison came into view, a squat structure sitting in a shallow basin. The surrounding land was rocky and brown, the color of old adobe, spiked with cactus and cedar bushes.

I realized that our earlier assumptions had been correct. There weren't forty thousand religious fanatics living in the desert. If there were four thousand, that was on the high end. There were no crops growing anywhere. The soil was thin and rocky, able to produce enough food for a family of jackrabbits, but that was about it.

The prison was similar to others I'd visited. Four watchtowers and twenty-foot walls around an open exercise yard. The walls contained cells.

Most prisons are gray, but the Sky of Zion facility had been painted white with a huge purple cross on the tower closest to the highway. The high fencing that normally would have formed a perimeter a couple hundred yards past the walls had been torn down, replaced with double-wide trailers positioned end to end in a circle around the structure. Beyond that was barbed-wire fencing running along the highway.

There were too many trailers to count but nowhere near enough to hold forty thousand people. Back in the day, the prison itself probably had a maximum capacity of only two thousand.

On a hill to the west of the prison sat several houses, also painted white. They were set apart and had probably been administration buildings.

Brother Ted's pickup slowed the closer it got to the front gate, an arched entranceway made from granite. The top of the arch was adorned with a golden cross about six feet tall.

A pair of DPS squad cars idled across the highway from the entry, a trooper in full uniform leaning on the hood of each vehicle.

"What's with the police?" Hannah said.

"I don't know."

Despite what Aloysius Throckmorton had told me about the Sky of Zion being a major economic factor in the area, one not to be trifled with, the Department of Public Safety obviously recognized the organization as a potential disruptor of the peace. Someone had thought it best to keep an eye on the group.

Or maybe I was wrong. Maybe Silas had hired off-duty state troopers for crowd control.

Brother Ted entered the property, turning off the highway and onto a gravel road. We followed, Ian's van right behind us. The three vehicles drove past the prison and its ring of double-wide trailers, past the cluster of homes on a hill.

We slowed as a man directed us to a parking area, a pasture where there weren't too many rocks. The parking area contained a handful of cars, maybe enough for a good night at a restaurant in Midland, but not even half of what it would take to form the support staff of a megachurch.

The man pointed me to a spot next to a dust-covered Honda with New Mexico plates. I parked where he indicated, and the van stopped on our other side.

Ian and his camera guy exited at the same time Hannah and I did.

Ted appeared behind my car. "We need to hurry. The service is about to start."

The camera guy began filming.

"Where are we headed?" I asked.

"There." Ted pointed to the whitewashed penitentiary.

"That's your church?" I said.

"It used to be a place of pain and suffering." He smiled, a joyful look on his face. "Now it's a repository for the wisdom of the Apostle."

The camera guy aimed his camera toward the prison.

"And what's up there?" Hannah pointed to the houses on the hill.

Brother Ted quit smiling. He frowned, the first time he'd appeared to be anything but friendly. He pursed his lips several times and said, "That's the sacred area."

"Sacred how?" Ian asked.

"The Apostle," Ted said. "He lives there."

We were all silent for a minute while the camera guy pointed his lens toward the hill with the houses.

Ted looked at his watch. "We're late."

"Will the Apostle be at the funeral?" I said.

The camera guy turned toward Ted's face, which was sweaty now.

"The Apostle's movements are not mine to explain." He sounded testy. "We must hurry."

"After you." I smiled at the man.

He stared at me like he was trying to figure out something, and I realized he probably wasn't going to buy my searching-for-hope scam for much longer. After a moment, he headed toward the old prison at a brisk walk.

The entrance to the structure had been demolished and then rebuilt. Gone were the narrow passageways and cubbyhole offices used to process incoming prisoners or supervise visitation.

Now, the main access point to the building had been replaced with a large, open area, an arched tunnel leading to the yard. The symbolism was clear: people could come and go as they pleased.

At the opening, there were no guards.

We followed Ted through the corridor and found ourselves inside the walls.

The area was large enough to hold a thousand inmates with room to spare, places for the various gangs to stake their turf, a section for the weight lifters, a patch of asphalt that used to be a basketball court.

All that was gone. Now, the focal point was a raised platform in the middle of the yard.

Silas McPherson, right hand in a cast, stood on the platform in front of a lectern. Behind him were a half dozen men, all dressed the same—dark suits, white shirts, no ties. The ruling council.

About fifty people sat on the ground in front of the platform. Men, women, and children. Lots of children. The men were hatless, wearing white shirts and jeans. The women were dressed like Molly had been, long dresses covering all their limbs.

Brother Ted led us to a spot at the rear of the audience.

Everyone turned and watched. The silence was overpowering.

Hannah grasped my hand while the camera guy trained his lens on the platform.

Silas stared at me from afar, a slight smile on his face.

Ted indicated we were to sit down, pointing to a patch of dead grass.

Ian and his camera guy didn't take the hint. Ian probably didn't want to get his khakis dirty. Hannah and I remained standing as well.

Silas spoke in a loud, clear voice, the sound booming against the walls, no PA system needed.

"Welcome, visitors," he said. "You honor us with your presence."

Brother Ted removed his hat and bowed before the platform.

"Today is a special occasion for the church," Silas said.

The crowd murmured.

"Not only are we here to bury our brother Felix." He paused. "But the Apostle has given me a directive."

The crowd grew louder. Several people shouted, "Speak to us!"

"Today we grieve for our brother." Silas looked right at me. "And to honor him, we shall make a sacrifice."

The crowd went wild, yelling, jumping up.

The camera guy looked away from his eyepiece, stared at Ian. Hannah clenched my hand tighter. Silas shushed the people and continued.

"Yes, my children, a sacrifice." He paused. "A blood offering to the Apostle."

The crowd erupted in joy.

- CHAPTER FORTY-FIVE -

From somewhere behind the platform, two men in Stetsons led a calf toward the area between where Silas stood and the crowd.

The calf was brown, a white spot on its forehead. It followed along docilely, tail swishing.

I recognized one of the men. He'd been the shooter who'd taken out Chigger the day before, the guy with the goatee. Now he carried an ax while his partner held the lead for the calf.

The two men stopped in front of Silas, one on either side of the calf. Silas motioned for the crowd to be quiet. They did so readily, settling down. He lifted his good hand and looked like he was about to begin the ceremony.

But he never got the chance.

Because Chester stood up.

Organizations are the same the world over, no matter what their purpose. Any time you have three or more people in a group, somebody is not going to get his or her way.

This is where politics comes into play, the art of deciding who gets what and when the getting will occur.

Politics is a skill set attempted by many but mastered by few. The electorate—in this case a bunch of brainwashed religious fanatics—is a moody bitch, always asking for something, her demands mercurial. When her needs aren't met, she sends people into the breach, demanding change.

In the case of Silas McPherson's church, I later found out the man doing the demanding was the leader of the New Mexico synod. Chester Ruibal, a third-generation lay preacher within the organization, about as powerful as you can get without being on the ruling council.

A silence fell over the yard as everyone stared at the man with the weathered face, standing in the front row.

Silas, head cocked, looked at him for a long moment. The gaze was a challenge, an alpha male attempting to exert control over the situation, no different from the minor dramas that had played out a hundred times a day when this patch of dirt had been part of the prison.

Finally, Silas spoke: "What say ye, brother?"

"Our synod has taken a vote." Chester's voice was loud, tone somber.

"A vote?" Silas said. He sounded mildly amused.

"As is our right, we ask for an accounting." Chester crossed his arms. "A reckoning of our tithes."

The people around him nodded. Several men stood in solidarity.

The rest of the crowd stared at them in rapt silence.

"A day of mourning," Silas said. "This is how you honor our dead brother's memory?"

On the other side of the crowd, another man stood up. He was older, in his sixties, and had a long gray beard. "We demand an accounting, too." He paused. "We want to know how Brother Felix died."

Several women gasped.

The old man continued. "I hear that he was in the city." A moment passed. "Among the unclean."

More gasps.

Ian looked at Brother Ted. "What the bloody hell is going on?"

"We should leave." Ted pointed to the exit.

"Now?" I said. "Before the sacrifice?"

Hannah tugged on my arm. She whispered, "Let's get out of here."

"This is church business," Ted said. "It doesn't concern you."

The camera guy was still filming.

Ted stood in front of his lens. "Turn that off."

Chester continued his speech. "Our people are hungry. Does the Apostle not hear our prayers?"

A man in the middle of the audience stood. He pointed a finger at Chester and shouted, "Blasphemer! The Apostle hears all."

The two guards by the calf looked at Silas. He nodded once. The guy with the goatee pulled a walkie-talkie from his pocket, held the mic to his mouth.

Silas spoke to the crowd. "I exhort you, brethren. Please calm yourselves."

The brethren weren't having any of that. It became obvious there were three groups—Chester and his New Mexico contingent, who wanted cash and food; the old man and his gang, who wanted the skinny on what had happened to their beloved Brother Felix; and everyone else, those loyal to Silas.

More guards appeared from the section behind the platform.

Chester was jabbing his finger at Silas, yelling about holy payments. The man from the middle of the crowd, face red with anger, fought his way toward the front, fists clenched. Even the women were shouting at one another.

The sun was bright and hot, beating down on the mass of angry people, and you didn't need to be a sociologist to see that a riot was about to break out.

Ted pointed to the exit. "You must leave. All of you. Now."

Hannah grasped my arm. "Arlo, please. Let's go."

The camera guy lowered his camera and turned to Ian for instruction. Ian nodded, a look of satisfaction on his face. He'd gotten killer footage. He and the camera guy began to back away.

I spoke to Brother Ted. "Before we leave, I need to ask you something."

Ian stopped, motioned for the camera guy to start filming me.

Ted looked at the camera and then at me.

"A woman who lived here at the compound. Her name was Molly," I said. "She had two children, Caleb and Mary."

A fight broke out near the platform. Men shouted. The calf bawled. Silas yelled for everyone to be calm.

Ted's eyes had grown wide and fearful. He ignored the degenerating situation and stared at me.

"Tell me where Molly lived," I said. "And then we'll leave."

Ted never got the chance to speak. From the main entry, a mass of men in Stetsons appeared, streaming through the archway.

Now I understood the significance of the trailers in a circle around the old prison. They served the function of a fence, filled with men loyal to Silas. The guards, the ones in the hats with the crowns low in the front.

They swarmed around us, heading toward the altercation that was centered at the platform. Ted took a last look at me and then followed the guards, swept along by events out of his control.

The four of us were alone.

"Who's Molly?" Ian asked.

"A woman who wanted out," I said.

"You're not really interested in joining the church, are you?" he asked.

"We're looking for Molly's children," Hannah said. "And my niece."

From the middle of the audience came the piercing shriek of a woman in pain. The general noise level grew louder.

"We've pushed our luck enough," Ian said. "We should leave now."

"Keep the camera rolling." I headed toward the exit.

Several guards stood at the mouth of the tunnel leading outside, including a hatless man with a bandage on his forehead and his index finger in a splint, the one I'd slammed against the wall of the bar two days ago.

He glared at me and reached for a walkie-talkie.

We'd have to pass him in order to get out, so I headed straight for him. The camera guy, Ian, and Hannah followed.

He watched us get closer, the surly look on his face slowly being replaced by confusion. He lowered the walkie-talkie.

I stopped in front of him, the camera guy by my side, still filming. "Where did Molly live?" I asked.

He gulped, looked at Ian and then the lens of the camera, only a foot from his face.

I grabbed the front of his shirt. "Where are her children?"

He shook his head frantically, held up his hands. He didn't appear very tough. He seemed scared and weak.

I slapped him in the face.

He yelped, held up his hands in a gesture of surrender.

"Where are Molly's children?" I reached under my shirt for the Glock. Hannah grabbed my arm. *"Stop."*

I looked around. Ian was staring at me, mouth agape. The camera guy was still filming.

Ian said, "Do you always go around beating on people like that, mate?"

I let go of the man with the bandaged head. He ran into the yard. The other guards who'd been with him were nowhere to be seen.

The four of us were alone again. The fight in the yard had gotten bigger, louder.

"She'll explain." I shoved Hannah toward the two Brits. "All of you need to leave now."

"What are you going to do?" Hannah asked.

There was a metal door on one side of the tunnel that ran from the yard to the outside. It was ajar and appeared to lead to the interior of the building.

"I came here to find out about Molly's children," I said. "I'm not leaving until I do."

She started to say something, but I opened the door and stepped inside the old prison.

- CHAPTER FORTY-SIX -

The interior of the former penitentiary hadn't been painted white. The walls were still gray, and the air smelled like damp cement and stale sweat.

Immediately inside was a small, dimly lit room that had probably been a guard's office. In the room was a desk. On the desk was a Stetson and a child's doll.

I tried on the hat. The fit was a little loose but not enough to worry about.

From the office, I strode down a narrow corridor and entered what had once been a cellblock, two stories of eight-by-ten rooms facing onto a large, open area.

The cell doors were all open. From somewhere not too far away came the sound of a baby crying.

A woman in her forties sat at a wooden picnic table in the open area, braiding a girl's hair. From high above, a shaft of light illuminated the woman and child. Shadows formed by the bars cut across their faces, dust motes dancing in the air above their heads.

The girl was about eleven or twelve but wore enough makeup to be a televangelist's wife. The woman looked like she hadn't been near a tube of lipstick since high school. The juxtaposition was odd—an unadorned, plain-faced, middle-aged woman next to a prepubescent child painted up like a Vegas showgirl.

They watched me as I approached, faces blank.

"Hello." I tried to look as nonthreatening as possible.

Empty stares.

"What's your name?" I asked the woman.

"Sister Rose," she said.

"My name is Brother Arlo." I remembered the Honda in the parking lot. "I'm from the New Mexico synod."

She cocked her head like she was having trouble making sense of my presence. She wasn't afraid, just unsure of how to react to me. After a moment, she resumed braiding the child's hair.

"You're not supposed to be in the matrimonial chamber, Brother Arlo."

I looked around, trying not to react. This place was about as matrimonial as a Waffle House.

"Your name," Rose said. "I didn't see it on the register for today, either."

The girl scratched at her hair. "That's too tight."

"Shh," Rose said. "This is the way it's supposed to be."

"I'm looking for a woman," I said. "Her name is—"

"Have you talked to the council?"

I didn't reply.

"If you seek a conjugal," Rose said, "you have to talk to the council."

"The council?"

"Of course." She frowned and looked up from her braiding. "How do they do it in New Mexico?"

The girl rubbed her nose, smearing some lipstick in the process.

"What is wrong with you, child?" Rose swatted the girl's backside. "Making a mess of your face like that."

The girl didn't react.

I smiled at the youngster. "What's your name, honey?"

Rose stopped braiding. She stared at me, a look of astonishment on her face. The girl's eyes grew wide.

"How dare you!" Rose said.

I didn't reply, trying to figure out what breach of protocol I had inadvertently performed.

"This girl is intended." Rose grabbed the child's arm. "She's pledged for a conjugal."

From one of the open cells on the ground floor, another girl appeared. She was older than the one with the braids but not by much, maybe twelve or thirteen. She wore the same style clothes but no makeup. Instead, her face was pale, with dark smudges of fatigue under her eyes.

She cradled an infant in her arms, a tiny bundle. The baby was maybe four or five months old and crying.

"The pledge is to one from the council." Rose shook her finger at me. "She can't talk to a man like you, a man who's not her intended."

The girl with the baby approached. "Sister Rose, he won't stop crying."

"Go back to your room," Rose said. "I'll bring some formula in a while."

"I'm hungry, too." The girl was whiny.

"G'on, girl." Rose slapped the tabletop. "I have business to attend to."

"Do you need food?" I asked. "I can get you some."

The girl with the baby stared at me. The infant let out a caterwaul, one skinny arm breaking free of the blankets.

"We don't need your help." Rose stood up. "The Apostle provides for our needs."

"Has that baby ever been to a pediatrician?" I asked.

"Who are you?" Rose said. Her tone was suspicious now, bordering on hostile.

I became aware of the others, peering from the doorways of the cells. All of them girls, some old enough to vote, some in their grade-school years. Several held babies. Several others had toddlers standing behind their legs. More than a few were pregnant.

They all looked pale and unhealthy.

"What is this place?" I said.

Rose crossed her arms. "You're not a member of the church, are you?"

I took off the Stetson, dropped it on the ground. "I'd tell you to call the guards, but they're all busy right now."

Several of the girls had joined Rose at the picnic table. They all stared at me. One, a child about nine years old, was crying softly.

"I'm not here to hurt anybody," I said.

"You are one of the unclean," Rose hissed.

"Filthy as a pig in mud. Except I don't go around raping children."

"Foul words from a foul man." She shook her head. "You have no concept of the Apostle's glory. Of his power."

"Oh, I think I have an idea."

"Go to your rooms, girls." Rose snapped her fingers.

None of them moved. They all appeared transfixed by my presence. I knelt by the youngest, the one crying. "What's wrong, sweetheart?"

The girl had thick blonde hair that needed brushing. Her dress was dirty, stained with something dark. She rubbed her nose. "I don't want to be married anymore."

Sister Rose shook her head but didn't say anything. Her face contorted with an emotion I couldn't guess at. It wasn't just anger or disgust, though. She looked to be in physical pain.

"Where are your parents?" I asked.

"They are apostates," Rose said. "They've chosen an unclean path."

The crying girl looked at the older woman for a moment and then back at me. A second passed. She nodded. "Yes, Mommy and Daddy are apa—apostates."

I realized one of the stains on the child's dress was blood and that it was at her crotch.

"Do you want to see your parents?" I asked.

The girl glanced at Sister Rose again. The woman wiped her eyes and looked away. The girl turned back to me and nodded.

"I'll take you to see them," I said. "Pretty sure I know where they live."

A spark appeared in her eyes, a glimmer of something that had been missing up to that point. Hope.

Rose motioned for me to follow her. We walked a few feet away, out of earshot if we talked quietly.

She stood between the children and me. She whispered, "Please don't take her."

I smiled, kept my voice low. "Go fuck yourself, Sister Rose."

She didn't react to the words. Instead, she touched my arm and said, "If you leave with her, that will be the end of this."

"Perhaps it's time for *this* to end." I struggled to control my anger. "How could you let these children be abused?"

"This is the Apostle's will," she said. "This is what God wants for us."

"You really believe that?"

A moment passed.

Rose said, "I have to."

I strode back to the table, took the girl's hand in mine. "She's going with me. I'll be back for the rest of them later."

"Please. Don't. I'm begging you." Rose was crying now.

I picked up the Stetson, put it on my head.

"What will happen to me?" Rose asked. "Where will I go?"

I looked around the old cellblock full of sexually abused children. She'd already been to a very bad place. I couldn't imagine where she might end up that could be worse.

- CHAPTER FORTY-SEVEN -

The nine-year-old girl with the bloody dress was named Anna.

I scooped her up and fled the dank prison.

Outside, in the corridor between the yard and the rest of the Sky of Zion property, the air felt fresh and clean.

I glanced toward the yard.

The platform was empty. Silas was gone.

Several people were thrashing about on the ground, injured, moaning. Several more were still, not moving. A handful of people stood in clusters, surveying the aftermath of the violence. But most of the small crowd was nowhere to be seen.

"W-what happened?" Anna asked.

"Just a little disagreement," I said. "Close your eyes and we'll be out of here before you know it."

She buried her face against my shoulder, clinging to my neck with her little arms.

I strode in the opposite direction, toward the front gate, maybe three hundred yards away. I could have gone back to the parking area, but that was away from the highway, and I was pretty sure that Hannah and the BBC guys had already left. The safest course of action was to get to the squad cars across from the entrance.

The two squad cars were still in place, along with at least a half dozen others.

In addition to the marked police vehicles, Aloysius Throckmorton's Suburban was parked under the archway leading onto the compound.

The Suburban couldn't proceed onto the grounds because of the people blocking the way, the remnants of the crowd from the yard, plus a number of men in Stetsons like the one I wore.

I jogged toward the exit, Anna bouncing on my hip. It had been a long time since I'd held a child. It felt good and sad at the same time.

"You OK?" I asked.

"Uh-huh."

"You scared?"

No answer. Then: "A little."

"You don't have to be," I said. "We'll find your parents before you know it."

"What if the Apostle finds us first?"

I sped up. "That's not going to happen."

Aloysius Throckmorton stood on the front bumper of his SUV.

Silas McPherson was at the head of the group facing the Texas Ranger. Only a few feet separated the two men in the area underneath the arch, a no-man's-land between the right of way for the highway and the start of the Sky of Zion compound.

Several guards stood behind Silas.

Instead of fighting my way through the people, I jogged around the flanks of the crowd, running along the inside perimeter of a barbed-wire fence that separated the highway from the church property.

With the Stetson on, I wasn't stopped until I got close to the archway.

Then the guy with the goatee saw me.

He touched Silas with one hand, alerting him, and drew a pistol from his waistband with the other.

That was the wrong move to make with a Texas Ranger standing five feet away.

Throckmorton pulled his Colt. "Drop your weapon, boy."

Behind him, several state troopers produced their pistols, too.

Mr. Goatee didn't comply. Instead he aimed at me, apparently not caring that I was holding a child.

The crowd gasped and stepped back.

I stopped and spoke in a loud, clear voice: "I am unarmed, and I am not making any threatening moves."

Silas came forward. "What do you call kidnapping one of my flock?"

Throckmorton had his weapon aimed at Mr. Goatee. "Put the gun down now."

Goatee's fingers grew white. He continued to aim at me.

Silas pointed to Mr. Goatee. "This man is a security guard licensed by the state of Texas. He is attempting to stop a felony in progress, the kidnapping of a minor."

Throckmorton said, "You want to help me out here, Baines? The man has something of a point."

Everybody looked at me.

"The girl's parents aren't on the premises. And there's evidence of sexual abuse." I paused. "Not just her. There're more inside in the same condition."

Stunned expressions on the faces of the troopers behind Aloysius. Followed by anger.

Mr. Goatee continued to aim at me.

Aloysius looked like he was about to say something, but Silas cut him off.

"The girl is under my guardianship," he said. "Any accusations of abuse are absurd."

"Yet your security man is aiming a gun at her," Aloysius said. "I'd be inclined to believe your concern for her well-being if he'd put down his weapon."

The anger coming off Mr. Goatee was palpable. He was shaking, his face red, lips a tight frown.

"He is trying to protect an innocent child," Silas said. "Perhaps a little too vigorously."

"Why don't we just let Child Protective Services sort everything out?" I asked.

Gasps from the crowd. A woman shouted for the Apostle to save them.

"That's a good idea." Aloysius nodded. "Taking care of kids. That's their job."

"Absolutely not," Silas said. "The church does not recognize the right of the state to interfere with the upbringing of our children."

"The girl says she's married," I said. "So technically is she still a child?"

"Married?" Throckmorton lowered his gun slightly. "How can someone that young be married?"

Silas hesitated. Then he said, "Our religious traditions allow for this type of, uh, arrangement."

"There's a bunch of babies inside, too," I said. "They need doctors and food."

The crowd murmured. Several people suggested that Mr. Goatee shoot me. Silas waved them quiet.

"The church's attorney, a state legislator, will be here within the next two hours." He glared at Throckmorton. "If you remove this child from the premises, then you are violating our First Amendment rights, and there will be severe consequences."

"Tell your boy to lower his gun," Throckmorton said. "And then we can talk about severe consequences."

"I will not." Silas shook his head. "He is within his rights to protect our sacred ground as well as members of our flock."

"Last chance," Throckmorton said. "Put down the gun and let Arlo leave with the girl."

Silas shook his head. Mr. Goatee grinned at me, fingers white on the grip.

Throckmorton shrugged. Then he aimed his Colt and fired.

Only a few feet away, it was hard to miss.

The bullet tore into one side of Mr. Goatee's thigh. A stream of blood erupted. Goatee screamed and dropped his gun. After a moment, he fell to the ground.

"C'mon out, Arlo." Throckmorton kept his weapon aimed at Silas. "Guess we better call an ambulance, too."

- CHAPTER FORTY-EIGHT -

From the compound side, a gray pickup now blocked the entrance. A group of church members formed a half circle around the truck, facing the highway. They held hands and sang hymns.

Behind the singers was a number of men in Stetsons, all of them armed with long guns—rifles and shotguns, several AR-style weapons.

Aloysius Throckmorton had moved his Suburban backward about ten feet so that the SUV sat in the middle of the road, its nose pointed at the entrance to the compound.

More state police vehicles had arrived, bringing the total to ten, eleven if you counted Throckmorton's Suburban. The squad cars were flanked out on either side of the Suburban, officers crouched behind open doors, their weapons drawn.

Throckmorton had offered medical attention to the wounded man, but Silas had refused. Other guards had taken Mr. Goatee inside the old prison. Silas had disappeared into one of the houses on the hill.

Throckmorton and I were standing at the back of the Suburban, away from the entrance, trying to find a little shade. Anna was in the squad car immediately to the right of the SUV, being tended to by a female state trooper.

It was a little after noon, and the temperature was pushing ninety-five.

"Where's Hannah Byrne?" I asked.

"Is it my day to watch her?" Throckmorton fanned himself with his hat.

I'd already spent fifteen minutes giving him the rundown of the situation inside the compound, at least as much as I'd seen. Now, I was eating a PowerBar and drinking a bottle of water that one of the troopers gave me. As I ate, Throckmorton called the commissioner of the Department of Family and Protective Services and told her that we needed as many CPS caseworkers as they could find, pronto.

"Hannah was with the news crew," I said. "Two guys from the BBC."

"Awesome. The media is here, too." He rubbed his eyes. "Just what we need."

"What made you show up, anyway?"

"That high school gym," he said. "It was a crime scene, like you described."

"Why were there DPS units here beforehand, then?" I asked.

Across the road, the singers began a new tune—"Rock of Ages."

"Not everybody thinks these Zion people are on the up and up," Throckmorton said.

I peered around the back of the Suburban and stared at the crowd. Throckmorton stood next to me, arms crossed.

"We've got probable cause to go in," he said. "But this has Branch Davidians 2.0 written all over it."

I didn't say anything.

"Nobody wins if there's a firefight," he said. "You understand that, don't you?"

"They're raping children."

"I get that. Believe me." He paused. "We've got a call in to the AG. This needs to be handled delicately."

Neither of us spoke. Across the street, the singing stopped as women from the old prison brought what looked like refreshments—bottles of water and sandwiches.

Throckmorton stuck his head in the back of the Suburban, returning with a map of the state. He unfolded the map and pointed to the southwest quadrant.

"This is about where their property ends." He tapped a thin gray line, a county highway eight or ten miles south of where we were standing. Above that, there were no marked roads of any sort until you reached the highway where the main entrance was located.

"If somebody wanted to get away from here and not use the front gate," he said, "he could go cross-country and hop on this road."

"You've got to cover a lot of territory to get there," I said. "Rough country."

Throckmorton nodded. "But if you make it, then you're on a paved road, and two hours later you can be in Del Rio."

The implication was clear. Del Rio meant freedom, just across the Rio Grande from Ciudad Acuña. Provided he had enough money, Silas McPherson could disappear into Mexico forever.

"I'm working on troopers out of San Antonio to patrol this section," he said. "But there's some damn music festival in Austin this weekend, and we're a little short staffed."

I studied the map and then looked down the road to the west.

The highway crested a small hill about three hundred yards away. Beyond that, the road was out of sight.

"The other side of that rise," I said. "That's right behind the cluster of houses on the hill, right?"

He opened a different map, one that was just this county. He looked at it for a moment and nodded.

"There's a creek that runs behind those houses," he said.

A creek meant trees, places to hide as you approached.

We stared at each other for a moment, neither speaking.

"Don't even think about it," Throckmorton said. "You need to stay put, wait for the investigators to get here and debrief you."

I didn't reply.

From the compound came the report of a rifle being fired, followed by the whine of a bullet ricocheting off something hard.

I ducked instinctively.

Throckmorton swore.

A barrage of gunfire crackled all around us.

- CHAPTER FORTY-NINE -

Throckmorton grabbed a bullhorn instead of his weapon.

He aimed the speaker toward the compound and told everybody to calm the fuck down and quit shooting.

Miraculously, that worked.

All of the shots appeared to have come from the compound.

A group of untrained people with semiautomatic rifles, a tense situation. It was a wonder it had taken this long for someone's finger to squeeze a little too tightly.

Throckmorton got on his radio and asked all the troopers to check in. Then he moved to the first squad car to the east and crouched at the rear of the vehicle, conferring with two officers. His back was to me, so I decided to take a little stroll.

First stop, the squad car on the west side of Throckmorton's SUV to check on Anna. A female state trooper sat next to the child, her body forming a shield between the compound and the girl.

I knelt by the open door. "You doing OK?"

No response.

"That was pretty scary, wasn't it, that shooting?" I said. "You sure are being brave."

She rubbed her nose with the back of her hand.

"Some people will be here soon to take you to see your parents," I said.

Anna nodded, the hint of a smile on her lips.

"The houses on the hill," I said. "Do you know what's there?"

She frowned but didn't speak.

"Have you ever been up to those houses?" I asked.

A moment passed. Then, her voice soft and timid: "That's where the conjugals are."

"That's where you go to get, uh, married?"

Anna hesitated. She looked at the trooper and then back to me. She nodded.

"Who's your husband?" I said.

"He's dead." Her voice was even softer, words hard to hear.

"Was Felix your husband?"

After a moment, she nodded, tears welling in her eyes.

The female trooper hugged the girl's shoulders.

"The Apostle blessed us," Anna said. "That's why it was a special marriage."

The trooper stared at me, a look of disgust on her face that no doubt mirrored my own.

"Anna, can you tell me who the Apostle is?" I asked.

"We don't see him," she said. "He's behind the glass."

The trooper spoke to me. "She shouldn't talk about this anymore—not now, anyway."

I nodded, patted the girl's knee. "You take care, sweetheart. I'll see you in a little bit."

● ● ●

No more shots had been fired, but Throckmorton looked like he was still busy.

After making sure he couldn't see me, I headed toward the last squad car to the west.

It was empty. Most of the troopers were now congregated around the back of Throckmorton's SUV. The ones who were nearby paid me no mind.

I leaned inside the squad car and found a walkie-talkie. I grabbed the radio and then took off jogging toward the rise in the road west of the compound's entrance.

The smart play was to wait for the state troopers to make their move, but with shots being fired, that was liable to take a while.

Throckmorton was going to make sure all the boxes were checked before sending in the cavalry. The shadow of sieges gone bad loomed over the whole affair, the ghosts of Ruby Ridge and Mount Carmel swirling in the sky like dust devils.

I didn't want to wait. I wanted to find Hannah and keep looking for Molly's children. Get them all out of harm's way before the bullets started flying.

It didn't make sense that Hannah wasn't around, especially since she was a reporter with a news crew, and a huge story was unfolding right in front of her. That meant she was probably still on the compound.

About a quarter of a mile later, sweat dripping from my face, I crested the small hill to the west of the entrance, and the line of squad cars behind me disappeared.

A few seconds later, I saw the navy-blue van, the one Ian and his camera guy had been driving.

The van was parked on the south shoulder of the two-lane highway, the compound side, a wide spot where there might have been a roadside stand at some point, a place to buy fireworks or beef jerky.

I started sprinting.

A creek ran north to south, passing through a culvert underneath the road. Trees lined the banks, cottonwoods and desert willows, the only growth of substance in the immediate area. There was an opening in the barbed-wire fence that surrounded the compound property and what looked like an old cattle trail running alongside the creek.

I stopped about thirty feet behind the van, panting.

The side door was open, facing away from the highway.

I pulled the Glock and approached the vehicle slowly, weapon aimed.

A swarm of flies buzzed in and out of the van, the first clue that things weren't as they should be.

Ian and his camera guy were in the cargo area, dead. They'd both been shot in the back of the head.

Their video equipment appeared to be missing. Various duffel bags had been emptied, the contents strewn about. Sitting amid the gear was the backpack that Hannah always carried.

I grabbed the walkie-talkie, called for Throckmorton.

An instant later, his voice rang out: "Baines? What are you doing on this channel?"

"There're two dead bodies in a blue van," I said. "A quarter mile west of your location."

"What the hell are you talking about? Where are you?"

"The BBC reporters I told you about. They're both dead. Looks like Hannah's been taken."

Silence.

"I'll call you on this frequency in ten minutes and let you know what the situation is."

The radio crackled. Then, Throckmorton's voice, low and gravelly: "Get back here now. Do not, repeat *do not* enter the comp—"

I turned off the walkie-talkie.

- CHAPTER FIFTY -

Nine Months Ago

After the car service dropped me where I'd left my pickup, I drove to the county lockup, Lew Sterrett Justice Center, to get my father-in-law.

Normally, with a federal charge like bank fraud, Frank would have been taken to the penitentiary in Seagoville, a suburb south of Dallas. Seagoville had holding cells and ran arrestees back and forth to the United States courts downtown every day. But the federal pen was full—a big RICO case involving several biker gangs—so the county was handling new arrests for now.

Frank was sitting on a metal bench at the rear of one of the intake areas, a large room with concrete floors and tile walls that smelled of bleach and sweat. Two counters, protected by bulletproof glass, were on the far wall. Normally staffed by sheriff department personnel, the counters were empty at the moment.

Frank's attorney stood next to him, arguing with a deputy as to why his client was released from custody but forbidden to leave the building.

The deputy was an acquaintance who owed me several favors. He nodded hello when I entered and then walked away.

Frank's attorney turned in my direction, an angry look on his face, rightly figuring that I was responsible for the holdup. He raised a finger like he was going to tell me how important his client was, that a man of Frank's stature shouldn't be held a second longer than necessary on these trumped-up charges, but I cut him off before he could speak.

"Save it for the jury. Right now, you need to give us some space."

He glared at me but didn't move.

"For your own good," I said. "Take a walk."

Frank told him it was OK, and the attorney stalked off to the other side of the room.

Frank's clothes were rumpled, his face ashen. He looked like what he was, a rich man experiencing the gritty end of the legal system for the first time. The typical holding pen at Lew Sterrett was a lot different from the dressing room at the country club.

"What happened?" he said. "They wouldn't tell me anything."

The intake area was empty except for the deputy and the attorney, both standing in separate corners, out of earshot.

I slapped Frank across the face, hard.

Frank resituated himself on the bench. He touched his lip, wet with blood and spit.

The attorney started toward us, but the deputy stepped in front of him. The attorney protested until two more deputies entered the room. The three law enforcement officers formed a wall between the attorney and me and Frank. The cameras in this room had already been turned off, so there wouldn't be any record of my encounter with my father-in-law.

I said, "They're dead, Frank. All three of them."

He stared at me like I was speaking a foreign language. His brow furrowed. He blinked several times.

"My children and my wife." I tried to keep my voice low, to control my fury. "Murdered. Because of you."

The un-slapped side of his face was white as bone. He hunched his shoulders, breaths coming in heaves. After a moment, he said, "Wh-what happened?"

I told him about Chloe and our conversation at lunch, about her mention of two partners—Keating and Boulay, I'd later find out.

He sat back down, clutched his stomach, looking like he was about to vomit.

"Get up," I said. "We've got an errand to run."

"An errand?" he said. "What the hell are you talking about?"

I smoothed a wrinkle in my shirt. The skin on my face felt tight and hot. "We're going to a little Cajun restaurant I know. Pirate Red's."

"A restaurant?" Frank lumbered to his feet. "Have you lost your mind? I need to see my wife. I need—"

I grabbed his arm, leaned close. "You need to shut the hell up and do what I say."

He gulped but stopped talking.

"I've reached out to some people. Chloe and her partners are going to be there in the next hour."

"That's good, right? We know where they are." He paused. "We should call the police."

"They are the police, Frank."

"Then what . . . how . . . I don't understand."

"Remember last week when we went to the gun range?"

He frowned. After a moment, he nodded.

"Your pistol is still in the lockbox in my truck."

His eyes went wide, jaw dropping open.

"You're gonna do what needs to be done, Frank. Or so help me God, you'll wish you were dead, too."

- CHAPTER FIFTY-ONE -

I stepped through the break in the barbed-wire fence and was on the Sky of Zion property.

The navy-blue van containing the bodies of Ian and his camera guy was a few feet behind me.

I figured it would take thirty minutes at a minimum before Throckmorton and the state troopers would be authorized to enter the compound. That meant I had a half hour to find Hannah before bullets started flying again.

I darted up the cattle trail, running at a crouch to avoid the branches from the trees growing on the creek bank.

The air was hot and still and smelled like stagnant water.

A couple hundred yards later, the trail ended at the base of a small hill, at the far side of a backyard area behind the three houses overlooking the old penitentiary. The lawn was freshly mowed, and there were several live oak trees that provided shade for the homes. An outbuilding contained the black Bentley, the only vehicle visible.

The houses were white clapboard, one story each, cheaply constructed sometime back in the fifties. The one farthest from me was the biggest, maybe three or four bedrooms. The one closest was little more than a shack. The middle structure was the nicest, the best maintained. The windows, covered from the inside, were clean, the paint fresh.

Between my location and the houses was a commercial-grade backup generator, like something you'd see at a hospital or an office building.

I stood on the edge of the tree line by the creek and surveyed the scene.

It was the hot part of the day, and there appeared to be no activity from any of the three houses.

I looked at my watch. Five minutes until my promised check-in with Throckmorton, twenty-five minutes at the soonest before the troops arrived.

Not very much time—or an eternity, depending on your point of view.

My weaponry—a Glock 9mm with one magazine and a pocket-knife—was not up to the task of clearing three homes. On the plus side, I did have the element of surprise.

The rear door of the house closest to me, the smallest one, opened, and a man I'd never seen before came out. He wore a black suit and white shirt with no tie, the uniform of someone on the council.

He sauntered to a spot near the generator and plopped down on a lawn chair beneath one of the live oaks. His back was to me.

As soon as he sat down, he pulled a pack of cigarettes from his pocket and lit one.

I crept toward him, moving as silently and as quickly as possible.

When I was a few steps away, he jerked his head around, cigarette dangling from his lips.

I lunged and tackled the man as he tried to stand up.

We fell to the ground.

He butted the side of my head with his forehead, and stars cascaded across my field of view. His legs were tangled in the chair, so he tried to crawl away using his hands.

I grabbed his jacket, pulled myself on top of him, and slammed my elbow into the spot just above his ear.

He stopped crawling, moaned softly.

I yanked off his belt and bound his hands behind his back. My vision was double from his blow.

He wore heavy black shoes, brogues. I removed the laces from one and bound his feet. Then I dragged him behind the generator and slapped his face several times, bringing him back to coherence.

He stared at me, breathing heavily.

"What's your name?" I blinked several times, trying to get my eyesight back to normal.

He didn't answer. His lips pressed together tightly as if to emphasize his decision to not speak.

With one hand, I jammed his head against the grass, wedging it in place. With my other, I placed a thumb over one of his eyes and pressed down. Not hard, just enough to remind him that the situation wasn't trending in his favor at the moment.

He yelped. "D-Daniel. My name is Daniel. P-please stop."

I removed my thumb.

He took several deep breaths, blinking away tears from the eye where I'd been pressing.

My vision was more or less back to normal, so I glanced toward the houses.

No one was visible.

"Where's the woman?" I described Hannah.

He glared at me but didn't reply.

I held up my thumb, wiggled it in front of his eyes.

"She's with Silas in the main house."

"Is that where the boss man is?"

"The Supreme Apostle resides there." He nodded, a peaceful expression on his face. "But you cannot see him because you are not chosen. You cannot comprehend the divine."

"Gotcha. So is that where you guys diddle little girls?"

Silence. Then: "You don't understand the Apostle's will. The bliss of a conjugal is from Elohim himself."

Anger swelled in my chest. I reached for his eye but stopped. The mission was not retribution. The goal was to rescue Hannah Byrne and wait for Throckmorton's troops. Then find Caleb and Mary and Hannah's niece.

So I pulled the Spyderco from my belt, flipped open the blade, slid the point inside one of his nostrils. The knife was brand-new, as sharp as sharp can be.

"Well, we certainly don't want to violate anything," I said. "But you're gonna look like a pumpkin carved up for Halloween if you don't tell me what I need to know. How many people are in each house?"

His cheeks bellowed with each breath, but he didn't speak. After a few seconds, I slid the blade in another quarter inch.

"Silas and a synod leader are in the main house with the woman you seek." A trickle of blood oozed down his upper lip.

"What about the other buildings?" I removed the knife.

"Two men. In the control room."

I looked at the structures. "Which one is the control room?"

He coughed. His face was pale. "The closest."

"What about the other one?"

He shook his head. "You're not allowed in there. That is holy ground."

"I thought all three houses were holy." I sighed. "I'm getting my doctrine confused."

He didn't say anything.

"The third house," I said. "Is that where the conjugals go down?"

A moment passed.

"We have been persecuted for decades. Survival is paramount." Tears filled his eyes. "We do what is necessary. You wouldn't understand."

I was about to ask what he meant, but I noticed the girl first.

She was standing on the other side of the generator, maybe ten feet away. I had no idea where she'd come from. I hadn't heard a door open or any footsteps.

Her face was made up like the child's back in the matrimonial chamber: heavy rouge, thick eye shadow, bright-red lipstick.

The air in my lungs felt hot and poisonous as I realized how much she looked like my daughter.

My skull felt like it was going to explode. My limbs shook, throat tightened.

It was my daughter.

I reached for her as sweat stung my eyes. I blinked, and she was gone.

A moment passed.

I looked at the man on the ground. "What the hell are people doing here?"

"The Apostle's will," he said. "I told you that you wouldn't understand."

- CHAPTER FIFTY-TWO -

I sliced a strip of cloth from Daniel's coat and gagged him with it.

The girl who looked like my dead daughter had disappeared. If she'd ever really been there at all.

The throbbing in my head was getting better.

There were three options.

The "control" room, whatever that meant—the smallest structure.

The Apostle's home, where Silas was holding Hannah.

Or the third place, the one that Daniel had called "holy ground."

I scrambled across the yard to the rear door of the middle house, the place where Silas had Hannah. I tried the knob. Locked. I dashed around the side of the structure.

The front of the home was plain and unadorned, a square concrete stoop, no landscaping, just lawn all the way up to the walls of the house.

Several four-wheelers sat nearby, the preferred backcountry mode of transportation.

I reached for the knob with my left hand, my right holding the Glock.

The door flung open, striking my wrist.

A lightning bolt of pain shot up my arm.

I stumbled backward and fell off the stoop as Silas McPherson dashed out of the house. His right arm was still in a cast, and a satchel was strapped across his back.

He didn't stop. He ran and jumped on one of the four-wheelers.

I pushed myself up with my left hand, ignoring the pain.

Silas struggled to crank the ignition, his movements awkward because of the cast.

He was twenty feet away, an easy shot with the Glock.

I thought about the last time I'd fired a gun. But not for long.

I aimed for the rear of the four-wheeler, at the mass of metal where the transmission and exhaust system came together. A large target, much bigger than trying to hit the man astride the machine.

The engine caught, and a cloud of blue smoke spewed from the tailpipe. The four-wheeler lurched away as the Glock fired.

The whine of the engine swallowed the noise from the Glock. Barely audible above everything was a slight ping, the round striking metal.

I got to my feet.

Silas McPherson was already fifty yards from the top of the hill, speeding down a trail that led south away from the old prison. The trail followed the contours of the terrain, a low groove in the land that disappeared from view when it curved behind a bluff.

The whine of the engine grew quieter, and a few seconds later, he was gone. If the bullet had managed to hit anything vital, he wouldn't get far. That was a big *if*, though.

I examined one of the other four-wheelers. The key was in the ignition.

My left arm hurt. I wiggled my wrist and fingers. Nothing appeared broken.

I stared at the key to the four-wheeler for a few seconds and then pulled the walkie-talkie from my back pocket, turned it on, and hailed

Throckmorton. He answered immediately, swearing at me because I hadn't responded to his last message to not enter the compound.

When he'd gotten that off his chest, I related what had happened and that the suspect was fleeing south, headed toward the road we'd seen on the map. He told me air support was at least an hour away. He said to find Hannah Byrne and then get out. I didn't reply, turning off the radio instead, again ignoring his orders to leave the compound.

The back door to the middle house was open.

I approached warily, Glock in hand.

Hannah Byrne was in the living room, the front portion of the house.

She was bound and gagged in a chair that had been placed in front of a large mirror on the back wall.

A man in his fifties stood beside her, one hand on her shoulder. He was barely five feet tall and wore a black suit and no tie. He looked at me as I entered, mouth agape. One of his eyes was milky white over the entire surface.

"Wh-who are you?" he asked.

"Think of me as the devil." I eased inside. "It will be easier that way."

The room looked like the Salvation Army had decorated it. Mismatched, worn sofas; rickety chairs; a tattered hook rug.

His limbs shook, breath coming in rapid gasps like a panting dog. He stared at the gun in my hand for a moment. Then he ran out the front door.

I looked at Hannah. "Are you OK?"

She nodded and shot her eyes toward the mirror.

I pressed my back against the wall and eased toward a door next to the mirror.

She watched me go, a terrified expression on her face.

The door was unlocked.

I flung it open and stepped inside what had once been a bedroom.

The Apostle was waiting for me.

He was alone, sitting in a wheelchair, hands folded in his lap.

I aimed at his chest, my finger tight on the trigger.

He wore a black suit, a white shirt with no tie, and dark sunglasses. His hair was gray and slicked back.

"Put your hands up," I said.

He didn't move. He appeared to be in his late seventies or older, and I wondered if he could hear me.

I stepped closer, and that's when I noticed the smell.

A chemical tang overlaid with cologne and the faint stench of decay.

I lowered the gun, felt my jaw drop.

Dust freckled the man's shoulders like a thin coating of snow.

I stepped in front of him and removed the sunglasses.

His eyes were closed.

I grasped the significance of the loose skin on his cheeks and the stillness of his body at the same time that I realized his chest wasn't moving.

The Apostle was dead.

He'd been that way for a long time.

They'd embalmed him and placed his corpse in a wheelchair, an easy way to move him into view for the masses.

Their actions were understandable.

Personality cults were hard to maintain if the personality went offline.

Lenin's body stayed on display at the Kremlin for decades, until the embalming started to wear off. More than a few popes and saints were preserved under glass, moldering in their vestments. The Church of Scientology managed to convince their membership that L. Ron Hubbard hadn't died but had merely transitioned to another plane of consciousness.

This was a descendant of the original Apostle, according to Hannah. I imagined there had been a power struggle upon his death, and preserving the body seemed like a way to buy time.

I ran back into the living room and cut off Hannah's gag.

"Silas got away."

She nodded, taking several deep breaths.

I cut the cords on her wrists and ankles.

"He said the Apostle wanted to watch me die." She looked at the glass. "That little guy was supposed to do it. Some kind of specialist. I was a sinner. I deserved the fires of hell."

"The Apostle's not watching much of anything these days." I put away my knife. "It's more a *Weekend at Bernie's* situation."

"What do you mean?" Hannah stood, wobbly. "Is he in there?"

I took her arm and led her to the door. She gasped, staring at the corpse for a long moment.

"Ian and his camera guy," I said. "They're dead, too."

Her face turned pale. She told me what had happened after I'd darted into the old prison.

They'd made a frantic dash to the van and then left the way we'd come in, easing their way through the people to the front gate. The troopers let them leave, and they had headed west to get away from the riot that was brewing at the entrance to the compound.

They'd stopped at the wide spot on the shoulder, debating their next move, when a gray pickup full of guards, obviously alerted to their escape, had appeared and taken Hannah. They'd transported her to the houses using the same trail along the creek.

"Why did they kill them but not me?" she asked.

"Women have value. They're a commodity." I told her about the matrimonial chamber.

"What the hell are they doing up here?" she asked.

I didn't say the obvious, what we both knew intuitively but were afraid to speak aloud.

Instead I stepped outside the house and looked across the compound below to check the situation at the gate. Hannah followed.

From the front stoop, we had a good view.

Squad cars clogged the highway, too many to count. Officers had massed by the entrance.

On the compound side, more guards had taken up positions. Sandbags had appeared, forming spots for snipers to shoot from.

"What should we do?" Hannah said.

"There are two houses left," I said.

"Let's start with the control room."

"Why there?" I asked.

"Because I'm not real sure I want to know what's going on in the third house."

We looked toward the control room as the ground shook like a minor earthquake had hit, and then the windows of the structure blew out and glass shrapnel spewed everywhere.

Hannah and I jumped back.

The control room began to burn, and we turned to the last place on the hill.

The holy ground.

- CHAPTER FIFTY-THREE -

I suppose we knew all along what had been happening at the compound even if we didn't give voice to our suspicions.

The girls, the underage marriages, a patriarchal organization, the rife sexuality implied by that combination.

I liked to think that people who claim to be part of something righteous and good might be different, not affected by the basest of human desires.

But that was a mistake. Men have been men since time began. Some have lusts best not described, for fear that others will fall prey to their particular strains of darkness.

I entered the third house, gun in hand, Hannah right behind me.

A guard stood in the foyer. He offered no resistance when I disarmed him. He was scared of what lay ahead. Within the next few seconds, I understood why and couldn't say that I blamed him.

The leaders of the church, we later learned, had used a unique interpretation of their scriptures as support for allowing cameras to record the blessedness of the wedding night, especially those nights involving young, attractive brides. The so-called conjugals.

At some point, the church hierarchy discovered there was a market for such images. They also figured out that the younger the bride was, the higher the price the pictures (and later videos) could command.

A variety of criminal organizations, the Russians most lately, handled the retail distribution, selling the images on the Internet. The money flowed through several different offshore accounts before eventually ending up in the electronic vaults of the First National Bank of Piedra Springs.

But I didn't know these details when I took the guard's weapon and bound his arms with his own belt.

I began to understand, however, when we entered the main part of the house.

A king-size bed dominated what used to be the living room. The bed was unmade, the sheets rumpled. A comforter lay bunched at the foot.

Except for the professional-grade lighting equipment and expensive video cameras, everything felt cheap and dirty. Dismal and pathetic, anything but titillating.

On one wall, out of view of the cameras, hung a series of photographs—men in white shirts and black suits, the leadership structure of the church, no doubt. Interspersed with the photographs were framed plaques of various Bible verses.

The implication was obvious. What happened here was sanctioned, even sanctified by the church.

Hannah stared at the pictures.

A shot of Silas was toward the end. His face appeared younger, but the clothes were identical to what he had been wearing today.

She walked up close to the bed and knelt so that the mattress was at eye level. She looked at me and said, "What the hell is this place?"

I couldn't tell whether she meant this room or the whole compound. Either way, it didn't matter.

"They're running a porn operation," I said.

"What?"

"They're filming themselves." I pointed to a camera. "With the girls. Having sex."

"I don't under—" She got to her feet. "How can they call themselves a church and, and—" She looked at the bed.

I didn't reply because there was nothing to say. I was tired all the way to my bones. My knee hurt, and there was a throbbing pain in my temple. After a moment, I headed for the hallway leading to the back half of the home. Together, Hannah and I explored the rest of the house.

Three bedrooms, two of which were empty.

The door to the last room was open.

A girl in a long-sleeve dress sat in the middle of a sofa, legs crossed demurely at the ankles.

She wore a thick layer of makeup, blue eye shadow, cherry-red lipstick, heavy rouge on her cheeks.

"Hi there," I said.

She didn't reply.

"How old are you?" I asked.

She looked at Hannah and then back to me. A moment passed. Then, she said, "I am twelve, sir. Are you here for the conjugal?"

I shook my head. "There's not going to be any of those today."

Hannah took her by the arm, led her from the room. A few seconds later, we were all outside, blinking in the sunshine.

I pulled the walkie-talkie from my pocket, turned it on.

Throckmorton's voice immediately rang out. "Baines, where the hell are you?"

I told him.

"You haven't left yet?" His voice was shrill. "I am giving you a direct order. That's a crime scene. You need to exit that location ASAP."

"You don't understand," I said.

Silence. Then: "What was the explosion? Looked like one of those houses blew up."

"The holy ground." I paused. "That's what this is about."

My voice, even to my own ears, sounded strangely hollow.

"What do you mean?" he asked. "I'm not following."

"There's a twelve-year-old girl up here with us." I told him about the cameras.

No response from the radio.

Hannah covered her mouth like she was going to be sick.

I stared at the smoldering control room.

The guards in the control room had tried to destroy the smallest structure, the place where the images were processed and stored, but they hadn't quite succeeded. Not that it would have mattered, with what was going on everywhere else. It would take weeks, but between the three houses and the old prison, a good forensics team could uncover a mountain of evidence.

"You need to get the feds involved," I said. "This is probably an interstate situation."

The radio crackled, but no response was forthcoming. The girl we'd rescued from the third house stared at the horizon and hugged herself.

I shielded my eyes against the sun's glare and peered at the front entrance. More police cars were on the highway, but other than that, nothing had happened.

Throckmorton spoke again, his voice sounding subdued. "What about the hostage?"

I looked at Hannah. "She's safe. What's your ETA?"

No response.

"Throckmorton? Are you still there?"

Static from the speaker. Then: "The AG is talking to the governor. The guv wants to bring in the DOJ."

"Good for the bureaucrats," I said. "Now tell me when you're coming in."

"Soon. We've got a bunch of CPS caseworkers on-site now at least, but air support had a mechanical issue. They're hours away."

Air coverage was critical. The compound and surrounding area were too vast to exert control without helicopters.

"Soon?" I said. "What the hell does that mean?"

"It means we're sitting on a leaky gas tank and nobody wants to give the go-ahead to light the first match."

I swore. Then I had an idea.

"There's a cattle trail by the creek. Just to the west of your location. It's unguarded. Send in CPS and some troopers that way."

A few moments passed. Then he said, "OK. That'll work. We'll put a sniper up there, too. That should help when the big push comes. Hold your position until they get there."

I lied to him and said I would do as he asked. Then I turned off the radio and gave the device to Hannah. "You stay here."

"Where are you going?"

I stared at the trail that ran south, the way Silas had gone. "He'll get away if I don't go after him."

"I'm going with you," Hannah said.

"What about your niece?" I pointed to the old prison. "She's down there somewhere."

"How am I going to find her in all that, especially with those people shooting at me?"

"You should stay with her, then." I nodded toward the girl we'd rescued.

The youngster stared at us like we were talking statues. Eyes wide, mouth slightly open.

I hopped on one of the four-wheelers.

"The troopers will be here in a couple of minutes," Hannah said. "She'll be OK."

I cranked the ignition. The engine caught, the fuel gauge indicating a full tank.

"Please." She stepped in front of the four-wheeler. "I don't want to stay in this place anymore. The girl is safe for the moment. There's nothing that can happen to her now."

I hesitated, foot on the gearshift. I understood. The houses on top of the hill made me feel dirty and ashamed, even though I'd had nothing to do with what had gone on here.

I looked at the girl. "Stay right here. You're going to be OK. People are on their way who will take care of you."

The girl nodded, a shy smile creasing her face for the first time.

I turned my attention back to Hannah and pointed to the rear of the seat behind me.

"Hop on."

- CHAPTER FIFTY-FOUR -

The trail that Silas McPherson had taken headed south, following a dry creek bed.

The vegetation was sparse—cactus and cedars, scrub oaks, tufts of creosote bushes that looked like olive-colored medicine balls.

I pushed the four-wheeler to its limit, bouncing along at nearly fifty miles per hour, a blisteringly fast pace when you're on the back of an open vehicle on rough terrain.

Hannah held on tightly, her arms around my torso.

The terrain grew rockier and more uneven, arroyos and narrow gorges overtaking the flatlands where the old prison was located.

We gradually climbed higher, making our way toward an escarpment covered in mesquite trees.

After a few minutes, the trail cut to the west, through a narrow canyon filled with chalky white boulders. Then it switched back and we found ourselves atop the escarpment, zipping through a grove of mesquites, the thorns on their branches clawing at us as we sped by.

Hannah saw the other four-wheeler first.

She squeezed my arm, pointed to a clearing just to the right of the path, a flash of painted metal.

The four-wheeler that Silas had used to escape sat under an old windmill.

I pulled off the trail, stopped behind the vehicle, and killed my engine. Away from the path and in the thicket of trees, visibility was minimal. I strained to hear any movement, but there was nothing but the whisper of the breeze and the creak of the old windmill.

The rear of Silas's four-wheeler was damp with transmission fluid, and the air nearby smelled like burned insulation.

I felt the engine block. It was warm but not hot. He had a head start but was now traveling by foot.

"He'd stay on the trail," Hannah said. "Let's keep going."

I nodded.

"How far to the road?" she asked.

We'd been traveling between forty and fifty miles an hour for nearly ten minutes. That put us about seven miles south of where we'd started.

I tried to remember the details from the map that Throckmorton had shown me. The highway to Del Rio couldn't be too much farther.

"Maybe a mile or so." I still had the two Glocks, one that I'd taken from the guard back at the third house, the second being the pistol I'd retrieved from the roof of Jimmy and Dale's.

I handed the latter to Hannah. "You know how to use a gun?"

"I can figure it out." She slid the pistol in her back pocket.

"Let's go." I cranked the ignition and threaded the four-wheeler back to the trail.

This time, I drove slower, wanting to be more aware of what was around me. The engine was noisy, signaling our presence, so I needed to keep an eye out for Silas or any possible attacks.

A few hundred yards later, the trees thinned out and the trail snaked across a plain covered with buffalo grass, green and healthy from the recent rain. At the end of the plain was a limestone bluff, and I sensed that the highway was on the other side, not very far away.

"There." Hannah pointed to a tiny figure in black, a smudge between us and the bluff.

A buzzard circled high overhead, and I wondered what the bird's presence signified—nearby carrion or wishful thinking?

The figure started to run. I sped up.

The bluff was not high, maybe thirty feet above the plain.

Silas scrambled up the limestone as we got closer.

The trail veered to the left, taking a more gradual slope to the summit.

I drove that way and circled around to meet our target when he made it to the top.

We arrived at the same time, a flat spot by a gravel road.

Sheriff Quang Marsh was already there, waiting for us.

- CHAPTER FIFTY-FIVE -

Nine Months Ago

The Frisella brothers were cold.

I knew this because they were banging on the door of the walk-in cooler at Pirate Red's, hollering about how they were freezing to death, demanding to be let out.

The restaurant was still closed for remodeling, meaning there was no food service, but the place was open for a certain type of customer. I'd known the patrons I was after would be there.

It was eight o'clock in the evening, the day my life changed. Seven and a half hours after Chloe sat down at my table at the diner and upended my world.

Now, Chloe and her two partners, Keating and Boulay, were going to pay for their crimes.

The three crooked cops were kneeling on the greasy floor of the kitchen, hands behind their heads.

I aimed my service pistol at Chloe.

My father-in-law cowered behind me. Frank held his revolver in one hand, a Smith & Wesson snub-nose, the gun he'd shot the week before that had been in the lockbox of my truck. A gun whose serial number was attached to his name. The weapon dangled from his fingers like he was afraid it might bite.

Frank was not having a good day. Arrested for bank fraud, slapped around by his son-in-law, informed that his daughter and grandchildren had been murdered, now forced to confront their killers.

His breath was coming in heaves, his face pale, limbs trembling.

I, on the other hand, was feeling remarkably calm. Considering the circumstances, I actually felt good, in control for once.

Chloe said, "You do get the fact that if you kill three cops, there won't be a rock big enough for you to hide under?"

"Three crooked cops who killed my family," I said.

"That's not how it's going to play out." Chloe shook her head. "Trust me."

Keating, the guy on the end, sneered at me, his eyes rattling in their sockets like marbles in an ashtray.

I walked to where he knelt and smashed the barrel of my pistol across his mouth.

He fell over. A couple of teeth scattered across the tile, blood pooling underneath his chin.

No one spoke. Frank whimpered in the background.

I looked at Chloe. "You gave me until five."

She cut her eyes toward Boulay, an angry expression on her face. Then she looked back at me.

"An unfortunate turn of events," she said.

I tightened my finger on the trigger, the muzzle aimed at her face. The anger inside me was a living, breathing thing, a mass of poisonous heat worming its way through my veins.

"Don't screw up any more," Chloe said. "Beat the shit out of us if that makes you feel better. But you're not shooting anybody."

"You think giving you a beat down will bring my family back?" I said.

She shrugged. "Do you think killing us will?"

I didn't respond. Instead I placed the muzzle against her forehead.

She didn't flinch. "Boulay was the shooter. Break his arms and legs. I'll help you."

Boulay looked at her. "What the fuck?"

Chloe stared at my eyes. "But you need to get over this idea that you can just kill three cops and get away with it."

"What if I don't want to get away with it?"

"You're a Texas Ranger," she said. "Not suicidal. You wouldn't last an hour in prison."

I moved the gun from her head. "You're right."

She smiled, appearing to relax just a tiny bit.

I pointed to my father-in-law. "Frank's going to do it."

Chloe quit smiling.

"He was arrested today for bank fraud," I said. "You killed his daughter and grandkids. He's out of his head. Doing you will probably get him only another year or two."

"Ah, shit." Chloe shook her head.

"He takes out three crooked cops," I said. "Bet they treat him like a king in prison."

A sheen of sweat had appeared on Chloe's upper lip. "Don't be stupid, Baines. They'll nail you as an accomplice."

"Maybe." I shrugged. "But probably not. I did try to stop him. Isn't that right, Frank?"

Frank appeared as if he was going to be sick. After a few seconds, he nodded timidly.

"He's not looking too good," Chloe said. "I don't see him actually pulling the trigger."

"We've been practicing," I said.

There was a low hum in my brain and a throbbing sensation in the soles of my feet. My skin felt like an electrical charge was pulsating just beneath the surface.

I struggled to keep the grief in check. There would be time enough for that later.

Frank aimed at Boulay. His arm shook.

"Do it," I said. "Just like we talked about. Avenge your family."

After a few seconds, he lowered his hand, dropped the gun.

"I can't, Arlo." He sobbed. "I just can't."

Chloe smiled like she'd just won the lottery.

I picked up my father-in-law's revolver, aimed at the guy on the floor, Keating.

"That's what I figured."

- CHAPTER FIFTY-SIX -

Sheriff Quang Marsh stood by his squad car at the top of the escarpment at the south edge of the Sky of Zion property. He was carrying a rifle, an AR15.

Hannah and I sat astride the four-wheeler we'd used to track Silas McPherson from the three homes on the hill where he'd kept prisoner an untold number of children.

Marsh aimed the rifle at my face. "Put your hands up."

I did as requested. So did Hannah.

Silas was on his knees a few feet away, struggling to catch his breath after climbing to the top of the bluff.

Marsh said, "Did you bring the money?"

Silas nodded, removed the satchel from around his shoulders.

"Open it," Marsh said.

Silas did so, displaying bundle after bundle of hundred-dollar bills.

"You're going to let him go?" I asked.

Silas stood. He smiled at me, a look of victory on his face.

I stared at Marsh. "Have you been listening to your radio?"

The sheriff didn't reply.

"God is on my side, Mr. Baines," Silas said. "You are part of the unclean. You will never triumph over me."

I spoke to Marsh. "They're filming their marriages, selling it on the Internet. Children having sex. That's where the money comes from."

Marsh lowered the rifle. He looked at the satchel and then at Hannah and me.

"Lies of the serpent," Silas said. "We had an arrangement, Sheriff Marsh. I expect you to honor it."

"The state police are about to storm the compound." I pointed to Silas. "The only reason they don't have him yet is because they're late getting air support. But it's coming."

Hannah slid off the back of the four-wheeler. She strode to where Silas stood and slapped his face.

"Where is my niece?" she said.

Silas didn't react. Marsh watched her like she was on a TV show that was only mildly interesting. He made no move to interfere.

She slapped him again, her face purple with rage.

Silas shoved her to the ground.

Marsh looked at me, a bewildered expression on his face.

"He's not going to get far," I said. "Even with your help."

Silas smiled. "I only have to get across the border, Mr. Baines. We have churches in Mexico."

I said, "What about your daughter, Sheriff?"

Marsh didn't say anything.

"Imagine her a prisoner at the compound." I paused. "Being filmed."

No one spoke.

"I saw you and your daughter yesterday," I said. "Standing in the window of your house. She looked like a nice kid."

"What are you talking about?" Marsh asked. "I don't even have a house just now. My wife left me. She wanted more than a sheriff's salary. She and my daughter live in Tyler with her new husband."

Silas chuckled.

"I live in a back room at the courthouse," Marsh said. "You're hallucinating if you think you saw me and my kid together."

I tried to imagine the scene from yesterday. Everything had been so clear. Marsh with his coffee mug, his daughter standing next to him. The rain falling.

Marsh slung the rifle on his shoulder, preparing to either pick up the satchel or walk away. I didn't care which. It was out of his reach for easy access, so I pulled the Glock from my waistband, aimed at him.

Marsh said, "Put the gun down, Baines."

"No." I tightened my grip.

"You gonna shoot me?" Marsh asked.

I didn't reply.

"You don't have it in you," he said. "I think the forensics people were right. Your father-in-law shot those cops, not you."

"You're wrong," I said.

A gun fired, and everything changed again.

- CHAPTER FIFTY-SEVEN -

The smell of bleach came to me at the oddest of times.

In the early hours of the morning when sleep was elusive. At the end of a long day on a bus, my muscles stiff from sitting. When I saw a hard-looking woman who reminded me of Chloe.

Or now, as Silas McPherson fell to the ground dead.

He'd been struck in the head by a bullet from the Glock that I'd given to Hannah.

The look on his face reminded me of the surprised expression in Keating's eyes when I pulled the trigger and the bullet from Frank's revolver punched a hole in his forehead in the kitchen of Pirate Red's.

I shot Chloe and Boulay immediately afterward, single rounds to their temples. Then I wiped my prints from the gun, manhandled a whimpering Frank, and forced him to fire into the wall so that gunshot residue would be found on his hands. The weapon was made from stainless steel, and I pressed his fingers all over the smooth metal, making sure his prints were everywhere.

Marsh jerked his pistol from its holster.

I said, "Put your gun down. Nobody's gonna be doing any more shooting."

He aimed at Hannah but stared at Silas's body, his mouth agape.

I walked over to where Hannah stood. I took the gun away from her and tossed it on the ground.

The stench of bleach filled my nostrils. I remembered washing my hands at the restaurant, using the Clorox I'd found underneath the sink, the cleaning solution removing all traces of gunshot residue from my skin.

Sheriff Marsh holstered his weapon as the buzzard circled overhead, and Hannah Byrne sat on the ground and cried.

"Children?" he said. "They were filming little kids?"

I nodded.

"I didn't know." He shook his head. "You have to believe me."

"I'm tired now, Sheriff. I don't really care what you did or didn't know."

He stared at me for a moment and then pulled a phone from his pocket.

• • •

Marsh said he was going to call the state police. He walked a few feet away, cell phone in hand.

As soon as his back was turned, I wiped down all the surfaces of the Glock I'd been carrying and placed the weapon in Silas McPherson's hand, making sure his fingers touched the metal frame where a good print could be obtained.

Marsh returned as I was finishing up with Silas. He obviously saw what I was doing, but he made no move to stop me.

Then he watched as I wiped down the other weapon and told Hannah not to talk about what had happened without an attorney advising her. She was in a state of near shock but agreed.

I stepped away from the immediate area near Silas's body.

Marsh stared at me. After a moment, he nodded like he approved.

The next day was a blur. Interviews with various investigators, a walk-through of the compound with Throckmorton, meetings with CPS caseworkers. I told everyone that I didn't know who had killed McPherson because I hadn't been looking. Technically true.

Sheriff Quang Marsh never gave a statement. He had disappeared along with the satchel of money soon after the arrival of the state troopers. His room at the courthouse had been emptied, and his whereabouts were currently unknown.

Hannah Byrne lawyered up. Her former employer, sensing a great story, hired a criminal defense attorney out of Dallas to serve as her counsel.

As the scope of the crimes at the compound became clear, the police became less interested in who had been responsible for Silas McPherson's death and more grateful that the leader of the organization was gone.

Throckmorton, to his credit, told the state and federal authorities that I had been instrumental in uncovering the operation. He also told his superiors that I had provided key details about the Russians who'd been selling the images on the Internet and the now-deceased president of the local bank who'd been handling the money.

For this, I was thankful, and I told him so.

The town of Piedra Springs was soon filled with state police, various federal agents, and more reporters than at a royal wedding.

The hardest work fell to CPS, tasked with finding foster care for the hundreds of children at the compound, most of whom had been abused.

For much of the day, I stood in the shade of a temporary tent by the front entrance of the compound and watched the parade of damaged souls being processed by the state workers.

Molly's children, Caleb and Mary, were found in a trailer on the back side of the old prison. Boone had been right; they'd returned to what was familiar. The people who lived in the trailer were part of an informal network of church members disillusioned by Silas's leadership. They were in contact with Boone and from time to time helped people like Molly escape.

There was an aunt in Tulsa who was not part of the church. She'd been notified and was on her way to pick up her niece and nephew and take them to what would hopefully be a better life.

Late in the day, I caught a ride to town with a state trooper and had her drop me off at Boone's. The old veterinarian was sitting on the front porch with Suzy. I walked across the lawn and sat next to him.

The squad car that brought me left. Several others drove down the street, followed by a couple of unmarked units.

"Lotsa traffic here in Piedra Springs," Boone said as a greeting.

"Your Crown Victoria is still at the compound," I said. "They haven't released any of the cars yet. Sorry about that."

He shrugged. "No place I need to drive to anytime soon."

"Where's your girlfriend?" Suzy asked.

"In her motel room, writing a story about what happened." I paused. "She's not my girlfriend."

"She was making goo-goo eyes at you," Suzy said. "Figured you two were doing the deed."

"You figured wrong," I said.

Another unmarked unit drove by.

Boone fanned himself with a copy of the *Midland Reporter-Telegram*. The front page was a color picture of children being led from the entrance of the compound.

"They're taking custody of the youngsters here in town, too," he said.

The neighborhood of apostates, the skinny people. Once the government got its wheels turning, it was hard to stop.

"We've been watching it all on the TV." Boone put down the paper. "That's a hell of a mess."

"One way to put it," I said.

We were silent for a while. Suzy disappeared inside.

"I didn't know what was going on," Boone said. "If I did, I would have tried to stop it."

"How?"

He didn't reply.

I went inside and got my stuff. I'd spent last night upstairs. Hannah had returned to the Comanche Inn, snagging one of the last rooms.

When I came back out, Boone said, "Where are you going now?"

Suzy appeared in the doorway, carrying a tray of iced tea.

"Not sure," I said.

"You could stay here." She put down the tray on a wicker table. "In Piedra Springs."

"Probably ought to keep moving," I said.

- CHAPTER FIFTY-EIGHT -

The day after the compound fell, I found Hannah at Jimmy and Dale's.

She was doing an interview with a reporter from one of the networks. They were standing by the dartboard where I'd first seen the two men from the Sky of Zion compound a few days before.

The place was full, about half locals, the rest reporters, various state officials, and hangers-on.

I found an empty spot at the bar. Jimmy brought me a beer without being asked, ignoring several other people clamoring for drinks.

"On the house," he said.

"Thanks." I took a sip, opened up Gibbon to kill time until Hannah was free.

"No." He leaned close. "Thank *you*. What I hear, it was you who saved this town."

I shrugged.

A guy who looked like Geraldo Rivera squeezed in next to me and slapped a twenty on the bar, asking if anybody knew how to make a White Russian. Jimmy said he'd try, by golly.

I started reading about the Romans.

The Geraldo look-alike left with his drink, and a few minutes later, Hannah took his place.

She hugged me. "Where have you been?"

I put down the book and told her.

"How many kids are they up to?" she asked.

"A hundred and fifty-three." I paused. "So far."

She shook her head. "I have a hard time believing that nobody in town knew what was going on."

"People see what they want to and ignore the rest. What about your niece?"

"They think she's in Mexico. I'm headed down there tomorrow; *20/20* is going with me."

I pointed to the guy in the corner. "Is that Geraldo Rivera?"

She ignored my question. "Why don't you come with me?"

"Where?"

"To Mexico."

The crowd got louder as another reporter with a video crew entered the bar.

I shook my head. In my pocket was a ticket for the six fifteen to Lubbock.

"What are you going to do?" she said. "Where are you going to go?"

The noise level ratcheted up another notch. Reporters talking to one another, half the locals trying to be interviewed, the other half trying not to be.

I took a last drink of the beer and picked up my rucksack. "Let's go outside."

Hannah followed me to the exit.

On the street, there was more traffic than all of the days before combined. Across the street at Earl's Family Restaurant, all the parking spots were taken.

"Are you staying in town?" Hannah asked.

"Leaving in about an hour." I held up the ticket.

"What's in Lubbock?"

I shrugged. "I'll know when I get there."

"What's that?" She pointed to an envelope in my hand.

The envelope and the ticket had been in my back pocket.

"I should get to the bus station."

Neither of us spoke for a few moments.

"Thank you for all your help," she said. "I think I might be dead by now if it wasn't for you."

"The reverse might well be true, too. We made a good team."

Another period of silence.

"You sure you don't want to go to Mexico with me? We're taking a chartered plane from Midland tomorrow afternoon."

I shook my head.

She leaned over and kissed me on the lips. Her lips were soft, her touch pleasant and warm.

She pulled back, head cocked just a little. "Good-bye, then." She smiled, ran a hand down my cheek. "It was very nice to meet you, Arlo Baines."

"Good-bye to you, too, Hannah." I headed toward the bus station.

About halfway there, a block past where Chigger had attacked me, I found a mailbox and dropped the envelope inside.

The envelope contained a card for my son, whose birthday would have been in two weeks. Inside the card was a picture of my family, a snapshot taken several Christmases ago.

The envelope was addressed to my father-in-law at the federal penitentiary in Beaumont.

As long as he was alive, I planned to send him cards on the birthdays of the family members. I wanted him to feel the pain as sharply as I did.

Six people were dead because of what we'd done, three of them utterly innocent.

In the weeks after their deaths, I'd blamed Frank exclusively. Now, with the clarity of time, I realized their fate had been in my hands all along. I could have said no to my father-in-law, but I chose not to.

In the distance, the station came into view.

I walked faster, eager to be on the road.

ACKNOWLEDGMENTS

Creating a work of fiction is a group experience. The raw material may have been mine, but the end result is a communal effort, thanks to a dedicated group of professionals who are as much responsible for what you hold in your hand as the author. To that end, I would like to thank everybody at Thomas & Mercer: Jacque Ben-Zekry, Dennelle Catlett, David Downing, Gracie Doyle, and Sarah Shaw. Also, many thanks to Richard Abate for helping to make this book possible at the outset.

For their help with the manuscript, I would like to offer my gratitude to Jan Blankenship, Victoria Calder, Paul Coggins, Peggy Fleming, Alison Hunsicker, Fanchon Henneberger, Brooke Malouf, Clif Nixon, David Norman, Glenna Whitley, and Max Wright.

ABOUT THE AUTHOR

Photo © 2013 Nick McWhirter

Harry Hunsicker is the former executive vice president of the Mystery Writers of America. His work has been short-listed for both the Shamus and Thriller Awards. He lives in Dallas. *The Devil's Country* is his seventh novel.